KNITTY GRITTY MURDER

"You don't really think it was okay for Dennis to be having an affair with Jenny, do you?" Pamela asked after the server had noted their orders and turned away.

"No." Bettina shook her head. "But I believe he really loved her—too much to kill her, for whatever reason. And I can't believe that, like we discussed, she could have been holding the affair over him and threatening to tell his wife. She wasn't that kind of person and he's a nice man."

"So we don't care if he has an alibi for the night Jenny was killed—because he's so nice?"

"We have other suspects," Bettina said. "Lots of other suspects." She raised a carefully manicured hand and began to count off on her fingers, beginning with her pinkie. "Calliope, Danielle—and remember she made sure to tell us she was home with her husband all Monday night, but then Wilfred said he was at the historical society. Why would she volunteer an alibi unless she was guilty? And—" Bettina moved on to the next finger, but Pamela interrupted her.

"Apparently Detective Clayborn doesn't think any of the gardeners are guilty, including Johan Friendly." Pamela tapped the finger Bettina had moved on to. "The murder weapon—"

It was Bettina's turn to interrupt. "—was a knitting needle, and a rather specialized knitting needle at that . . ."

Books by Peggy Ehrhart

MURDER, SHE KNIT

DIED IN THE WOOL

KNIT ONE, DIE TWO

SILENT KNIT, DEADLY KNIT

A FATAL YARN

KNIT OF THE LIVING DEAD

KNITTY GRITTY MURDER

CHRISTMAS CARD MURDER
(with Leslie Meier and Lee Hollis)

Published by Kensington Publishing Corp.

KNITTY GRITTY MURDER

PEGGY EHRHART

KENSINGTON
PUBLISHING CORP.

www.kensingtonbooks.com

For my sweet husband, again

ACKNOWLEDGMENTS

Abundant thanks to my agent, Evan Marshall, and to my editor at Kensington Books, John Scognamiglio.

CHAPTER 1

Pamela Paterson was enjoying her coffee, her crumb cake, and the welcoming atmosphere of her best friend's kitchen. She was not, however, enjoying the conversation.

"We agreed," she said at last, "that you would never again bring up the topic of Richard Larkin."

Bettina Fraser stopped in mid-sentence, and the cheer that usually animated her mobile features vanished. "I was just saying that Wilfred had a chat with Rick this morning about gardening," she said. "It's May and everyone's thinking about their yards and Richard Larkin lives right across the street. Wilfred and I can hardly avoid him. I wasn't saying anything about . . . you know . . ." Bettina shook her head sadly. "I've given up on that."

Pamela sighed. "I know. It's just . . ." She stared into her coffee mug.

Richard Larkin was a handsome single man who had bought the house next to Pamela's a few years earlier. His interest in Pamela had been immediate and obvious, but despite Bettina's encouragement and even Pamela's own daughter's approval, Pamela had resisted his overtures. No one, she believed, could replace the dear husband she'd lost in a tragic accident long ago.

As the ensuing silence threatened to become uncomfortable, Bettina leapt up from her chair. The sudden motion startled Woofus the shelter dog, who had been napping in his favorite spot, sprawled against the kitchen wall. He watched for a moment as Bettina leaned toward Pamela, then lowered his shaggy head and closed his eyes again.

"Let me warm up your coffee," Bettina chirped, reaching for Pamela's mug. "And I'm ready for another piece of crumb cake. How about you?"

Pamela had eaten barely half the piece already on her plate. She let Bettina take her mug and she picked up her fork and teased off a bite of crumb cake as if to acknowledge Bettina's peacemaking gesture. "It's delicious," she said, "but I'm still working on this."

Bettina carried Pamela's mug and her own past the high counter that separated the eating area of her kitchen from the cooking area. "I'll just warm the carafe a bit," she murmured from the stove, and she returned a few minutes later with two steaming mugs.

"I don't see how you can drink it black," Bettina observed as she added a liberal amount of sugar to her own mug and followed with a generous dollop of heavy cream.

"Habit, I guess." Pamela shrugged.

"That's why you're thin and I'm not." The comment was more a statement of fact than a lament. Bettina wasn't thin, and she wasn't tall, but she loved clothes. Though she and Pamela lived in a small suburban town, Bettina's wardrobe would have delighted even the most devoted fashionista. This morning she was wearing a stylish jumpsuit in crisp lavender cotton, accessorized with dangly earrings made from antique gold coins. The effect was striking with her scarlet hair, which she herself described as a color not found in nature. Pamela's lack of interest in the clothes her tall, slim body could have displayed to such advantage was a constant mystery to her friend.

Bettina stirred her coffee and added a bit more cream, then helped herself to another square of crumb cake from the platter before her. But before she could take up her fork again, the doorbell chimed. Woofus raised his shaggy head and cast a troubled glance in Bettina's direction.

"It's okay, boy," she cooed in a soothing voice as she rose and headed for the doorway that led to the dining room and the living room beyond. The next moment, her powers to soothe were put to a more demanding test.

Pamela heard the front door open, and from the living room came Bettina's voice, tinged with alarm, saying, "Oh you poor dear! Whatever is the matter?"

The response was an indistinct high-pitched muddle followed by a pause. The words that followed the pause were, however, enunciated clearly: "And she was dead!"

Pamela had been holding her coffee mug, just about to take a sip, when the doorbell chimed. Now she noticed that the jolt she'd received when she heard those words had roiled the coffee's dark surface into a tiny tsunami. She set the mug down, lowered both hands to the table's surface, and took a deep breath.

Bettina's voice took over then, murmuring disjointed phrases having to do with sitting down and drinking coffee and explaining again what on earth had happened. In a moment, Bettina reappeared, leading the woman Pamela recognized as Marlene Pepper. Marlene was a fixture of the Arborville community, the same age and shape as Bettina, a genial woman who Pamela chatted with when her trips to the Co-Op for groceries overlapped with Marlene's.

At the moment, though, Marlene barely resembled herself. Instead of the tidy pants outfits or suit skirts she was normally seen in, she was wearing a pair of dirt-stained and baggy jeans, topped with a dirt-stained flannel shirt, untucked. The smooth gray-blond hair that normally curved around her plump cheeks was in disarray, and instead of the placid cheer that suited her round face, her expression combined shock and grief. Her eyes had the red and watery look of someone who had recently cried and was likely to cry again.

Woofus stared at the newcomer for a second, seemed to decide she wasn't a threat, and resumed his nap.

Bettina settled Marlene into a chair, paused to give her shoulders a gentle rub, then hurried toward the stove to fetch a mug of coffee.

"It's nice and hot, and here's cream and sugar," she said as she set the mug in front of Marlene. She gestured at the cream pitcher and sugar bowl and hurried off again to fetch a spoon. "And there's crumb cake from the Co-Op," she added when she returned.

Marlene shook her head and left the coffee untouched. "I just keep seeing her," she whispered, "stretched out on the ground, right across a row of tomato seedlings. And at first I just thought she'd fallen, so I bent down to ask if she was okay and to help her up. But she was . . ." Marlene shuddered. "Her eyes were wide open, just staring. And there was"—she shaped a lopsided circle with her hands—"one of those knitting things that's like a loop of wire with two ends that look like knitting needles . . ." Her voice modulated into a wail. "It was around her neck."

Marlene buried her face in her hands. Bettina rose from her chair and resumed rubbing Marlene's shoulders, making comforting sounds.

"It's just a blessing I found her before her mother did," Marlene went on when she'd recovered a bit, though her cheeks were now slick with tears. "Jenny and Janice share the garden plot and they're both . . . they *were* both . . . such early birds, up there digging away first thing in the morning."

Bettina darted away again and returned with a fresh kitchen towel that she'd dampened at the sink. The damp towel and Bettina's ministrations restored Marlene to something like her normal self, though with quavering voice and weepy eyes.

She explained that of course she'd called 911 immediately—thank goodness she had her phone with her—and the police had come and she'd been at the community gardens for the past two hours telling the same story to more than one officer and finally to Detective Clayborn. They'd put the yellow tape up and turned away everyone who showed up expecting to spend a pleasant few hours planting seeds and setting out seedlings from the garden center. And soon the news that the body of Jenny Miller had been found in her garden plot would be all over Arborville. That was for sure. And Bettina agreed.

"I wanted you to hear about it first," Marlene explained, directing her words at Bettina, "since you write for the *Advocate*." The *Advocate* was Arborville's weekly newspaper. "People are going to blame the community garden program, and I'm the chair, and . . ." Marlene began to weep again and lowered her face into her hands.

CHAPTER 2

By that evening the news was indeed all over town.

Bettina steered her faithful Toyota toward the curb in front of Holly Perkins's house and she and Pamela climbed out only to be hailed by Nell Bascomb, arriving on foot from farther up the hill. They paused on the sidewalk as Nell hurried toward them, her white hair floating in the slight May-evening breeze.

"What a sad, sad thing!" Nell exclaimed, panting slightly. "And to happen at the community gardens, of all places, just when everything's coming alive again."

"Very sad," Bettina and Pamela agreed in unison.

"I almost wondered if we should postpone our Knit and Nibble meeting tonight," Nell said, shaking her head and gazing bleakly at nothing. "Because everyone will be so—"

"Upset," Bettina supplied.

"Curious." Nell finished her sentence. "And you know how I disapprove of the gossipy chatter that events like this give rise to."

Arborville, New Jersey, was a pleasant town inhabited by pleasant people. Yet over the years a shocking number of murders had taken place within its borders.

Pamela touched Nell's arm comfortingly. "I'm sure everyone will want to just focus on their knitting," she said. "I know I do."

Pamela was just finishing up an ambitious project she'd started right at the new year—a sweater for her daughter, Penny, with the yarn and pattern chosen by Penny as a Christmas present. Penny would be arriving home from college for the summer in just a few days and Pamela hoped to have the sweater ready—though Penny would need to wait for cooler weather to wear it.

The three women started up the walk that led to Holly's broad front porch. Her house, like most of the houses in Arborville, was old and charming, a wood-frame house with clapboard siding. Pamela rang the doorbell and in a moment the door swung back to reveal Holly, dressed in black leggings and a slouchy black shirt with a cowl neck, but she had added a perky cotton apron that would have suited a 1950s housewife.

"Come in, come in!" she greeted them, cordial but not quite her usual vivacious self.

Nell was the first to step over the threshold. As Bettina followed, a male voice called from partway down the walk, "One more coming!"

Pamela turned to see Roland DeCamp advancing toward the porch, dressed as usual in an expertly tailored pinstripe suit and carrying the elegant leather briefcase that he used in place of a knitting bag. She paused to greet him as he climbed the steps, and she smiled at the courtly gesture with which he waved her through the door.

The balmy May evening hadn't required coats. With no need to divest themselves of outerwear, the knitters proceeded directly to Holly's living room, where two people already occupied the streamlined ochre sofa that was the focal point of Holly's midcentury modern décor. Tossed over the back of the sofa was the color-block afghan that had been Holly's Knit and Nibble project for many months, a dramatic juxtaposition of squares and rectangles in shades of orange, turquoise, and green.

Karen Dowling looked up with a timid smile and seemed about to introduce the woman who was her sofa-mate, but Holly stepped forward quickly. "We have a visitor," she said, "a potential new member."

Pamela and Bettina looked at each other. Visitors were one thing, but a new member would have to be approved by the whole group. Was it wise to let this woman think she'd be welcome, only to turn her down later?

As Pamela's mind, sometimes overactive, occupied itself with this worry, Holly went on. "Knitters," she said, "meet Claire Cummings. She's married to Dennis, from the hardware store—my home away from home."

"Mine too," Karen murmured.

Holly and Karen, and their respective husbands, were recent owners of old houses in need of renovation. They'd met while poring over paint chips at Arborville's hardware store and become fast friends, despite their quite obvious differences. Holly was as outgoing as Karen was shy, and Holly's vivid good looks, with her dark hair—which tonight sported a bright pink streak—and quick smile, offered a striking contrast to Karen's pale blond prettiness.

Holly gestured in turn toward Nell, Bettina, Pamela, and Roland and listed their names, then added, "Sit down, everyone, please."

Nell headed for one of the angular chairs that flanked the coffee table, but Holly took her arm and steered her toward a more comfortable choice, a love seat upholstered in fabric that featured abstract flowers rendered in shades of bright orange and chartreuse. Pamela joined Nell there, and Bettina and Roland ended up in the angular chairs as Holly took a seat on the sofa.

Karen had already been at work on her project when they entered. From its delicate apricot-colored yarn, it looked to be another garment for her daughter, Lily, who was now nearly one and a half. And after the introductions, Claire had gone back to studying a knitting magazine, apparently contemplating what to do next on the project waiting in her lap.

Wasting no time, Roland snapped open his briefcase and extracted an in-progress back, or front, and the skein of charcoal-gray yarn to which it was tethered by a long strand. Pamela was happy to join the other three in their industry.

The sweater for Penny was a simple crew-neck pullover made special by stripes in shades of pink, blue, pale green, and brown. The width of the stripes varied in a random way, from just a few knitted rows to several inches wide. Pamela was just finishing up the last sleeve, which featured a long stretch of pale blue at the shoulder interrupted by a narrow band of dark brown. She was switching from pale blue to dark brown when Holly's voice disturbed her concentration.

"Such a shocking event in our little town," Holly commented. "We're all thinking about it, I know."

Many people, though perhaps not all, were indeed thinking about it—because no sooner had Holly finished speaking than from either side of her on the sofa and from one of the angular chairs came words of agreement: from Karen a meek "So sad," from Claire a more assertive "Terrible," from Bettina an expansive "Marlene Pepper is in a frightful state."

"Have you heard anything more than what the *Register* reported online?" Holly asked, leaning forward.

"I talked to Detective Clayborn this afternoon," Bettina said as Nell closed her eyes and gave a resigned sigh.

"Jenny Miller was our tenant, you know," Claire cut in. "She rented one of the apartments above the hardware store—a lovely person, such a shame."

Sitting next to Karen and Holly on the sofa, Claire seemed the average between them, though more than a decade older. Neither as fair and retiring as Karen nor as vivid and outgoing as Holly, she was a pleasant-looking, medium-sized woman with soft brown hair worn in a casual style.

She rummaged in her knitting bag and pulled out a circular knitting needle, like a length of flexible wire twisted into a loop, with ends like conventional knitting needles. "Was that really true—what the *Register* said about the murder weapon?" She tugged at the ends to tighten the loop, then grimaced, and said, "I guess you could choke someone with it."

"It was," Bettina said, "but Clayborn's not planning to interview all the knitters in town, though he did ask me if circular needles are common."

"Well, that's a relief." Holly smiled, but too faintly to evoke her usual dimple.

"However, he *has* been talking to the other gardeners," Bettina added.

"Resentments simmering in the garden plots?" Roland spoke up suddenly. "I've never thought the community gardens were a good idea. People are all for socialistic ideas like sharing public land for free until they actually do it."

Nell stirred and opened her eyes, which had been closed ever since Bettina first spoke. "The community garden program has been going for decades," she declared. "This . . . horrible event . . . could have happened anywhere."

"But it happened in one of the garden plots." Roland set his knitting down, obviously warming to his topic.

"The community gardens enable people who don't have land of their own to grow their own fresh vegetables," Nell said firmly.

"And Jenny was writing that book," Claire chimed in. "*Grow, Cook, Eat*, all about healthy food and growing your own."

"Does Detective Clayborn think one of the other gardeners did it?" Karen whispered, her pale eyes wide.

"No suspects yet," Bettina said, "but of course he wanted to find out if anyone saw or heard anything."

"And did they?" Roland asked.

"Apparently not." Bettina shook her head and her earrings swayed from side to side. "A few people were still working in their plots at sundown and no one saw or heard anything suspicious. But the murder seems to have happened *at* the garden plot—because there was evidence of a struggle. Some of the tomato seedlings had been uprooted."

"She was still at work past sundown, then? And the

killer somehow knew she'd be there?" Holly leaned forward again.

Bettina nodded, and her earrings swayed from front to back. "It happened sometime after sundown but before Marlene Pepper showed up the next morning. Clayborn said the ME might be able to give a more specific time, though it makes sense she wouldn't have kept working once it really got dark." Bettina twisted her brightly painted lips into a rueful smile. "It's just a blessing, like Marlene said, that Jenny's mother wasn't the one to find her."

"A blessing," Claire agreed. "They shared the plot, but Jenny liked the idea of living on her own. What twenty-something wants to have to tell Mom where she's going and what she's doing all the time? And she was supporting herself quite well, working for that local caterer."

"Poor Janice!" Absent the good cheer that so suited her features, Bettina scarcely resembled herself. "Losing a child . . . I just can't imagine . . ."

"Do you think it was a random killing?" Holly's large eyes grew larger. "Or could Jenny have had an enemy?"

Claire gasped. "A jilted boyfriend, perhaps! She was so *very* pretty, beautiful even—"

Sitting next to her, Pamela had sensed Nell growing more and more restless. Now Nell lowered her knitting to her lap and half rose. "This is not constructive," she said sternly. Her faded eyes, which were usually kind, had become stern too, and she shifted her gaze from Bettina to Holly to Claire and back to Bettina.

It was hard to tell which of them appeared more chastened, but Claire resumed studying her knitting magazine and Bettina made a great show of picking up her needles, from which dangled the beginnings of something fashioned from taupe-colored yarn, and launching a new stitch. Nell lowered herself back onto the love seat and returned to her knitting, which Pamela recognized as one of her do-good projects.

When Nell wasn't knitting winter scarves for the Guatemalan day laborers, infant caps for the hospital, or Christmas stockings for those forgotten by Santa, she created knitted animals for the children at the women's shelter in Haversack. At the moment she was working on what Pamela recognized as an oval that would form the body of an elephant, wrought from fuzzy lavender yarn.

For a time there was silence, not a companionable silence but an awkward silence, during which Pamela considered and rejected several conversational gambits. The others were presumably doing the same, searching for just the right fresh, interesting idea to replace the grim topic of Jenny's murder.

CHAPTER 3

It was Holly who spoke first. "It's getting to feel so summery," she observed, looking brightly from person to person.

It was not the freshest idea or the most interesting, but it would serve. A bird in the hand is worth two in the bush, as Bettina's husband, Wilfred, would say.

"Yes, indeed," Roland said. "Good point"—his lean face was as intense as if he was seconding an opinion expressed by one of his corporate lawyer colleagues—"though it won't be officially summer until June 21."

"True," Holly agreed. "And that is a ways in the future."

Everyone nodded sagely.

"It will be here before we know it, though." Claire seemed eager to atone for upsetting Nell by doing her conversational part. "And then"—she paused with eyes

wide and mouth agape as if suddenly taken by surprise—
"Fourth of July will be upon us."

"Ohh!" Holly crooned. She clapped and smiled the
smile that displayed her perfect teeth and brought her
dimple into play. "Fourth of July is almost my favorite
holiday in this amazing town."

"I love it too," Claire agreed. "The parade down
Arborville Avenue—"

"The fireworks—" Holly interrupted.

"The dogs terrified out of their minds." Roland looked
up from his knitting and scowled.

"Oh, Roland!" Bettina turned toward Roland and
scowled back. "You are such a spoilsport. For heaven's
sake, lighten up."

"No," Roland said, and his scowl became more pronounced. "The Fourth of July in Arborville is a huge
waste of taxpayer money. Money for fireworks—which
just goes up in smoke, literally, and extra police on duty,
with extra pay, for the parade. Does anybody at Borough
Hall ask the taxpayers what they think? If they asked me,
I'd tell them." He lowered his knitting into his lap.

"I'm sure you would." Bettina's tone was dry.

"The *Advocate*!" Roland swiveled to face her. "I'll
write a letter to the editor."

"Well, you just do that." Bettina's annoyance gave her
words a taunting edge. She aimed a scowl at Roland that
rivaled his own and tightened her lips into a sarcastic
smile.

"Not that anyone reads the *Advocate*." Roland tossed
off the words as if this were an accepted fact.

"That's not—" Bettina opened her eyes so wide the
whites were visible around the irises. She paused and her

face grew red. She panted slightly as if struggling to contain herself.

"*I* read it," Holly sang out. "Lots of people read it." She looked around eagerly. "We all do—almost all—and . . . and . . . Nell!"

Pamela felt the love seat jiggle as Nell gave a startled twitch. Holly took a deep breath. Her dark eyes flickered here and there. She's trying to change the subject, Pamela said to herself.

"Gardens!" Holly exclaimed. "It's that time—" She halted, closed her eyes, and raised a pretty hand to her forehead. Her nails, painted metallic blue tonight, glittered.

Karen's lips parted and she inhaled, like a breathy hiccup.

"Not *those* gardens," Holly amended quickly. "Nell, I mean *your* garden."

Nell was a skilled gardener, and a large portion of her backyard was devoted to her craft: rows of root vegetables, beans and peas climbing on poles, bushy tomato plants, rampant vines bearing squash of all sorts, and sweet-smelling clusters of herbs.

"Well"—Nell smiled, understanding Holly's aim—"not much is happening yet. But I do have rhubarb, just about ready to cut. It reappears in the same spot every year whether I want it or not."

"*Rhubarb!*" Holly exclaimed, as if the word was magic. "And I'll bet you have a million recipes . . ."

"Not a million"—Nell smiled again, indulgently—"and it takes a great deal of sugar to make it palatable. But in the old days, before supermarkets carried every fruit and vegetable at every season, people were happy enough to see it—after a winter of potatoes and onions and things like rutabagas."

Holly was gazing at Nell with something like adoration.

"I have plenty," Nell said, "so if anybody wants rhubarb . . ."

"Oh, I do!" Holly clapped her hands. "Yes, please. And a recipe."

"Anyone else?" Nell looked around.

Bettina had recovered from her pique and eagerly claimed a batch for Wilfred, and by the time everyone had spoken, Nell had promised rhubarb to all the Knit and Nibblers except Roland.

Roland, however, appeared resolved to be on his best behavior. "I'll look forward to tasting your creations," he said. "That is . . . I don't mean that you have to . . ."

Pamela was happy to help Roland work toward redemption. "I'll make something for Knit and Nibble," she proposed. "The next time we're at my house."

"Pies," Nell said. "Pies are what people usually make."

Knitters took up their knitting again, all but Pamela. Her eyes strayed to the retro sunburst clock that gleamed against the dramatic graphite color of Holly's living room walls. Roland was usually such a conscientious time-keeper, checking his watch on the stroke of eight p.m. and reminding everyone that it was time for the nibble portion of the evening. But the clock's minute hand indicated that eight p.m. had come and gone five minutes earlier, and Roland was still laboring industriously at his project.

Holly glanced up at the clock then too, and suddenly she was on her feet, hurrying toward her dining room and the kitchen beyond. Roland paused his knitting then and pushed back his immaculate shirt cuff to consult his impressive watch. He looked up with such a forlorn expression that Pamela, had she been sitting closer to him, would have given him a comforting pat.

The clatters and clunks coming from the kitchen made it clear that Holly was preparing to serve the coffee, tea, and sweet treat that the person whose turn it was to host Knit and Nibble customarily provided. Bettina was on her feet then, and Pamela followed her through the dining room, but Holly met them in her kitchen doorway.

"It's all under control," she said with one of her dimply smiles, "and it's going to be amazing." She gestured toward her dining room table, which was pale wood with Scandinavian-inspired lines. "We'll eat in here instead of holding plates in our laps, because it's going to be kind of . . . saucy." In the center of the table, a matching cream and sugar set waited, chrome like Holly's elegant chrome coffeepot, and a large serving fork and spoon. The table was set with cups and saucers, and forks, spoons, and napkins, all arranged on turquoise placemats, with a stack of small plates next to the place setting at the head. Based on the smells coming from the kitchen, it was also going to be sugary and buttery, with a hint of orange.

The dinnerware was different from the Melmac that Holly, who loved all things from the 1950s, had proudly brought forth on previous occasions.

Holly noticed Pamela studying the stack of small plates. "Awesome pattern, isn't it?" she exclaimed. "EBay, of course." She glanced toward the kitchen. The sugary and buttery smells were getting more intense. "I've got to get back," she said, and darted away.

The plate was a simple glazed pottery disk that curved up slightly at the rim, but over its surface careened abstract shapes that resembled tiny spacecraft or flying saucers.

"Please tell them to come to the table," Holly called from the kitchen as the rich aroma of brewing coffee mingled with the other smells, and a teakettle hooted.

Pamela stepped into the arch that separated Holly's living room from her dining room—the layout of Holly's house, like many houses in Arborville, was just like Pamela's—and announced that people were invited to put their knitting aside and take seats at the table.

"At the table," Claire murmured as she rose and followed Karen around the back of the sofa and through the arch. "So fancy."

Roland had risen too but he stood aside with a gallant air as Nell made her way to the dining room. Holly peeked from her kitchen doorway as they seated themselves, leaving the spot at the table's head for their hostess. Then she stepped back into the kitchen and emerged carrying her sleek chrome coffeepot in one hand and a squat teapot in the other. She set the teapot before Nell, commenting, "It may need to steep a bit more," and circled the table pouring coffee into the streamlined cups that matched the vintage eBay plates for the coffee-drinkers.

The buttery-sugary aroma with its hint of orange was almost overwhelmingly seductive at this point. Holly darted back to the kitchen. When she emerged again, she was carrying a curious brass stand—four curved legs supporting a ring into which something was obviously intended to fit. Suspended beneath the ring was a small metal container above which a blue flame blazed.

"Oh my goodness!" Nell exclaimed with a chuckle. "A chafing dish. They were all the rage when I was a young married in the fifties. And I can guess what you're about to serve"—she raised a finger to her lips—"but I won't spoil your surprise."

Holly rewarded her with a particularly dimpled smile and a heartfelt "Nell, you are awesome!"

She darted back to the kitchen and returned bearing an object like a particularly elegant skillet, gleaming copper with a wooden handle. She lowered it into the brass stand and Pamela got a glimpse of the contents—delicate crêpes folded to form triangles, overlapping one another in a pattern like the spokes of a wheel. They were golden brown and bathed in a buttery sauce that gave them a seductive luster.

Holly produced a long wooden match from somewhere, struck a light, and touched the match to the surface of the crêpes. With a poof, flames leapt up and hovered, blue at the base and flickering orange at the tips.

"Crêpes suzettes," Holly exclaimed gleefully. "Flambé! With Grand Marnier!"

"I thought I smelled orange," Bettina commented.

"Wherever did you get that . . . what is it? Chafing dish?" Claire asked as the flames subsided.

"A tag sale," Holly said, "at a grand house in Timberley." Incomes rose as one traveled north, and Timberley was directly above Arborville. Nice as Arborville was, Timberley was nicer.

Holly scooped two of the folded triangles out of the chafing dish and deposited them on a plate from the stack in front of her, then she dipped the spoon back into the chafing dish and added a generous portion of the buttery sauce. She handed the plate to Karen, who was sitting on her left. Karen passed it to Claire, who passed it to Nell.

Holly continued to serve as people oohed and aahed

and held out their hands as plates with their tantalizing cargo made their way down one side of the table and then the other.

When she'd nearly finished serving, Holly paused and, with a sly smile, remarked, "Sometimes crêpes suzettes are served with a dollop of vanilla ice cream."

Bettina's eyes widened and her brightly painted lips— a vibrant pink that contrasted with her scarlet hair— parted. Holly had resumed scooping crêpes from the chafing dish, but she tipped her head toward Bettina, who was sitting on her right, closest to the kitchen door, and said, "It's in the freezer, and there's another big spoon out on the counter."

An hour later, Bettina pulled up in front of Pamela's house. "I don't know why people speak of the 1950s so scornfully," she commented. "Those crêpes suzettes were incredible. And flambé! So dramatic!"

CHAPTER 4

On this May morning, Pamela opened her eyes as sunlight set the white eyelet curtains at her bedroom windows aglow. Her bedmates, burrowed deep into the shadowy coziness of her bedclothes, continued to slumber. Only as she pushed herself into a sitting position with her pillow scrunched against her brass headboard did she feel a whisper against her ankle that told her at least one other being was stirring in the Paterson household.

The stealthy softness made its way along her leg and in a moment a pair of amber eyes were gazing at her from a furry black face.

"Catrina," she murmured. "Where's your daughter?"

As if in answer, a second pair of eyes joined the first, jade green this time, as the head of Catrina's ginger-colored daughter—named Ginger, of course—emerged from beneath sheet and blanket.

"You're hungry, I suppose." Pamela addressed them both. Their lithe bodies slipped from beneath the covers and they stepped daintily over their mistress and leapt to the floor. Pamela pulled her summer robe over her pajamas, slid her feet into her slippers, and followed the cats out into the hall. They all proceeded down the stairs to the kitchen, where the soft yellow walls glowed even more yellow in the morning sunlight.

The first order of business was to open a fresh can of chicken giblet blend and scoop it into a fresh bowl to be placed in the corner of the kitchen where the cats were accustomed to receive their meals. Then Pamela refreshed their water bowl and measured water into her kettle for her morning coffee. Once the kettle had been placed on the stove with a flame alight under it, she hurried out the front door and down the walk to fetch the *County Register*.

The *Register*'s ace reporter, Marcy Brewer, was indefatigable, but Pamela doubted that she'd been able to extract any more details from Detective Clayborn than Bettina had, and Bettina had told the Knit and Nibblers everything she knew the previous evening. Besides, she and Bettina had heard the crime-scene details firsthand from Marlene Pepper, who had discovered the murder. So she left the *Register* shrouded in its flimsy plastic wrapping as she set about preparing her breakfast.

She measured coffee beans into her grinder and set a paper filter in the plastic cone that fit atop her carafe. The kettle began to whistle as she pressed on the grinder's cover to set it in motion. For a few moments, the whir and clatter of coffee beans in the grinder's chamber supplied percussion for the kettle's melody. She tipped the grinder's fragrant contents into the filter and followed up with the now boiling water from the kettle, which hissed as it flowed from the spout. As the water dripped and the coffee brewed, Pamela slipped a piece of whole-grain bread from the Co-Op Grocery into the toaster.

Soon she had poured a cup of coffee and buttered a piece of toast and she was sitting at her kitchen table with her usual breakfast before her. The meal was simple, but the cup and saucer for the coffee and the plate for the toast were from the rose-garlanded set that had been Pamela's wedding-gift china. She saw no point in having nice things if the things seldom came out of the cupboard and were only to be left behind once one was gone. Besides, most of her other nice things were treasures salvaged from tag sales and thrift stores.

She took a cautious sip of the coffee, which was still very hot, and slipped the *Register* from its flimsy plastic. As she'd anticipated, the "Arborville Community Garden Murder" took up a few generous columns on the *Register*'s front page. She skimmed the article as she nibbled her toast. All the details she already knew about were there—the victim's identity, the murder weapon, the fact that the murder happened after sundown right in the garden plot where "fellow gardener and chair of the Arborville community garden program Marlene Pepper" found the body the next morning. The *Register* had, however, tracked down a photo of the victim as she had been in life, a tall young woman with strikingly attractive features and dark hair.

She sighed and tried to distract herself by setting Part 1 aside and turning to Lifestyle, which always had a food feature on Wednesday. RHUBARB, the headline announced, IS NOT JUST FOR PIES. This indeed was a distraction and she read the article with pleasure. One could make relishes, it seemed, and rhubarb pickles. And on the subject of food—she glanced at the grocery list held fast to the door of her refrigerator by means of a magnet in the shape of a mitten—Penny would be arriving home from college for the summer that Friday and a special meal had to be planned. Maybe—

Pamela jumped from her chair, startling Ginger, who had been playing with a catnip mouse. The mouse had long since lost the aura of catnip that had made it a particularly enticing toy, but its long tail still twitched in an interesting manner as the mouse was batted here and there over the black and white ceramic tiles of the kitchen floor.

Penny would know about the murder. Many of her fellow students at her college in Boston were from Arborville's environs, and Penny's high school friend Lorie Hopkins was away at another college but kept close tabs on doings at home.

Back upstairs in her office, Pamela brought her computer to life, clicked on SYNC, and watched as the tally of emails in her inbox rose to seven.

Yes, as she had expected and feared, a message from Penny Paterson awaited. "Mom," Penny wrote, "I just found out about that woman being strangled with a knitting needle in Arborville. I know none of the people in Knit and Nibble would do such a thing but I hope that detective won't decide they could. And I especially hope that since there's a knitting needle involved you and Bettina won't decide you can do a better job than the police."

Curiously, Pamela and Bettina had on occasion puzzled out solutions to crimes that had mystified Detective Clayborn and the Arborville police force. But in response to Penny's message, Pamela wrote, "You do not need to worry, and I'll see you this Friday and the sweater is almost finished. Love, Mom."

The other emails included a message from the college Pamela had graduated from announcing that the current president was stepping down and a search for a replacement was in progress, an offer of coupons from the hobby store, and a solicitation from a charity that rescued orphaned elephants. The only one that required immediate attention, aside from the one from Penny, was the email marked with the paperclip symbol that indicated it included attachments.

That message was from Pamela's boss at *Fiber Craft*, the magazine for which Pamela worked, mostly from home, as associate editor. Her main tasks were to help evaluate submissions and copy-edit the articles selected for publication, and from time to time she was asked to review a book. Today was one of those times.

Her boss's message read, "Please read the attached articles and let me know by Monday which ones you think are suitable for *Fiber Craft*. Also I'm sending you by FedEx Alison McDermott's new book on sustainable fashion for review. I want to run the review in the upcoming issue so get busy as soon as it arrives because I need that back Monday too."

Only three articles were attached, something about paisley, something about rayon, and something about mathematics, to judge by the abbreviated titles ranged with the paperclip symbols and Word logos across the top of the message. The application of mathematics to knitting seemed curious—though of course knitters did have to be able to count—so Pamela opened the file to see the full title: "The Mathematics and Mechanics of Knitting: Untangling the Web." The author was a woman who identified herself as a professor of physics in her byline. Definitely a change from most *Fiber Craft* submissions, Pamela reflected. That one sounded especially intriguing, but the first item on the agenda was a trip to the Co-Op Grocery. And there were tomatoes and basil to be planted, fetched from the garden center the previous weekend and waiting on the back porch. The tomatoes would go in the one spot in Pamela's yard that got a reliable amount of sun. If she had more sun, she would grow more things, but the appeal of homegrown tomatoes harvested just before eating was so great that she devoted her entire sunny spot to her tomato crop.

Back in her bedroom across the hall, Pamela exchanged her robe and pajamas for a pair of jeans and a simple blouse, and her slippers for a pair of sandals. She stepped into the bathroom to comb her hair, which was brown and straight and which she wore hanging loose to her shoulders or pulled back with a clip.

Catrina was a creature of habit. If the day was bright, she claimed the patch of sunlight that reliably set the colors of the thrift-store carpet in the entry aglow each morning. Now she looked up as Pamela descended the stairs, then closed her eyes till they were only amber slits, and yielded again to the pleasure of her nap.

Pamela collected her shopping list from the refrigerator door, her purse from the kitchen counter, and a few canvas bags from the closet. The bags were gifts from Nell, who had long ago impressed on her friends the importance of eschewing paper and plastic. She still hadn't decided what the welcome meal for Penny would be, but she would ponder menu possibilities on her walk uptown.

* * *

Arborville was small, and walkable. Its commercial district, anchored by the Co-Op at the south end, stretched along a few blocks of Arborville Avenue and could be reached on foot from Orchard Street, where Pamela and Bettina lived, in about fifteen minutes. As young marrieds looking for a place to settle, Pamela and her husband, Michael, had been charmed by the town's hundred-year-old houses and tree-lined streets, which had reminded them of the college town where they met and fell in love.

Michael's architectural training had helped them restore a fixer-upper to its former glory. When he was gone Pamela had stayed on in the house, raising her daughter in an environment as close as Pamela could manage to the one Penny had known when both her parents were alive.

As she walked up to the corner where Arborville Avenue intersected with Orchard Street, Pamela enjoyed the balmy May day. The past week had transformed her neighbors' yards. The shrubs that bordered expanses of newly green grass now bore drifts of blossoms in shades ranging from palest pink to deep maroon.

At the corner where a stately brick apartment building faced Arborville Avenue, she detoured into the building's parking lot. A discreet wooden fence shielded the building's trash cans from the eyes of passersby, and it also hid larger objects, like cast-off chairs or interesting pottery, that apartment dwellers no longer wanted. Pamela had rescued various treasures over the years and her daily walks often included a peek behind the fence to see what was new. Today, however, there was nothing of note and she continued on her way.

The Co-Op Grocery, with its cramped aisles and creaking wooden floors, recalled an earlier era, but it suited the atmosphere of Arborville's small commercial district. Narrow storefronts with awnings and old-fashioned signage offered basic goods and services, like hair styling, stationery supplies, and liquor. Their second floors—none was higher than two stories—housed apartments and offices.

The Co-Op's automatic door, a modern touch that had been added long after the Co-Op was founded, swung open as Pamela approached, and soon she was wheeling a shopping cart toward the produce section. From among leafy, bulbous, elongated, and knobby offerings, she chose collard greens, cherry tomatoes, a cucumber, and several potatoes.

It had occurred to her on her walk uptown that a pork tenderloin would make a tasty welcome-home meal, with scalloped potatoes and cooked greens. The tenderloin would provide meals beyond Friday's dinner as well.

Accordingly, the next stop was the meat department, from which Pamela went on her way with a tenderloin from a New Jersey farm, swaddled in a sheet of white butcher's paper. At the fish counter, she picked out a piece of salmon for her own dinner that evening. She ventured into the inner aisles then, crossing staples like cat food off her list, and paused at the cheese counter where she debated between Swiss and cheddar and came away with half a pound of each.

She was waiting her turn at the bakery counter when a voice behind her said, "Pamela Paterson?"

She turned to face a woman taller than herself, with gray hair that flowed untamed past her shoulders. A close-fitting, sleeveless T-shirt showed tan and muscular arms to advantage, though the gauzy skirt that swirled

around the woman's ankles hid her legs. She looked somehow familiar and in a moment Pamela realized why.

"You're Bettina's friend, aren't you?" the woman said.
"And I think you know Marlene Pepper."

Pamela mustered her social smile and commanded her
brain to produce a name. But the woman spoke again before Pamela's brain responded.

"Calliope Drew," the woman said, and Pamela nodded.

"Such a shocking thing," Calliope went on. "Poor
Marlene—she's beside herself. And I don't blame her. Of
course a murder doesn't reflect well on the community
garden program. A community garden should be a place
of peace and love. And people will think another gardener killed Jenny—as if we can't get along with each
other."

"I don't think that," Pamela murmured, but Calliope
seemed not to have heard.

"It's an open secret that I had run-ins with Jenny." Calliope's throaty voice faded to a whisper, though obviously an open secret was not much of a secret. Pamela's
glance strayed toward the bakery counter. She had previously been almost next in line to be served but now two
additional people had edged in front of her.

"So I'm afraid"—Calliope continued whispering and
looked around as if to make sure no one nearby was pay-
ing attention—"I'm afraid Clayborn suspects *me*."

"Why would he suspect you?" Calliope was obviously
eager to talk, and now that she had lost her place in line,
Pamela thought she might as well let the woman have her
say.

"The run-ins!" Calliope seemed irritated. "Pay attention! I just said it was an open secret that I had run-ins with Jenny."

"Ummm?"

"Territory!" Calliope exclaimed. "Isn't that the whole history of the human race? Land, land, land. Everyone wants more land."

"Those garden plots seem large enough to grow a lot of food," Pamela said.

"Some of us aren't growing *food*." Calliope's tone implied that growing food was for lesser beings. "Some of us are trying to clothe ourselves without aiding and abetting the fashion industry in its destruction of Mother Earth."

The word *flax* popped into Pamela's mind. She had recently copy-edited an article about processing home-grown flax into usable fibers.

Echoing the voice in Pamela's brain, Calliope sang out "Flax!" Then she lowered her voice. "But it takes a lot of flax to make anything useful and a lot of flax takes a lot of land. And meanwhile Jenny, who hadn't been in the garden program nearly as long as I've been, grabbed up an unclaimed plot in March, even though she already shared one plot with her mother, and planted enough tomato plants to feed an army." Calliope reared back and raised her voice again. "An *invading* army! Because she's writing a cookbook. What's more important? Sustainable clothing or a cookbook?"

"Both?" Pamela ventured. "People do need to eat."

"Well"—Calliope lifted her chin and straightened her spine—"I would never kill a person or any living creature." She leaned close to Pamela again and said in a confiding tone, "I was going to do silkworms, then I realized that you have to kill the silkworms to get the silk. I couldn't do that—murder a silkworm. Could you?"

Pamela shook her head no.

Calliope leaned closer and Pamela took a step back. Calliope was really very tall. "If Clayborn wants to pursue the murderous gardener angle, he should look more closely at Johan Friendly."

A spot opened up at the counter and Pamela edged into it, gesturing toward the loaves displayed along the counter's top and smiling apologetically at Calliope. By the time she had requested a loaf of whole-grain bread and waited while it was sliced and bagged, Calliope had finished her own bakery transaction and gone on her way.

Pamela chose the checkout line for people with fewer than ten items and watched as the conveyor belt transported her groceries into the hands of the checker, who scanned them and passed them along. Then with groceries paid for and apportioned between her two canvas bags she stepped through the automatic door and out onto the sidewalk.

The Co-Op Grocery provided its community with information as well as food. Mounted on its façade was a bulletin board where anyone with an event to promote, a service to offer, or an object to sell (or give away) was welcome to post a notice. Despite the fact that Arborville now had its own Internet chat group, Access-Arborville, the bulletin board persisted, and grocery shoppers and passersby still lingered on the sidewalk to scrutinize the colorful collage formed by its overlapping cards and flyers.

As the automatic door glided closed behind her, Pamela nearly collided with Marlene Pepper, who had evidently been studying the bulletin board and was now heading toward the Co-Op's entrance. Marlene had recovered considerably since the last time Pamela saw her. Her gray-blond bob was tidy and her eyes were no longer red, though her plump features were uncharacteristically mournful.

She mustered her social smile once again, a consoling version of it, and transferred the bag in her right hand to her already burdened left hand so she could offer Marlene an encouraging pat.

"How are you doing?" she inquired.

"Oh, Pamela!" Marlene didn't smile but her expression changed in a way that suggested she was grateful for Pamela's concern. "I know *you* don't blame the community garden program for the"—she paused, closed her eyes, and tightened her lips—"the . . . what happened. But other people do. And on AccessArborville"—she gulped and swallowed—"they're saying it was one of the other gardeners, and I'm sure Clayborn thinks it was one of the other gardeners, and the committee assigns the plots, and sometimes two gardeners want the same plot . . . and . . ."

Pamela nodded sympathetically, tugged Marlene out of the path of a shopper who seemed in a great hurry, and shifted her second bag back to her right hand.

"Calliope Drew is afraid that Clayborn will decide she's the guilty one," Pamela offered, "because she wanted an extra plot for her flax but Jenny grabbed it for tomatoes instead."

"Calliope did make a fuss." Marlene sighed. "But Danielle Hardy is the real troublemaker."

"Oh?" Pamela wasn't a nosy person, but it was hard to resist such a provocative statement.

Marlene grabbed her arm. "You've been up to the community gardens, haven't you?"

Pamela nodded. She'd inspected the garden plots a few times with Bettina when Bettina was reporting on the program for the *Advocate*.

"The plots all get equal amounts of sun, wouldn't you say?"

Pamela nodded again.

"Well!" Marlene twisted her lips into an annoyed knot. "Danielle and Jenny always enter—or, in poor Jenny's case, *entered*—their tomatoes in that tomato competition the *Register* sponsors every year."

Pamela knew about the contest but, not being the competitive type, she'd never entered her own tomatoes. Apparently, though, Danielle *was* the competitive type and Jenny had been—because Marlene went on.

"Jenny's tomatoes always won," she said. "And Danielle was convinced that it was because Jenny's tomatoes got more sun—and then Jenny even claimed the extra plot but absolutely refused to trade plots, or even let Danielle put a few tomato plants in a corner of the extra plot. You should have heard them squabbling—honestly, just like children. Or mean girls in high school."

Tomatoes did like sun. Pamela knew that. Her backyard had only one spot that was sunny enough for her small crop. She pictured the tomato plants waiting, with the basil, on her back porch. She really would have to get busy very soon.

Marlene gazed up at Pamela with a beseeching look that reminded her of her daughter's long-ago entreaties—to stay up a bit later or have one more cookie.

"But they were just squabbles," she insisted. "Nothing to kill a person over. I hope Clayborn will realize that and look elsewhere for the killer. Maybe you and Bettina could . . ."

Burdened again with a bag in each hand, Pamela couldn't accompany her words with an encouraging pat. But she strove to make up for that with an expression that creased her forehead and softened her mouth.

"I'm positive Detective Clayborn will soon get to the bottom of things," she said, though secretly she *wasn't* positive at all. But Penny was coming home Friday and didn't approve of her mother's sleuthing, so the mystery would have to remain in the hands of Arborville's police.

Seeming consoled, Marlene continued in the direction she had been heading and disappeared through the Co-Op's automatic door. Pamela set out along Arborville Avenue toward Orchard Street.

CHAPTER 5

The canvas bags were growing heavy and Pamela sped up her pace as she turned the corner onto her own street. She passed several attractive houses the same vintage as her own, with their wraparound porches and little dormer windows up above and their wide yards shaded by huge trees like those in her yard.

As she approached Bettina's house, which as an original Dutch Colonial was even older than its neighbors, she prepared to cross to her own side of the street. But a voice accosted her from Bettina's front porch.

"Pamela! Oh, Pamela!" the voice called.

Pamela paused and turned. The figure calling to her wasn't Bettina, or Wilfred. She had to think for a minute to bring a name to mind. Then she realized—yes—the person calling to her was Danielle Hardy. The tomato-grower Marlene had just been telling her about.

Danielle scurried down Bettina's driveway and in a moment she was standing breathlessly at Pamela's side, her slender body vibrating with energy.

"I was just talking to Bettina," she trilled. Her speaking voice was curious, almost operatic, rising and falling in pitch like an aria.

"The *Advocate*, you know, and she has Detective Clayborn's *ear*. So I wanted to make *sure*—" Danielle gazed at Pamela, her large pale eyes open unnaturally wide. "I know everyone thinks I *hated* Jenny, but I *didn't*. Not at *all*."

"The tomatoes," Pamela heard herself murmur, though she was longing to escape from Danielle, cross the street to her own house, and deposit her grocery bags on her kitchen table.

"I would *not* kill a person because of *tomatoes*!" Danielle's body tensed and she clenched her fists, as if offering to box. Pamela took a hurried step back. "And besides," Danielle added, "I was home with my husband from sundown *Monday* night to midmorning *Tuesday*."

Pamela nodded and edged toward the street.

But Danielle hadn't finished. "*So*"—her voice soared—"the police should look more closely at *Johan Friendly*." She grabbed Pamela's arm. "I told *Bettina* and now I'm telling you. It's all about that corn of his."

And she was off, scurrying up the sidewalk with her head erect and her arms swinging rhythmically at her sides.

It's all about that corn of his? Pamela felt her brow wrinkle. The mystery was drawing her in despite her best intentions. Instead of crossing the street, she made her way up Bettina's driveway.

Bettina opened the door before she had a chance to ring.

"I was watching through the window," Bettina said by way of greeting, as she held out her hands to relieve Pamela of her grocery bags. "Danielle does go on." She set the grocery bags on a nearby chair.

Bettina was wearing one of her tunic-and-leggings outfits, in a springlike shade of green with cheerful bands of daisies at hem, cuffs, and neckline. A whisper of eye shadow in the same shade of green accented her hazel eyes. Her lips and nails were a bright scarlet that nearly matched her hair.

"I think there's still some coffee left." Bettina glanced toward the arch that led to her dining room and the kitchen beyond. "Or I could make more."

"I've got to get home with these groceries," Pamela said, "but who's Johan Friendly? Danielle thinks he could be a suspect."

Bettina shrugged. "The name sounds familiar, but I can't think why. Maybe something to do with the *Advocate*."

"I guess he grows corn up at the community gardens," Pamela said.

Woofus peeked around the corner from the dining room and then retreated toward the kitchen.

Bettina nodded. "According to Danielle, it's his main crop. And Danielle says she overheard a huge argument between him and Jenny about whether he planned to plant it again this year. Jenny called it his 'evil' corn."

"Evil?"

"According to Danielle." Bettina shrugged.

"How can corn be evil?"

Bettina shrugged again.

"Did Danielle tell Detective Clayborn about the argument?" Pamela asked.

"If she did, he didn't take it seriously. He interviewed all the gardeners and he didn't have any suspects when I talked to him."

A scuffle of feet and the clicking sound of a dog's toenails against the floor drew Pamela's and Bettina's attention toward the dining room. Wilfred Fraser was just stepping through the arch, dressed in the bib overalls he had adopted as a uniform when he retired. At his side was Woofus, the dog's large shaggy body pressed against Wilfred's thigh. In his hand Wilfred held a leash.

"How are you, Pamela?" Wilfred's genial expression became even more genial as a smile transformed his ruddy face. He bent his gaze toward Bettina. "Woofus and I are heading out for our morning constitutional, dear wife. However—I couldn't help overhearing—I can answer one of the questions that is vexing you."

"How can corn be evil?" Pamela's voice was hopeful.

Wilfred shook his head no. At his side Woofus gave a restless twitch and Wilfred calmed him with a pat. "But I do know who Johan Friendly is. He has an office above one of the shops on Arborville Avenue. He's a lawyer, but not like Roland. Just wills and deeds and things like that."

He and Woofus started toward the door, with Woofus casting nervous glances at Pamela all the while. But Wilfred paused with his hand on the doorknob.

"Curious," he observed, raising an eyebrow, "that Danielle was so eager to point out that another gardener might have a motive for Jenny's murder too."

"It is curious," Pamela agreed.

"She has an alibi, though—that is if Clayborn wanted

to follow up." Bettina's slight frown suggested she wasn't impressed with his handling of the case so far. "She was home Monday night with her husband."

"Not *all* of Monday night." Wilfred shook his head. "Danielle might have been at home, but her husband was at the historical society meeting till nine. I came home then but I suspect he went out for beer with the guys afterward."

"Danielle is little," Bettina commented, "but I'll bet she's strong. She's always inviting me to sign up for one of those martial arts classes that she takes." She tipped her head to survey her ample waistline. "I suppose the exercise might do me some good."

"Dear wife!" Wilfred sounded genuinely alarmed. "You could not be more beautiful!"

Woofus was getting genuinely restless now, whimpering and nudging at the door with a paw. Wilfred gave the doorknob a twist and tugged the door open. Woofus sprang out onto the porch and with a wave Wilfred followed him.

"So," Pamela said as the door closed behind Wilfred and his shaggy companion, "at least three of the gardeners have motives—Danielle with the tomatoes, Johan Friendly with the corn, and Calliope Drew." She quickly described her encounter with Calliope at the Co-Op. "And Detective Clayborn talked to all the gardeners. Numerous people must have told him about the squabbles over plots."

"I know." Bettina nodded. The tendrils of her scarlet hair vibrated and her earrings, jade pendants the same shade of green as her outfit, swayed. "But for some reason he's not considering any of them suspects."

"They all had a motive," Pamela said, feeling a wrin-

kle form between her brows. "And they all had opportunity too. They could easily have known that Jenny often
stayed to work on her plot after everyone else had gone
home."

"There's means, though." A matching wrinkle formed
between Bettina's brows, which were more carefully
shaped than Pamela's. "Why would a killer choose a circular knitting needle for a weapon unless the killer was a
knitter?"

"That's what I was thinking." Pamela sighed. "Detective Clayborn must have satisfied himself that none of the
gardeners are knitters. And luckily none of the town's
knitters—at least those we know of—have plots at the
community gardens."

"But why would a person get so agitated about corn?"
Bettina asked, twisting her lips into a curious knot. Her
expression brightened. "My editor might like a story
about the community gardens for the *Advocate*—after
Clayborn has brought the killer to justice, of course. But I
could get a head start."

"Of course," Pamela agreed with a conspiratorial
smile. "Johan Friendly will probably be in his office tomorrow morning. How about ten a.m.?"

At home, Pamela put her groceries away, checked her
email, and made a grilled cheese sandwich with some of
the cheddar she had just brought home. Once she'd finished eating, two contrasting tasks beckoned. There were
articles to evaluate and there were tomatoes and basil to
plant. The following day would most likely bring a
FedExed copy of the book on sustainable fashion that she

was to review, so she really shouldn't dawdle over getting the articles read.

But the day was so bright, and Mother's Day—which gardeners in New Jersey recognized as the start of the tomato-planting season—had come and gone. So she'd devote an hour or so to transferring her basil to a larger pot and giving her tomato plants a good start in the yard. Then she would settle down at her computer with "The Mathematics and Mechanics of Knitting: Untangling the Web."

Pamela plunged her garden trowel into the ground and turned over a small heap of moist soil, fragrant with a dark earthiness and complete with an undulating worm. She shaped the hole deeper and wider, and blended in a bit of composted manure from a sack stored in the garage. Then she freed a tomato plant from its plastic pot, nestled it into the hole, scooped soil around its root ball, and pressed the soil into place with her fingers.

She worked meditatively, enjoying the feel of the sun on her back. This was the same sun that would encourage her small tomato garden to produce the homegrown tomatoes that, starting in late summer, would add their seductive acidity to her meals.

The sunny spot in Pamela's backyard was only large enough for five tomato plants and a stand of daylilies that returned year after year with no encouragement at all. Huge trees cast their shade over most of the lawn, and the borders of azaleas and rhododendron were happy with a few hours of sun in morning and late afternoon.

When Pamela had finished, four spindly plants formed a square with the fifth in the center. She lowered a wire tomato cage over each. Each plant now had only a few of the hairy leaves with their delicate scalloped lobes. But she knew that soon the tiny plants would shoot up and out and long vine-like branches would trail on the ground if they weren't supported by a cage.

Later, hands scrubbed of dirt, Pamela worked at her computer until Catrina appeared at her office door to remind her that it was dinnertime for both humans and cats. While the cats got their favorite chicken-fish blend, Pamela herself ate unalloyed fish—salmon, with brown rice and a green salad. The leftovers would be plenty for the next night.

After dinner she settled onto her sofa, a cat at each side, with her knitting. As a British mystery unfolded on the screen before her, she took up the sweater sleeve she'd been working on the previous night at Knit and Nibble. A few inches remained to do at the shoulder, in the pale blue that formed one of the stripes, and she set to work.

Once the sleeve was done, all she'd have to do was sew the pieces together, and the sweater would be ready to present to Penny when she arrived home on Friday afternoon.

The next morning, Pamela was sitting at her computer enjoying once again the illustrations that had made "Paisley Power: A Decorative Motif's Journey from Persia to the Beatles" so appealing. She reread her enthusiastic recommendation that *Fiber Craft* print the article, along with her recommendation of "The Mathematics and Mechanics of Knitting." The author of "Rayon: Silk for the Masses" had taken on a topic that deserved a book and tried to do justice to it in twenty pages, and Pamela suggested that the article be focused on the discovery of the process that turned wood pulp into silklike fibers, with perhaps future articles to come.

She had just clicked on SEND to dispatch her comments to her boss when the telephone's ring startled her. She swiveled in her chair to reach for it, and that motion caused Ginger to spring from her lap.

"Pamela?" The voice on the phone was familiar but not immediately recognizable—though perhaps it was only the urgent tone that made the caller hard to identify.

Before Pamela had a chance to say "Yes," the voice went on. "It's Marlene Pepper, Bettina's friend. She said I should call you—that maybe you could help. Because Woofus, you know, has his problems . . ."

Pamela felt her brow wrinkle. Where could this be going? But she mustered the vocal equivalent of her social smile and said, "I'll try. What—?"

Marlene interrupted, words flowing out as if she was eager to include all the details before her listener could object that perhaps she wasn't the best choice for the task at hand.

"There's a cat," Marlene said. "Poor Jenny had a cat, and her apartment is a crime scene, and her neighbor, Helen, has been taking care of it but she can't, any longer. And Jenny's mother, Janice, is too sad to take it because it would just remind her of poor Jenny. And Bettina"—Marlene was becoming a bit breathless—"has Woofus and Punkin, and Woofus gets nervous when there's more than one cat in the house." She was silent then, except for a gasp and a few pants.

"The cat needs a place to stay?" Pamela inquired, though she suspected she knew the answer.

"Its name is Precious." Marlene's confident tone suggested she took Pamela's question for an answer to her own unspoken plea. "I'll let Helen know you'll be over this morning."

CHAPTER 6

"I was going to come and warn you as soon as I got dressed." Bettina greeted Pamela at the door wearing a silky robe in a delicate floral print. Her face was free of makeup and her hair was a mass of careless waves. She studied Pamela's expression. "I guess Marlene couldn't wait. It's an imposition, I know."

Pamela hadn't been aware that her expression suggested anything more than pleasure at the sight of her friend. She didn't think she had been frowning. But perhaps the impending errand—for, yes, she did intend to give Precious a temporary home—had lent her features an unaccustomed intensity. So she smiled.

"I don't mind," she said. "But you'll come with me, won't you? We can stop by there on our way to Johan Friendly's office. It's right in the same block."

"I'm not walking, though." Bettina looked down at her

fetching satin slippers, pink to match the blossoms on her robe, as if Pamela was about to propose they leave right then and there. "And we'll be carrying a cat back with us besides."

"I'll drive." Pamela laughed. "And we'll take my cat carrier."

Bettina said she could be ready in fifteen minutes and Pamela crossed the street to her own house, where she found a FedEx parcel on her porch. Once inside, she opened it to find the book she was to review, *The Future of Fashion Is Slow: How Fast Fashion Is Destroying the Planet*, by Alison McDermott.

Though Bettina's toilette had been hurried, she appeared at Pamela's front door fifteen minutes later looking chic in a pistachio-green linen ensemble, composed of cropped pants and a belted jacket. She had accessorized it with dark green wedge heels and her jade pendant earrings. Every scarlet hair was in its usual place and her makeup was flawless.

The first words out of Bettina's mouth as Pamela swung the door back were, "I forgot to tell you what else Marlene said."

"What?" Pamela stooped for the cat carrier, which she had staged on the carpet in the entry, causing Catrina to abandon her favorite sunny spot and scurry away. Both cats associated the appearance of the cat carrier with journeys to the vet.

"Jenny's funeral." Bettina stepped back as Pamela crossed the threshold, her purse over her shoulder and the cat carrier in her hand. "It's Friday. Marlene thinks I should go—and I think *we* should go—to see who all turns up and how they act."

"Like Calliope and Danielle?" They had reached Pamela's serviceable compact. She unlocked the trunk and settled the cat carrier inside, then unlocked the passenger-side door for Bettina. "Or Johan Friendly?"

"Marlene doesn't want the killer to turn out to be one of the gardeners," Bettina said as she slipped into her seat.

"I know," Pamela responded. "But the only people who will be at the funeral will be people who had some connection with Jenny—or her mother."

Bettina waited until Pamela circled the car and took her place behind the steering wheel to say, "We'll just have to see what we can see."

"And hear," Pamela added.

They headed up Orchard Street, past yards made glorious by drifts of azaleas and rhododendrons in every shade from palest yellow through salmon, pink, and fuchsia, to deep maroon. At the corner, Pamela turned left, and soon (very soon—the distance was one Pamela could walk in ten minutes) they were cruising past the Co-Op and nosing into a parking space in front of the hardware store.

Their destination was an inconspicuous door between the hardware store, with its window display of gardening tools and sacks of potting soil, topsoil, and fertilizer, and the neighboring nail salon. The two doorbells in the doorframe offered a choice between J. Miller and H. Lindquist. Bettina rang the bell for H. Lindquist and a moment later a low buzz and a click indicated that H. Lindquist had approved her callers.

The door opened onto a steep and narrow stairway that

was nonetheless freshly painted, with carpeted steps. They emerged at the top to find a young woman standing in an open doorway at the end of a short hall. The hallway's other door was crisscrossed with yellow crime-scene tape.

"Thank you, thank you so much," the young woman said as she caught sight of the cat carrier. "I'd love to keep her but I just can't."

She stood aside, beckoned Pamela and Bettina to enter, and followed them into her apartment. The living room was sparsely furnished but pleasant, with a small sofa made cheerful by the addition of a patchwork quilt cleverly draped and folded to hide most of its worn up-holstery. Other furniture included a square wooden table with four wooden chairs arranged around it and a tall wooden bookcase that held books, stacks of magazines, and some interesting pieces of pottery. A coffee table that looked like it had been someone's woodworking project was piled with odds and ends that a desk might have ac-commodated, had the apartment's furnishings included a desk.

Helen Lindquist was quite striking, tall and slender with jet-black hair that fell unimpeded nearly to her waist. Her outfit—leggings and an oversized T-shirt with holes in it—suggested she hadn't yet dressed for anything that would require her to venture outdoors.

"Please sit down," she said, gesturing toward the sofa, "and I'll see where Precious has gotten to." She paused. "Or would you like coffee first? I can make some coffee. It's just instant, but—" She turned and took a step toward an open door through which Pamela could glimpse a stove. Through an open door in the opposite wall an un-made bed was visible.

"No, no." Pamela waved the hand that wasn't holding the cat carrier as if to banish the idea, but gently. "You don't have to. Really."

Helen swiveled. "You're sure? It won't be any—" She interrupted herself to sigh and then sank into one of the wooden chairs. "This has all been so . . . the police . . . and poor Jenny. I didn't know her that well, but . . ." She closed her eyes and breathed deeply, in and out. "And her poor, poor mother. Do you think the police will ever figure out who did this awful thing?"

Pamela could sense that Bettina was about to hurry across the room and engage in some very Bettina-like comforting. But at that moment, a pale streak darted from the kitchen in pursuit of a ball of yarn, which rolled under the coffee table and then disappeared beneath the sofa.

The creature skidded to a halt and was revealed to be a gorgeous Siamese cat whose luminous body was accented by a sable-colored face, legs, and tail.

The focus of Bettina's attention changed and she stooped to where the cat now stood on the carpet that covered most of the floor. "You must be Precious," she cooed, extending a hand.

The cat regarded her suspiciously and raised a dark paw to bat the hand away. Then it veered off and retreated to the bedroom.

"She can be a little shy," Helen said, "but for some reason she took to me right away, even though I hadn't ever spent much time in Jenny's apartment."

Pamela, meanwhile, had set the cat carrier down near the coffee table and accepted Helen's invitation to have a seat. Instead of joining Pamela on the sofa, Bettina moved one of the wooden chairs closer to the chair occupied by Helen and lowered herself into it. She reached for the hand that Helen had rested on the table and gave it a squeeze.

"Even when you don't know someone well it's a terrible shock to hear they've been murdered." Bettina gave a shudder. "And when you're a pretty young woman and the someone is another pretty young woman who was your actual neighbor, well . . ." Bettina squeezed Helen's hand harder and leaned over to put an arm around her shoulder. "Of course you're upset," she murmured.

Helen *was* pretty, beautiful even. Her face was a perfect oval. Her dark brows arched over expressive eyes almost—it seemed to Pamela—the same amber shade as Catrina's. Even without lipstick, her lips were rosy and well-shaped, with a pronounced bow.

They sat like that for a few minutes and the room was silent. Perhaps thinking that the intruders had gone, Precious emerged from the bedroom and crept cautiously toward Helen's chair.

"That is one beautiful cat," Bettina whispered. Helen nodded. "It's a shame you can't keep her," Bettina went on. She retracted her arm from Helen's shoulder and drew back. "You're not allergic or anything, are you?" She studied Helen's face as if searching for the telltale itchy eyes or runny nose of an allergy sufferer.

"No." Helen shook her head. "It's just that I don't know how long I'm going to stay in Arborville. I'd hate to have her get used to me only to have to be put up for adoption again."

"Arborville is fine for us old folks." Bettina's expression brightened. "But the kids who grow up here often head for the city as soon as they can, or some city at least. My oldest lives here but the younger one is in Boston."

Helen nodded. "That's my goal. New York. When you

grow up in a tiny town in Minnesota, and you want something more out of life . . ."

"You're close," Bettina said encouragingly.

"The city is so expensive, though. I'm working on it—a job across the river and a place to live, or a place to live and then a job . . ." She sighed. "I've got a job at the mall now, odd hours but that's okay."

Precious had remained sitting on the carpet at Helen's feet, seemingly undisturbed by the voices as long as none of the intruders made a motion in her direction.

Pamela spoke up from the sofa. "I can certainly offer her a home. It might be a bit of a challenge to entice her into the cat carrier, though." She gestured toward where the cat carrier sat near the coffee table.

Bettina relinquished Helen's hand. "We have another errand in town," she said, "then we'll be back." She started to rise. Precious watched her warily.

Pamela stood up too.

"I'll see what I can do," Helen said as they moved toward the door. She rose too and scooped up Precious, who nuzzled her sable-colored muzzle against Helen's arm. "Maybe I can coax her into the carrier with cat treats."

The journey to Johan Friendly's office was not a long one. They walked past the nail salon to reach a door similar to the one they had entered to reach Helen's apartment, and a directory to the left of the door listed the tenants of the four offices on the floor above the salon. As soon as Pamela pressed the doorbell opposite *Johan Friendly, Esq.*, an answering click announced that the door was now unlocked.

Johan Friendly was not standing in the doorway of his

office to greet them, but a knock on the glossily varnished door with its impressive brass plaque identifying THE LAW OFFICES OF JOHAN FRIENDLY, ESQ. brought forth a cordial "Come in." They entered to find a portly gentleman with rosy cheeks and thinning but carefully trimmed brown hair rising to his feet behind a desk so grand it seemed to take up half the room.

"Was I expecting you, ladies?" he inquired pleasantly as he leaned forward to rummage through the pages of a calendar. "Today's the . . . let's see . . . May 13." He looked up, squinting through rimless glasses, and repeated "May 13," then went on, "But today's Thursday, not Friday. We're in luck." He laughed briefly and consulted the calendar again. "Nothing listed here for this morning—so, a walk-in. What can I do for you?"

With that, he sprang from behind the desk, pulled two chairs away from the wall, and bowed slightly as he waved Pamela and Bettina into them.

"What can I do for you?" he repeated after he had taken his seat again and they were facing him across the broad expanse of his gleaming desk. "Buying a house? Looking to update a will?"

"Actually . . ." Bettina produced one of her most flirtatious smiles, made all the more flirtatious by the bright pink lipstick she had chosen to complement her pistachio-green ensemble. "It's not a legal matter."

She had recently acquired business cards identifying her connection with the *Arborville Advocate*, and now she extracted one from her handbag and leaned across Johan Friendly's desk to deposit it in his outstretched hand.

"Please call me Bettina," she said. "And this is Pamela Paterson."

"Pamela," Pamela murmured, accompanying her name with a tip of the head and her social smile.

"You may have read my work in the *Advocate*," Bettina explained, but went on without waiting for an answer. "We're doing a feature on the community gardens. This week will be too soon to run it after this sad, sad, *tragic* thing, of course"—her expression became serious, as befitted the shift of topics—"but people's thoughts turn to gardening this time of year and I'm getting a head start. And I know you're a long-time participant in Arborville's community garden program—as well as a leader in Arborville's business community."

Was Bettina actually batting her eyelashes? Pamela couldn't be sure, but the flirtatious smile had definitely returned.

Johan Friendly smiled back. "Gardening is one of the joys of my life," he responded. "Nothing takes a person's mind off the stresses of a demanding profession"—he gestured around his small office as if the very walls might bear witness to those stresses—"than sinking one's hands into the earth." He leaned back and his leather-upholstered swivel chair squeaked. "So, yes, questions welcome. Fire away." He gazed at Bettina expectantly. "And please call me Johan."

Bettina was seldom at a loss for words, but in the short time it took her to formulate her first question, Johan was on his feet again. A moment later he was pulling open the top drawer of a handsome wooden filing cabinet, one of several that lined the wall behind his desk. From the drawer he took a liquor bottle and a bakery box, which he opened to reveal cookies. He turned to deposit the bottle and box on the desk and then dipped into the drawer again for two glasses.

"May I offer you a little refreshment?" he inquired as he set the glasses on the desk and reached back into the drawer for another.

"Oh, no thank you," Pamela said. "Please do go ahead, though." Her words overlapped with Bettina's "Nothing to drink, but I'll take a cookie or two."

Johan leaned across his desk to extend the box toward Bettina, who reached in and pulled out two large, round cookies, with a texture that suggested they involved oatmeal. Small depressions in the centers glistened with red jam. Pamela recognized them as an item from the Co-Op bakery.

Johan took two cookies for himself and poured a goodly portion of liquor—which from the label appeared to be scotch—into one of the glasses. He immediately lifted the glass to his mouth and took a healthy swallow. Then he bit into one of the cookies.

"What are your favorite things to grow?" Bettina asked, after she had sampled a cookie.

Corn! Pamela said to herself. *But let's see what he says.*

Johan took a meditative sip of his scotch, then another and another, followed by another bite of cookie and another sip of scotch to wash it down.

"Corn is my prize crop—superior corn, if I do say so myself." He raised his chin, looking the very picture of contented self-confidence with his hands before him on the desk, one holding his glass and the other holding his half-eaten cookie. "I plant a strain that produces an outstanding ear, a large juicy ear, with regular kernels, and resistant to blight, mildew, and garden pests." He pounded the desk with the hand that held the cookie. "Science! I believe in science. None of this wild mongrel corn with its little weevils and—*ick*—crawly things, infecting other people's gardens and—"

He was interrupted by a chiming sound. He reached a hand beneath his desk and in a moment feet were heard on the steps.

The visitor felt no need to knock. She simply turned the knob, pushed the door open, and strode into the room.

"What?" she said. "You have clients?"

"No, Mom, I'm—" He jerked a drawer of the desk open and quickly swept the box of cookies into it, but in his haste to also hide the bottle of scotch and the glass, he tipped the glass over. Fortunately it was empty except for a tiny dribble. He waved toward Bettina and Pamela. "These are—" He patted his pockets as if searching for a handkerchief.

Bettina was on her feet then, leaning over the desk and dabbing at the spilled liquor with a tissue from her purse. That task accomplished, she turned to face the visitor.

"I'm Bettina Fraser, from the *Arborville Advocate*," she said, summoning her best professional manner. "You may have read my work." She extended a hand toward Pamela and added, "This is my associate, Pamela Paterson."

The visitor resembled her son in her portliness, the rosiness of her cheeks, and her tidy brown hair. But whereas his expression conveyed a hapless geniality, her face seemed primed for disapproval. Nonetheless, Bettina's self-introduction had evidently impressed her. A sound like "hmmm" escaped her lips. She blinked a few times, allowed herself a small smile, and said, "I'm Frederica Friendly."

"We're doing a feature on the community gardens," Bettina explained, "not, of course"—she raised a fastidi-

ously manicured hand as if to forestall the obvious comment—"as a murder scene, but . . ." And she repeated
what she had told Johan about people's thoughts turning
to gardening in the spring and her desire to get a head
start.

Then she added, with a toss of the head and a flirtatious wink at Johan, "It's a real thrill for me to be interviewing your son. I understand he has one of the most
impressive gardens in the program."

"He does?" Frederica Friendly wrinkled her nose.
"Well, perhaps." She glanced from her son to Bettina and
back at her son. "I just stopped in because I was on my
way to the Co-Op," she said. "I'm serving dinner at six
p.m. sharp and I expect you to be on time."

"Will you make the pork chops like you said you
would?" Johan asked in a hesitant voice.

"We'll see," she said in a severe tone. "Leave that bottle of scotch in the drawer and don't fill up on cookies all
day if you expect me to cook special things for you."

With nods at her son and at Bettina and Pamela, she
was on her way. No sooner had the door closed behind
her than the cookies and the bottle of scotch reappeared
on Johan's desk.

CHAPTER 7

He filled his glass halfway up and, with a questioning lift to his eyebrows, extended the bottle toward Pamela and Bettina.

"I might have just a drop," Bettina said as Pamela smiled but shook her head no.

Provided with considerably more than a drop, and another cookie, Bettina took a sip and then a bite. "These are delicious cookies," she commented. "Such a nice midmorning treat." She waited as Johan took considerably more than a sip of his own scotch and then went on. "Have you ever tried the Co-Op's crumb cake? That's one of my favorites." She finished up the comment with a smile.

Johan returned the smile, rolled his chair closer to his desk, and leaned forward. "Is it?" he inquired with an expression more serious than the topic would seem to warrant.

"Oh, yes!" Bettina exclaimed. "And they make it fresh every day."

Pamela, meanwhile, was asking herself where Bettina was going with this change of topic. Wasn't Johan's garden the stated premise for their visit? And weren't they actually wondering what his corn might have to do with Jenny's murder?

But Bettina had her ways. She chatted on about the Co-Op's bakery offerings, taking an occasional small sip of scotch and helping herself liberally to the cookies. She and Johan discovered a shared love for the Co-Op's cinnamon rolls and Johan listened, mesmerized, as Bettina described Wilfred's pie-baking talents. The level of scotch in his glass sank and his speech began to reflect the amount of liquor he had imbibed.

"This isn't typical," he said at last, nodding toward the bottle and his glass, which was now empty. "Usually this time of day I'm hard at work, but I like to offer visitors— especially such attractive visitors as you—a little something. Unless they're here on legal business, of course."

"Of course." Bettina had pulled her chair closer to the desk as they talked. Now she leaned across it and murmured, "You were telling me about your corn. Your *superior* corn." Pamela couldn't see Bettina's face, but she recognized the head tilt that Bettina used to signal her rapt attention. "I know you're a master gardener," Bettina went on, "and so of course your corn is superior, but what, exactly . . . ?"

Johan pounded on his desk. "Because it's not that damn mongrel corn that Jenny Miller grows—*grew*, I mean." His fist came down on the desk again. His face had grown even rosier with drink. "She called it *heirloom* but it was *mongrel*, with pollen drifting all over the place, *mongrel* pollen. And she had the nerve to accuse *my* corn of infecting *her* corn with my pollen, my superior pollen. And she—" He half rose and in the process bumped his chair, which spun away. "She was trying to get me expelled from the community gardens and obviously she just wanted to take over my plot." He reached out a hand to corral the chair, sat back down, and leaned toward Bettina. "But that won't happen now," he said with a satisfied smile. "Will it?"

As if realizing that he had spoken a bit too freely, Johan suddenly sat up straight. He cleared his throat and consulted his watch.

Bettina took the hint, as did Pamela. Both stood up, and a few minutes later they were standing on the sidewalk in front of the nail salon. Through the large window, manicurists in pink smocks were visible at their stations, bent over the extended hands of their clients.

"Well," Pamela said. "He certainly has a motive."

"I kind of liked him, though." Bettina's lips shaped a rueful smile. "And those cookies were delicious. I'll have to remember to look over the Co-Op's cookie selection now and then, instead of always getting the crumb cake." She paused, leaned closer to the window, and murmured, "I'm not sure about this fashion for making each nail a different color." She held out both her hands to appraise her current manicure, featuring bright pink polish, the same on each finger. "What do you think?" she inquired, turning to Pamela.

Pamela studied Bettina's nails for a minute and

laughed. "I think that even though Johan has a motive, it would be odd for a non-knitter to think of using a circular knitting needle as a murder weapon."

"It would be," Bettina agreed, withdrawing her hands and curling her fingers inward as if aware that she and Pamela had more serious things to discuss. "But I can see why he'd want to hang onto his garden plot when his corn is so important to him."

"His corn certainly is important to him." Pamela nodded. "Superior corn, not mongrel corn, with no weevils or crawly things." She tried to approximate the horror with which Johan had uttered those last few words. Then she chewed on her lip for moment, feeling her forehead pucker as she stared at the busy manicurists. "It might be helpful," she said at last, "to figure out exactly why Jenny had such an objection to Johan's corn. Could there have been more at stake even than the threat of losing his garden plot?"

"It *would* be helpful." Bettina nodded too. "The police aren't making any headway in finding Jenny's killer, at least judging by the reports—or lack of them—in the *Register.*"

They turned away from the window and began to walk toward the door that led to Helen's apartment. But Bettina seized Pamela's hand as she raised it toward Helen's doorbell.

"While we're here, I'll pop in and see if Clayborn has any late-breaking news on the murder," she said. "I'll tell him there's just time to get it in before the *Advocate* goes to press, and people will be impressed that their police department is working so hard to keep them safe."

They continued past the hardware store and crossed Arborville Avenue at the light. Between the hair salon and Hyler's Luncheonette, a narrow passageway led from the sidewalk to the library, the police department, and the town park. Pamela and Bettina proceeded down it single file, and when they emerged at the other end, Bettina headed toward the brick building that housed the police department and Pamela took a seat on one of the benches that faced the kiddy playground.

Once settled, she took out her smartphone and keyed in *superior corn*. Normally her Internet searches were done while sitting in her comfortable desk chair, fingering her familiar keyboard and contemplating her search results on the large screen of her office computer. But despite the sun glare and the distractions of children screaming with delight, by the time Bettina returned she had something quite interesting to report.

Bettina spoke first, however, if only to say that Detective Clayborn had sent a message out to the front desk to say that he had no new information for the *Advocate*.

"I found out something interesting." Pamela motioned to Bettina to take a seat next to her on the bench. A page was still up on the tiny screen of her smartphone but she'd absorbed enough that she didn't need to refer to it.

"I think Johan has been growing genetically modified corn," she explained. "It can resist pests like corn borers and weevils, and its proponents argue that it's more nutritious and can even solve world hunger. But"—she held up a finger—"it's really controversial, for a lot of reasons. And the reason that might have struck a particular nerve with Jenny is that if you're trying to preserve heirloom strains—and that's good because biodiversity is good—the pollen from genetically modified corn can drift onto your corn and create a hybrid that you don't want."

"Oh, my!" Bettina raised her fingers to her lips. "Does the same thing happen with tomatoes? Those heirloom tomatoes Wilfred brings home from the farmers market in Newfield are amazing! They really taste like tomatoes. I'd hate to think people growing genetically modified tomatoes were ruining the chance to ever eat those again."

Pamela nodded. "Probably the same thing can happen with tomatoes. But with corn it's a special problem because the pollen drifts far and wide. I can see why Jenny would have been upset."

"I can too." Bettina stared at Pamela bleakly, perhaps still contemplating the prospect of never being able to eat heirloom tomatoes again. When she rallied, however, it was not to smile but to frown. "But wouldn't it be more likely that Jenny would want to murder Johan, and not vice versa?"

Pamela frowned too. "Well," she said slowly, "he did say Jenny was trying to get him expelled from the community gardens."

"But maybe she was only trying, and not succeeding"—Bettina shook her head, setting her dangly jade earrings in motion—"whereas killing him would eliminate the threat of his genetically modified corn for good."

"So are you thinking she attacked *him*, but then he ended up killing her in self-defense?"

Bettina shrugged. "We don't know if Jenny was a knitter, but it would be more likely for a woman to have knitting supplies handy than for a man to."

"It would," Pamela agreed, "but were there signs of struggle in the garden plot? I can't remember if the *Register* said."

"There were," Bettina said. "That was part of what I

heard from Clayborn when I talked to him Tuesday afternoon. It's what made the police determine that Jenny had been killed there and not brought there after she was dead. The ground was scuffed up and some tomato seedlings had been uprooted."

"It does make sense that Jenny might want to kill him." Pamela nodded slowly. "And I believe she was quite athletic . . . and he obviously isn't . . . so she might have thought it was possible." She had been staring at the kiddy playground, watching a child go down the slide, but she turned to Bettina. "We can ask Helen if Jenny was a knitter."

"Yes!" Bettina had cheered up a bit, now that it seemed progress on the murder case was possible. "And we'll see Jenny's mother at the funeral tomorrow. We can ask her too."

Helen had managed to coax Precious into the cat carrier, which was now sitting on the otherwise bare coffee table. The stacks of paper and other odds and ends that had littered the table's surface were strewn about on the carpet. The cat was visible through the mesh panels in the cat carrier's sides as a luminous presence settled into the serene pose that Pamela thought of as the furry meatloaf—front paws tucked beneath the chest and tail curled nearly to the nose.

"I did have a bit of a time"—Helen gestured toward the mess on the carpet—"but cat treats ultimately did the trick." The mess included bills and other mail, handwritten notes on scraps of paper, pages torn from magazines showing sweaters and other cozy creations—even souvenirs like a theater program, a faded photograph of a handsome dark-haired man posing in what looked like Manhattan's Washington Square Park, and a menu.

Pamela crouched near the coffee table and peered through the cat carrier's mesh. A pair of deep blue eyes, seemingly lit from within like opals, gazed back at her. "Do you want to come home with me?" she whispered. "And meet Catrina and Ginger?"

The cat's expression didn't change. She didn't, however, seem troubled by whatever change of status her transference to the cat carrier might portend.

Meanwhile, Bettina had segued from complimenting Helen on her success in persuading Precious to enter the cat carrier to wondering how soon "poor Janice" would be up to sorting through her late daughter's possessions. "So sad," Bettina commented. "Usually it's the children who are left with a household's worth of their parents' things to find homes for."

Pamela stood up and joined the conversation. "Yarn," she said. "I've stockpiled enough for several lifetimes. I hope there are still knitters in the world when I'm gone and that my daughter finds homes for it."

Bettina laughed. "There will still be knitters," she said. "Think of Holly and Karen in our Knit and Nibble group." She detoured for a moment to fill Helen in on the details of Arborville's knitting club, winding up with the question, "What about you? Do you knit? Did Jenny?"

"Oh, I'm hopeless." Helen lifted her hands, fingers wide, as if to emphasize that they were unencumbered by needles or yarn. "No talent at all in that direction—and I don't know about Jenny. Like I said, I hardly knew her."

They chatted a bit longer, and Pamela assured Helen she'd take good care of Precious and thanked her for her concern for the animal. Then Pamela picked up the cat carrier, eliciting a mild squeak from its inhabitant, and she and Bettina made their farewells and set off down the stairs to the sidewalk, the car, and home.

Catrina and Ginger approached curiously. Pamela had set the cat carrier down on the carpet in the entry, and she let them investigate as she stepped back onto the porch to collect her mail. When she returned they had both retreated—not altogether from the room but to the arch that separated the entry from the living room. From that vantage point they watched as she knelt to unzip the mesh panel that formed the carrier's door.

Opalescent blue eyes gazed up at her as Precious lowered her body into a tense crouch. "It's okay," Pamela whispered, rocking back onto her heels and leaning away from the exit she'd created by unzipping the panel. "This is your new home."

Precious came slinking out, looking from side to side. She caught sight of Catrina and Ginger, who were hovering uncertainly at the edge of the living room. Before her was the barrier presented by the closed front door. To her right was Pamela. To her left were Catrina and Ginger. She spun around and sped in the only direction that seemed clear—toward the kitchen.

Pamela climbed to her feet, picked up the cat carrier, and rezipped the front panel. She waited a bit. Then she tiptoed into the kitchen, but once there she saw no sign of a svelte creature with pale, luminous fur and dark face, feet, and tail.

She glanced down the hallway that led past the laundry room. After being adopted by Pamela as a pitiable stray, Catrina had spent the first few days hiding behind the washing machine. But the laundry-room door was securely closed so Precious hadn't taken shelter there.

A doorway connected the kitchen with the dining room, and Pamela glanced into that room as well. Precious wasn't under the table or any of the chairs. It was possible that she had squeezed under the sideboard, though the clearance between sideboard and carpet was barely three inches, if that.

Well, she was somewhere. Pamela would put food and water out for her, separate from where Catrina and Ginger were accustomed to taking their meals. And in time Precious would become adjusted to her new home.

Pamela headed back to the entry to look through the day's mail. But on her way she paused. Just beyond the kitchen doorway was the door that opened to the basement stairs. That door was slightly ajar. Pamela couldn't remember what errand had taken her to the basement, but she recalled doing something down there the previous day. Obviously Precious had taken advantage of the open door and was now feeling safe, if not exactly cozy, in the depths of Pamela's basement.

She'd wait a bit and then stage food, water, and a makeshift litter box near the bottom of the basement stairs. For the present, she'd tend to her own stomach, which was demanding lunch.

After a quick grilled cheese sandwich, Pamela settled onto her sofa with *The Future of Fashion Is Slow*.

The final lecture in Wendelstaff College's 2019–2020 lecture series hadn't been a lecture at all. It had been a fashion show that fit right in with the book Pamela was reviewing for *Fiber Craft*. Students from the Sustainable Fashion class had modeled the garments they created from the raw material of thrift-store finds. Pamela had enjoyed comparing the "before" images that flashed up on a screen—young women swallowed up in shoulder-padded 1980s frocks that flowed to their ankles—as the same young woman modeled the chic transformations they had wrought.

Now she was standing next to her car in the Wendel-staff parking lot wondering how quickly Triple A would come to her aid. She had lingered to chat with a few of the students who had modeled their creations—"refash-ions," they called them—and only a few cars had re-mained in the parking lot when she reached her own.

She had climbed into the driver's seat expecting to be back at home in fifteen minutes or less, but nothing had happened when she stepped on the gas pedal and turned her key in the ignition. The May night was balmy, the moon was bright, and the Haversack River was at high tide, its waters lapping at its grassy bank rather than in the low-tide retreat that exposed mossy rocks littered with detritus. Enjoying the night air and the view seemed preferable to sitting inside the car while she waited, and that was exactly what she was doing.

She hadn't noticed headlights turning in from the road that served the parking lot, so she was surprised to be hailed by a friendly male voice calling "Hello there!" She swung around toward the voice, which was coming from the direction of the Wendelstaff quadrangle, and noticed a shadowy figure making its way across the asphalt.

CHAPTER 8

He called "Hello there" again and continued to advance. When he was close enough to speak in a normal tone of voice, he added, "Is everything okay?"

"Fine, yes," Pamela answered. She was sure whoever Triple A had dispatched would arrive any minute. A number of service stations were within a few miles of the Wendelstaff campus.

"Just enjoying the view of the lovely Haversack River?" The man stopped when he was a few yards away. Between the moon and the lights on tall poles placed here and there around the parking lot, Pamela could see him quite plainly. Since the bulging leather satchel dangling from one hand identified him as someone connected with the college, there was no need to be alarmed by his presence. So she studied him a bit more closely. The blue jeans and denim shirt were suitable professor garb, and the dark hair was a bit long but tidy. The slight wolfish cast to his handsome features was offset by the gentle smile that had accompanied his last question.

"Not quite," Pamela said. "My car won't start, but I called Triple A."

"I wouldn't want to say the Wendelstaff parking lot is a dangerous place," the man said, "but we're not that far from Arborville and . . ."

"There's a killer on the loose." Pamela finished the thought for him, then hoped she hadn't seemed to be mocking his concern.

They looked at each other for a minute. Pamela would be fine, she was sure. She was convinced the Arborville killer had chosen his victim for a reason, whether the reason had to do with resentments among the gardeners or something else.

"You don't have to wait, really," she said. "Triple A is very dependable, and I don't live far."

But he seemed inclined to linger. "Do you take classes here?" he asked in a conversational way, his pleasantly interested expression more suited to a social gathering than a deserted parking lot.

"No." Pamela twisted around to glance toward the parking lot entrance. No headlights in sight. "I was at a lecture . . . well, not exactly a lecture. It was a fashion show. A *re*fashion show."

"Ah—Callie Davenport's project." He nodded. "My colleague. How was it?"

"Inspiring," Pamela said. "Such a good approach to sustainable fashion. And ideas like that are really catching on. My daughter and her friends do more shopping at the thrift store than at the mall."

"And how about you and your husband?" the man—

evidently a professor, as she had surmised—inquired. "I'm definitely in tune with that philosophy. People don't need half the stuff they buy." He'd been focusing on Pamela's face but now he stole a look at her shoes and worked his way back up. Her sandals, jeans, and simple cotton blouse hadn't come from a thrift shop, but they certainly didn't identify her as a fashionista.

"Oh, I'm . . . I'm . . ." Even after so long Pamela hadn't gotten used to thinking of herself as a widow. "My husband died," she said at last.

She was grateful for the distraction when headlights announced that aid had arrived. A van with the logo of a local garage on the side made a wide circuit around the parking lot and then slowed and pulled up next to her car. The door opened and a young man jumped out.

"Dead battery, I expect," he said without preamble. "That's usually why they won't start. Did you forget to turn the lights off when you parked?"

"They weren't on," Pamela said. "It wasn't dark yet."

"Probably need a new battery." He darted around to the back of the van and returned with a set of jumper cables. "They don't last forever. I can give you enough of a charge to get you home, though."

The other man, the man she now thought of as "the professor," was still lingering and spoke up now to say, "I could have given you a jump."

"It's okay." Pamela gestured as if to wave the idea away. "I'd already called Triple A."

"So . . . it looks like you're all set." He started to say something else but was interrupted.

"Ma'am!" The man from the garage was standing in front of her car. "Do you want to get in and pop the hood for me?"

"I . . . yes . . ." Pamela responded, then she turned back to the professor. "I guess I'd better . . ."

But he had opened his briefcase and was fumbling around in it. He came up with a small card, a business card, and handed it to her. "I'm Brian Delano, by the way," he said. "I teach photography here. Maybe you'd like to have coffee . . . or lunch . . . or something . . . some time."

"Pamela Paterson," she murmured as she accepted the card.

When she got home, Pamela made a note to take her car to the garage in town the next day. It probably did need a new battery. She couldn't remember the last time she'd replaced it. She worked a bit on the sweater for Penny, sewing up the long seams that turned the sleeves into sleeves.

Brian Delano's card sat on the mail table where she'd put it when she came in.

"You're here!" Bettina sounded both surprised and re-lieved. "I thought you'd gone ahead without me. Where's your car?"

Pamela swung the door farther open and Bettina stepped into the entry. Catrina looked up from the sunny spot on the carpet.

"It's at the garage," Pamela said. She described the previous night's adventure, concluding with, "And when I tried to start it this morning the battery was dead again, so I guess the man last night was right and I need a new one."

Their destination was St. Willibrod's church, where Jenny Miller's funeral was to be held. Bettina had dressed for the occasion in her smart black linen skirt suit, accessorized with a triple strand of pearls and matching earrings. On her feet were sleek black patent pumps and she carried a black patent clutch.

The day was too warm for Pamela's usual funeral standby, a brown-and-black striped jacket she had bought for a long-ago job interview. She had pondered the contents of her closet and settled on black cotton slacks and a crisp white shirt. She'd added simple silver earrings and gathered her hair at the nape of her neck with a wide barrette, and hoped the overall effect was sufficiently formal to convey her respect for the bereaved.

She stepped into the kitchen to retrieve her purse, and when she returned Bettina was fingering the business card that had been sitting on the mail table since the previous night.

"I don't think this is from the garage that took your car away this morning," Bettina said, looking up from her scrutiny. "Who's Brian Delano, MFA, Professor of Photography at Wendelstaff College?"

"Oh, just"—Pamela closed her eyes and shook her head—"someone."

"Someone who gave you his business card." Bettina's scrutiny now focused on Pamela's face, which Pamela willed to remain expressionless.

"Is he someone you met at the lecture last night?" Bettina could be persistent.

"No," Pamela said. "He wasn't at the lecture, and anyway it wasn't really a lecture. It was more of a fashion show." Her voice speeded up. "In fact, you would have liked it. It—"

Bettina set the card back on the mail table and reached out to seize Pamela's arm. "Whoa," she said. "You're trying to change the subject, and that tells me there's something interesting about Brian Delano."

"Not really. He . . . while I was waiting for Triple A to send someone, he was on his way to his car and he just stopped for a minute to see if I was okay."

"And he gave you his business card." Bettina got a certain look when she sensed romantic possibilities for her friend, and she had that look now.

"It doesn't mean anything." Pamela tried to extricate her arm from Bettina's grasp.

"Yes, it does." Bettina nodded so vigorously that the bright tendrils of her hair vibrated. "It means he's very gentlemanly. He's interested in you, obviously, but he didn't want to seem forward—especially meeting you under those circumstances—creepy, in the dark, in a parking lot. So he gave you his card, and he probably said something like 'Maybe you'd like to have coffee . . . or lunch . . . or something . . . some time.'"

In fact that was exactly what he had said. For some reason, Pamela remembered the exchange quite clearly.

"So it's your choice," Bettina went on. "And he wanted to show you that he doesn't think the man always has to be in charge, making the date and so on. But I'm sure he's hoping you'll get in touch. And you've already lost—"

Pamela controlled the urge to growl. Yes, she'd already lost Richard Larkin, and Bettina had sworn never to mention his name again. But now Bettina had a new name to invoke whenever the topic of Pamela's solitary state arose. *Brian Delano.*

Pamela looked at her watch. "We're going to be late," she said.

Bettina nodded meekly and they proceeded out the

front door, across the porch, and down the steps toward where Bettina's faithful Toyota waited at the curb.

After the funeral service ended, Pamela and Bettina had followed the sad procession of cars out of St. Willibrod's parking lot. The procession had wended its way up to the cemetery at the crest of the hill that formed the backside of the cliffs overlooking the Hudson River. They had watched as Jenny's coffin was laid in the ground, the somber mood of the occasion soothed by the lush green of the cemetery's grass and shrubbery, the soft May breeze, and the occasional lilt of birdsong.

Now Bettina was pulling into one of the spots in the lot set aside for visitors at the town-house development where Jenny's mother, Janice, lived.

"It looks like we're in for a treat," she commented, pointing toward a van occupying another parking spot. Lettering on the van's side read DEBBIE DOES DELICIOUS in a fanciful script. The lettering was surrounded by a wreath made from fruits, vegetables, and flowers. "She's local," Bettina added. "Based right here in Arborville. Does an amazing job, I've heard."

"Didn't we hear somewhere that Jenny worked for a local caterer?" Pamela asked.

Bettina nodded. "Maybe this is her. That would be a nice gesture—providing food for the funeral reception."

The town-house development was relatively new, and it occupied land near the border with Meadowside that had once been the site of a grand house with spacious grounds. The owners had died and the house, dating from an era when families were much larger, had sat vacant for years, falling further and further into disrepair. Rezoning had allowed the heirs to find a buyer for the land, if not for the house, and within less than a year, an attractive town-house development of twelve units had replaced the sadly derelict structure.

The new construction echoed the woodframe and clapboard of the typical Arborville house, and several Arborville empty nesters had been happy to trade their too-big dwellings for smaller dwellings in a style they were familiar with.

Pamela and Bettina strolled along the sidewalk until they found the address they were looking for. They climbed a few steps to find the front door already ajar and the buzz and hum of conversation coming from within.

Bettina entered first. From the narrow porch Pamela could hear the swoop and glide of Danielle Hardy's voice, greeting Bettina with "Isn't this just *too sad!*"

Pamela followed her friend into the crowded room, decorated with simple furniture, probably new, that suited its compact floor plan. But in her downsizing, Janice had clearly preserved the possessions that meant something to her. A tall white bookcase that had an Ikea look displayed photos on its upper shelves—formal studio photographs, snapshots of a young Jenny and her handsome dark-haired father, and even a toddler Jenny posing with Santa at the mall.

She was relieved when Danielle continued to focus on Bettina, which gave her a chance to get her bearings and keep her social smile in reserve. As Danielle, in a black sheath dress that flattered her lean body, poured out her distress at "poor Janice's *tragedy*—and it's not that *long ago* that she lost her *husband* too," Pamela searched for other familiar faces.

There was Marlene Pepper, in a navy blue pants suit,

waiting to pay her respects to Janice, who was chatting with someone else near French doors that led to another room. And she recognized other community gardeners. Calliope Drew, in a homespun-looking garment that drooped nearly to the floor, was standing next to Johan Friendly, dressed as if for the office. Both seemed more occupied with what was on the plates they were holding than with each other.

Danielle was then accosted by a man Pamela didn't recognize, though the snatch of dialogue she overheard—something about compost being ready—suggested that this man was also a gardener. Bettina detached herself from the conversation and edged toward Pamela.

"I think the food is in there." She nodded toward the French doors, which stood open. "Little sandwiches it looks like—those Scandinavian things. Some people already have plates."

The thought of food was appealing. It had already been past lunchtime when they left the cemetery and Pamela's stomach had begun to remind her of that fact. They proceeded toward the French doors, but Marlene Pepper stopped them when they were almost there. She put a coaxing hand on Bettina's back and beckoned Pamela to follow.

"Come and say hello to poor Janice," she said. "I'm not sure either of you have met her before."

Janice Miller was a petite blond woman, in her fifties Pamela guessed. Her wide blue eyes and heart-shaped face tapering to a delicate chin gave her a particularly forlorn look, like a child puzzled by an unfathomable turn of events.

Marlene performed the introductions, then stepped aside as Bettina seized both of Janice's hands. "I am so, so sorry," Bettina said, her mobile face making her sincerity clear. "What a tragedy—to lose a daughter."

Janice nodded, and an almost inaudible "Thank you" emerged from her quivering lips.

Pamela took her turn then, echoing Bettina's sentiments. She found social chatting difficult at the best of times, and at the worst of times . . . what could you say to a woman who had lost a daughter not that much older than Penny?

Bettina was more adept. "Jenny was such a lovely young woman," she went on. (The funeral had included many testimonies to this effect.) "So talented with the gardening, and the cooking, and all those long-lost household crafts. I confess, cooking was never my strong point, and when it comes to gardening, that's my Wilfred's job." Bettina had continued to hold one of Janice's hands. Now she took the other hand up again.

"All I can do is knit," Bettina said. "But I imagine Jenny did that too."

Pamela felt an involuntary laugh welling up, and she struggled to suppress it and maintain her serious expression. Bettina was absolutely incorrigible. Yes, they had agreed it would be useful to know if Jenny was a knitter, and could thus have decided to squelch the spread of Johan Friendly's evil GMO corn pollen by garroting him with a circular knitting needle—only to have him turn the weapon back on her. But was a post-funeral conversation with a grieving mother really the time for sleuthing?

Curiously, Janice hadn't seemed to find it odd that the conversation had veered onto the topic of knitting. In fact, she had cheered up somewhat. "No," she said, even mustering a small smile, "she didn't knit. She sewed, though, even as a child—making clothes for her dolls. I still have some of them." She glanced from Bettina to Pamela and back.

Suddenly she stiffened. Her lips parted and Pamela heard a quick intake of breath.

"What is it?" Bettina whispered. "You look like you've seen a ghost."

Janice was staring at a spot near the front door, which had just opened to admit some new arrivals, including Claire Cummings, Helen Lindquist, and several other people. Janice continued staring for a moment, then seemed to make an effort to relax. She even laughed, feebly. "Oh, I—" She detached a hand from Bettina's grip and covered her eyes for a moment. After she uncovered them and blinked a few times, she continued. "For a moment I imagined I saw my daughter," she said. "I guess I'll imagine I see her everywhere from now on."

At that moment, a server in black slacks and a white shirt strolled through the French doors bearing a tray containing glasses of wine in a choice of red or white. Janice shook her head no when offered a glass, but gestured to Bettina and Pamela to help themselves. "Or have some food first," Janice suggested. "Deb's staff has done a beautiful job with the refreshments."

"I wouldn't say no to a bite to eat," Bettina said. After all, that had been their destination when they paused for a word with Janice. She gave Janice's hands an affectionate squeeze and with a "You take care now" stepped toward the wide doorway.

Pamela murmured a few words of condolence and followed Bettina into a room that offered a view of a sloping lawn and meticulous landscaping. A long table parallel to the window had been spread with a starched white cloth and on it were arranged platters and platters of tiny sandwiches, all open-faced. Some featured smoked salmon decorated with sprigs of dill, while others featured paper-thin slices of rare roast beef with dabs of what looked like freshly grated horseradish. Still others, ovals of crusty French bread, held pâté garnished with minuscule gherkins.

Several people who had already filled the small plates available at each end of the table were standing around talking in quiet tones. Pamela nodded at a few women she had met in the company of Marlene Pepper or recognized from Hyler's. Then she took up a plate and followed Bettina, who had begun working her way along the buffet, selecting one each from the bounteous assortment.

As they both turned away from the table with plates full enough to last them for some time, they were greeted by Helen, who waved from the threshold of the French doors and said, "I'll just grab some food and join you."

CHAPTER 9

Pamela had noticed Helen at the funeral—dressed in a slim dark skirt and a pale fluttery blouse, with her hair in a sedate bun. When she appeared next to them bearing her own plate of food, the first thing she said was "How is that sweet little kitty doing?"

Pamela had just sampled one of the salmon sandwiches and was enjoying the pairing of the dense brown bread and the delicate salmon, with its hint of sea and salt.

"Hiding in my basement, I'm afraid." Pamela offered a regretful smile. "But I'm putting food and water down there for her and I fixed up a litter box. I hope she'll get to be as comfortable with me as she was with you. She really took to you right away."

"I hope so too," Helen said. "She's a beautiful cat." These last words were murmured somewhat abstractedly.

Helen's eyes were no longer on Pamela and Bettina. Instead they were roving here and there, surveying the groups chatting near the buffet table and then gazing at the people crowding the town house's living room. "I hardly recognize anyone here," she commented, "though of course I haven't lived in Arborville very long." She glanced toward the living room again. "I wonder why Dennis didn't come, and he wasn't at the funeral either."

"Busy at the hardware store, I guess." Bettina paused in the act of lifting a sandwich garnished with caviar and grated egg to her mouth. "His wife is here, though—Claire." Bettina nodded toward where Claire was standing near the French doors. "She came in right after you did."

"*What?*" Helen's amazement—with staring eyes and open mouth—was so extreme as to be almost comical. "Dennis has a wife?"

"You didn't know he had a wife?" Bettina returned the sandwich to her plate. "They were your landlords."

"Dennis was the only person who ever came around, if there was a problem with the plumbing or whatever—and I guess she never helped out in the store because I never saw her there." Helen seemed flustered, but apparently feeling she had to explain her reaction, she went on, if hesitantly. "He was . . . he and Jenny . . . I thought . . ." She swallowed. "He seemed a little old for her, but I didn't know her that well, and it was none of my business."

"Oh, my!" Bettina's amazement was nearly as comical as Helen's had been.

Helen, however, no longer seemed amazed. Now her pretty mouth was twisted in disgust. She narrowed her amber eyes. "Men!" It was almost a hiss. "Why am I surprised? Aren't they all cheaters?"

"My Wilfred would never do anything like that." Bettina sounded as affronted as if Helen's condemnation had named Wilfred particularly.

"Well, you're lucky, then." Helen looked from Bettina to Pamela, then addressed herself to her plate of food, selecting a salmon sandwich for her first nibble. After an awkward few moments of silence, and as Pamela was ransacking her brain for a topic less fraught than the perfidy of men, Helen smiled valiantly and said, "I'm so envious of you both with your knitting and your Knit and Nibble group."

"It's not so hard," Bettina said encouragingly. "I didn't learn until after I joined the group."

"She used to crochet," Pamela added in an aside.

"I could teach you," Bettina went on. "It's such a good hobby—and a lot of young women, like you, are getting interested in it now."

"Oh, I'm really"—Helen held up both hands in protest—"not crafty at all. Genuinely hopeless."

Marlene Pepper suddenly appeared at Helen's side. "I'm going to steal this young lady and introduce her to a few more people," Marlene said, putting an arm around Helen's waist. "Just bring your food right along with you." She addressed these words to Helen as she led her away, adding, "It was so thoughtful of you to come today. I know it means a lot to Janice, that so many people cared about Jenny."

Pamela was just as glad to focus on her plate of food, standing with Bettina in companionable silence—though the buzz of conversation, even occasional laughter, meant that the room itself was not silent at all. When her plate was empty, she accepted a glass of white wine from a passing server and contemplated the view from the town house's back window as Bettina made another visit to the buffet table.

"Nice and sunny out there," Bettina commented when she returned to Pamela's side. "A person could grow vegetables just as well there as up in the community garden plots." Pamela nodded and Bettina went on. "But I guess the town house management probably wouldn't take too well to a vegetable garden on the common land."

"The landscaping they have is very elegant," Pamela said. "And Janice probably enjoyed sharing a community gardening plot with her daughter."

"I wonder if she'll keep it." Bettina turned to Pamela. "I'd think it would just be too sad to go back there now."

Both resumed staring out the window. Nary a dandelion or a sprout of crabgrass marred the perfectly manicured lawn. Its far edge curved around a bank of greenery that mingled hosta and luxuriant ferns against a background of hydrangea, crape myrtle, and viburnum, as well as the Arborville standbys, azalea and rhododendron. So far only the azaleas were in bloom, and the landscaper seemed to have eschewed some of the gaudier colors azaleas offered in favor of pure white, which showed to crisp advantage against the various shades of green.

A strangled groan behind them caused both to turn away from the window. One of the servers, a slight young blond woman, had gathered up more empty platters than she could manage. The platters' differing shapes and the presence of serving tongs, spatulas, and large forks made for an unsteady pile, and the topmost platter, which still bore a few sprigs of dill, was in imminent danger of slipping off and crashing to the floor. With both hands needed to support the load, there was nothing she could do to stop it.

With a few quick steps, Pamela was at her side and with a few quick motions she had seized the renegade platter and a fancy serving fork as well. She lifted a few more platters from the ungainly pile and followed the young woman, who was murmuring grateful thank-yous, toward the doorway that led to the kitchen.

The server who had been circulating with trays of wine was now standing at the sink with her back to the doorway. Next to her was another young woman, holding a dish towel. They were engaged in conversation, speaking loud enough to be heard over the gush of water as the first young woman lifted a platter from the sudsy bath in the sink and rinsed it. A hum from the dishwasher suggested it was in action as well.

"It's turning out nice, don't you think?" the young woman with the dish towel was saying.

Platters of petit fours waited on the kitchen table, charming squares and circles and rectangles iced in shades of white, pink, and yellow, and the rich cocoa-brown of chocolate. Nearby, coffee was brewing in a large chrome coffee urn. Cups and saucers and fresh plates for the petit fours were staged for delivery to the buffet table.

"Deb likes us to bring everything back clean," the young woman Pamela had helped explained as she proceeded toward the counter with her load.

"Deb's catering always gets rave reviews," the first young woman said, her voice loud in the silence between bursts of water from the faucet. "But I was amazed when she offered to do this for free."

"Really?" the young woman with the dish towel said

as she reached for the now-rinsed platter. "Jenny worked for Deb a long time."

"Too long." The first young woman turned toward the young woman with the dish towel and Pamela got a glimpse of a knowing smile. "You've heard of trade secrets?" The young woman with the dish towel continued drying the platter and the first young woman went on. "Deb has a lot of secret recipes—her specialties—and she believed Jenny was stealing them for *Grow, Cook, Eat*. And that Jenny's next step would be to set up her own catering business and steal Deb's best clients. And wait till you hear this—"

Now it was the young woman with the dish towel who turned. A fresh burst of water made her voice inaudible, but Pamela could tell from her expression that she hadn't had a clue that there was bad blood between Jenny and her erstwhile boss.

The young woman Pamela had helped stepped up to deposit her stack of platters and serving utensils near the others waiting to be washed. She glanced back toward Pamela, who was lingering near the doorway and uncertain about where to put the few platters she had carried. Then the young woman edged sideways, tapped the dishwasher on the shoulder, and leaned close to whisper in her ear.

The dishwasher swiveled her head to glance quickly at Pamela. She picked up a few dirty platters, slid them into the sink, and bent over them in a show of great industry. After a few moments, Pamela approached the counter, placed her platters with the others, and hurried from the room. She hadn't been intending to eavesdrop. It had just happened.

Back in the other room, Pamela looked around for Bettina. Her friend was no longer standing near the buffet table and gazing out the window but had wandered through the French doors and joined a cluster of people that included Marlene Pepper. Pamela arrived at Bettina's side in time to hear Danielle Hardy revisiting the theme of "poor Janice's *tragedy*" and the fact that she had recently lost her *husband* as well, such a sweet man, never lost his Minnesota nice.

The aroma of coffee emanating from beyond the French doors exerted a magnetic pull, and soon the living room was nearly empty as people made their way back to the buffet table. Pamela and Bettina were almost the last to help themselves to petit fours and accept cups of coffee from the young woman who Pamela had helped with her teetering platters. They stood aside as people who had reached the buffet table earlier and were now finished with their petit fours and coffee formed a ragged line to thank Janice for her hospitality and repeat their murmured words of sympathy.

As the line dwindled, they joined Marlene Pepper and Danielle Hardy, and the four of them paused one by one to squeeze Janice's hands or, in Marlene's case, give her a hug. From the next room came the subdued clatter of the servers as they labored to clear away.

"You just call me tonight if you need to talk," Marlene urged Janice as she released her from the hug. "And I'll be over first thing tomorrow to do whatever needs doing." Marlene's plumpness gave her features a gentle cast that made this assurance seem all the more comforting.

*   *   *

"We have things to talk about." They had reached the visitors' parking lot, but Bettina whispered nonetheless.

"Yes, we do." Pamela cupped a hand to shield her mouth and whispered back, just to tease her friend. She added, "More things than you know. Ask me what I heard about Debbie Does Delicious and Jenny when I carried those platters to the kitchen."

"What?" Bettina abandoned the whispering. She'd been about to unlock the passenger-side door but she stepped back, curiosity enlivening her features. "Tell me!"

"First things first," Pamela said. "Let me in the car, then we'll talk about Dennis."

Yes, they agreed, as Bettina steered the Toyota toward the road that served the town-house development, the news that Jenny had been having an affair with Dennis was quite stunning and opened up new possibilities for suspects.

"Clayborn must have interviewed Dennis," Bettina pointed out, "if for no other reason than that he was Jenny's landlord. But did Clayborn realize that the connection was deeper?"

"It's not something Dennis would have volunteered," Pamela said.

"He must have interviewed Helen too." Bettina paused for a break in the traffic and turned onto Arborville Avenue. "But she didn't seem to think Jenny's relationship with Dennis was any of her business—and she didn't know he was married. So there's no reason she would have said anything about him to Clayborn."

"So"—Pamela felt herself frown and she raised a hand to rub the little furrow between her brows—"are we thinking Claire found out about the affair and decided to remove her competition?"

"She *is* a knitter." Bettina nodded sadly. "But she's such a nice person and she doesn't seem like the murdering type."

"Why would Dennis do it, though—if he was in love with Jenny?" Pamela was still rubbing the furrow, staring out the window as they passed the well-groomed yards of the grand houses along this stretch of Arborville Avenue. Some people had pruned their azaleas into tidy geometrical shapes that now blazed crimson, orange, and neon pink.

With a shudder, she realized that she could answer her own question. "Maybe Jenny threatened to reveal the details of their affair to his wife," she suggested. "And maybe she said she'd keep quiet in exchange for a break on the rent."

"Oh, Pamela!" Bettina's hands twitched on the steering wheel and the car swerved. "How could she? Such a sweet young woman? Marlene Pepper will just be horrified if that turns out to be true. One of her gardeners trading . . . trading her . . . her *affections* for . . . for . . . rent? And Jenny's poor mother!"

"I'm not saying that was necessarily the reason he did it." Pamela tried to sound soothing. "But a love triangle is a much more likely motive for murder than garden rivalries. And given what we know, Dennis could have had both motive and means—because Claire is a knitter."

They had reached the corner of Orchard Street. Bettina paused to let a van with TREE DOCTOR—WE MAKE HOUSE CALLS painted on the side pass before she made her turn.

"We know the murder happened after sundown Monday night," she said as they neared her driveway. "We have to find out whether Dennis was home all night that night, but we can't ask Claire because we can't tell her why we want to know."

She pulled in next to Wilfred's ancient but lovingly cared-for Mercedes and turned to Pamela. "Now," she demanded, "tell me what you heard about Deb and Jenny."

Pamela described the conversation between the dishwasher and the dish-dryer in Janice's kitchen. If it was true that Deb feared Jenny was stealing her best recipes and aiming to steal her clients, Deb could have a motive for murder too.

Love and work, Pamela reflected, as she watched Bettina ponder this new information. Hadn't Freud said those were what it was all about? And if something gets in the way? Did Freud say we might resort to murder? She wasn't sure.

Bettina opened her car door and swung her feet onto the asphalt of her driveway. On her side of the car Pamela did likewise.

"Okay," Bettina announced as they faced each other over the Toyota's roof. "We're all set for tomorrow, then."

"We are?" Pamela murmured, but Bettina didn't hear her.

"First the hardware store and then Deb Holt's." Bettina nodded decisively, setting the tendrils of her hair in motion.

"What will we ask them?" Pamela inquired.

"Deb is easy." Bettina laughed. "I'm looking for a caterer for my upcoming do, of course."

"And Dennis?"

Bettina laughed again. "I'll think of something."

Pamela was sure she would. Bettina did indeed have her ways.

They walked together to the curb just in time to see an olive-green Jeep Cherokee approach and turn into the driveway of the shingled house next to Pamela's.

"I won't say anything." Bettina pressed her fingertips against her lips.

"Come for coffee tomorrow morning," Pamela said. "Penny will be home and I know she'd like to see you. Then we'll go to the hardware store. If my car is done, we can walk uptown and I'll pick it up while we're out."

"Always the walking!" Bettina rolled her eyes. "Call me in the morning so I know whether to wear my sneakers."

Pamela started to cross the street but Bettina called her back with an urgent "Pamela!"

"What?" Pamela hesitated a few feet from where Bettina stood.

"Have you called Brian Delano yet?" Bettina nodded toward where Richard Larkin was just disappearing through his front door.

"Bettina, *please*!" Pamela sighed.

"I won't say what I *want* to say."

Something about how she had missed her chance with Richard Larkin, Pamela was sure. Bettina folded her hands primly, looked away as if anticipating the scowl that Pamela felt taking shape, and went on. "I'll just say"—Bettina focused once more on Pamela's face—"that you're too young to resign yourself to being alone for the rest of your life. And soon Penny will be—"

Pamela squealed. She knew Penny would soon be out on her own. The squeal was involuntary but effective. With a startled gulp, Bettina left off.

"I'll call you in the morning, about the sneakers." Pamela set out across the street.

Bettina's voice, contrite, floated after her. "I'll never mention Brian Delano again."

CHAPTER 10

A few minutes later, Pamela entered her own house to find a large suitcase parked in the middle of the entry. Catrina and Ginger, who usually greeted their mistress at the door, were nowhere to be seen. But then Penny appeared in the kitchen doorway with Ginger snuggled against her chest and Catrina at her heels.

"You got here earlier than you thought!" Pamela studied her daughter closely. Satisfied that Penny's eyes were no less bright, her complexion no less blooming, and her smile relaxed and genuine, Pamela held out her arms and welcomed Penny home with a hug that included a sleek cat.

Penny explained that Kyle Logan, who lived in a neighboring town and was a frequent source of Penny's rides between Boston and New Jersey, had been ready to leave the campus sooner than he expected, and they had made good time, and here she was.

"Shall I carry your suitcase up?" Pamela asked, reaching for the handle.

"It's all laundry," Penny laughed, "and if I want to wear clean clothes tomorrow I'd better get it started right now."

A bit later, Pamela and Penny sat at the kitchen table sharing a snack of Swiss cheese and apple slices. From down the hallway came the rhythmic slosh of Penny's laundry.

Penny had transferred her laundry from the washer to the dryer and retreated upstairs to the room that Pamela had freshened and tidied a few days before. She was returning to her previous summer's job at an upscale home furnishings store in Manhattan on Monday, and Pamela was sure she wanted to arrange some weekend face-to-face time with her Arborville friends.

Pamela glanced at the clock and was startled to see that it was nearly five p.m. There had been the funeral at St. Willibrod's, and then the burial, and the reception where she and Bettina had lingered until the end. And she'd arrived home to find Penny and they had chatted— and now it was time to start dinner.

She took the pork tenderloin from the refrigerator and settled it into an oblong roasting pan after drizzling a bit of oil in the pan to keep the tenderloin from sticking. It would roast for forty-five minutes, and the scalloped potatoes would take about the same time, but it was too soon to turn the oven on. She also measured out a cup and a half of milk and set it in an out-of-the-way spot on the counter. She'd need it for the scalloped potatoes and didn't want it to be refrigerator cold.

Pamela's early exploits with scalloped potatoes had been disappointing. She would replicate the procedure she had observed while watching her mother cook—layering sliced potatoes and onions in her Pyrex casserole dish while sprinkling the layers liberally with salt and fresh ground pepper and sifting a bit of flour over them, dotting them with butter, garnishing them with grated cheese (sometimes), and bathing them in milk. But in Pamela's attempts, the potatoes would still be crunchy after an hour's baking, and the onions' piquancy barely mellowed. Instead of forming a rich sauce with the flour and butter, the milk would have pooled in the bottom of the casserole, as liquid as ever.

Her subsequent experiments had established that steaming the potatoes in advance, slicing the onions so thin they were nearly translucent, and making sauce in advance, rather than relying on the milk, flour, and butter to understand their roles, resulted in scalloped potatoes that met her expectations and even attracted compliments.

Accordingly, Pamela took four large potatoes from the basket where she kept her potatoes and retrieved her peeler from its spot in the utensil drawer. She washed the first potato, then with long strokes began carving the earth-colored peel from the pale flesh beneath.

The work was monotonous but soothing, in the way that knitting was soothing. She finished the first potato and pushed the peelings into a little stack at the side of the cutting board. She held the second under the tap and rubbed at it with her hands while she absentmindedly gazed out her kitchen window. Sunset was a few hours away, but a light was on over the sink in the kitchen window across the way.

The light illuminated the lustrous black hair and glowing olive skin of Jocelyn Bidwell. As Pamela watched, a pair of hands landed on Jocelyn's slender shoulders and Richard Larkin's shaggy blond head bobbed in the background. Then Richard bent forward and nuzzled the back of Jocelyn's neck.

The sound of dribbling water summoned Pamela back to her task. She glanced down. The potato was certainly clean enough by now. Peeler in hand, she attacked it with more vigor than was strictly warranted.

Once the potatoes were all peeled, quartered, and sliced, Pamela arranged them in her steamer basket, which she had placed in her largest saucepan. She added a few inches of water and lit the burner under the saucepan. They would steam only until they were almost soft enough to poke with a fork.

It was time to set the oven to 350 degrees now, and as Pamela listened to the whoosh and hum that signaled it had begun to heat up, she peeled back the dry outer skin of the large onion that would be sliced and layered in with the steamed potatoes.

The light was still on over Richard Larkin's sink, but the two figures had vanished. Probably in the living room drinking wine, Pamela reflected as she took up her sharpest knife and began the delicate task of carving the onion into the thinnest possible slices without including bits of her fingertips.

Onions never made her cry—she had read somewhere that, like some people's aversion to kale, it was one of those curious traits ruled by genetics. And anyway, the tears onions provoked in the susceptible had nothing to do with sorrow, so certainly the lump that had invaded her throat couldn't have anything to do with the stack of onion slices, with their neat concentric rings, that was accumulating before her.

She sighed, set down the knife, and closed her eyes. Bettina was right, of course. She didn't want to resign herself to being alone for the rest of her life. And soon Penny would be out on her own. And she *wanted* Penny to be out on her own, and not worry about her mother.

The lid on the saucepan containing the potatoes was jiggling, a sign that the boiling had become intense, perhaps too intense. She checked the potatoes, turned the burner off, and let the saucepan sit uncovered while she quickly finished slicing the onions and then grated a small heap of cheddar.

The white sauce took five minutes and she'd made it so often she didn't need a recipe. Melt the butter, whisk in the flour and stir for a minute, add salt and pepper and then the now room-temperature milk. Continue watching, and whisking occasionally until it thickened, whisk in the grated cheese, and that was that.

Brian Delano had seemed nice, she reflected as she buttered the round Pyrex casserole dish that had been a wedding gift so long ago and began layering the potatoes and onions. He was a professor at Wendelstaff. It wouldn't be like following up with a person she'd met in the mall parking lot. And he was a photographer, probably interested in some of the same things she was interested in. Maybe she would call him.

But what to say? "Hi! Remember me? In the Wendelstaff parking lot?"

What if he didn't?

Penny's voice brought her back to the reality of her

kitchen and the scalloped potato recipe coming together beneath her busy fingers. She was grateful for the distraction and turned to see Penny standing in the doorway.

"What should I do to help?" Penny asked as her eyes darted here and there around the kitchen.

"You don't have to do anything," Pamela said. "It's your welcome-home dinner." She reached for the saucepan containing the cheesy white sauce and poured it slowly over the potatoes and onions, watching through the clear sides of the casserole as the sauce filled the crevices between the stacked potato and onion slices. Then she opened the oven door, leaned into the waft of hot air to pull the top shelf out, and arranged the casserole with the soon-to-be scalloped potatoes side by side with the roasting pan containing the pork tenderloin.

"Are these collards?" Penny took up the bundle of dark greens Pamela had set on the table as she was assembling the ingredients for that night's meal. Also in wait were two small cucumbers—the kind she'd recently come to prefer because of their edible skin, and a plastic basket of mini tomatoes.

It was much too early for locally grown Jersey tomatoes, and Pamela had discovered that the mini tomatoes, with a nice acidic bite to them and a texture that wasn't disappointingly mealy, tasted much more real than the sad off-season tomato pretenders flown in from who knows where.

"I know how to do collards." Penny joined her mother at the counter and freed the huge leathery leaves from the wire twist that bound them. She cut the long vein from the center of each, then she stacked them up, folded them in half lengthwise and in half again, and began to slice through the bulky roll at inch-long intervals. The result was collard strips in a tangled mass, to be transferred into the salad spinner for washing and drying and then set to cook in the large double-handled pot Pamela used to boil pasta.

Meanwhile, Pamela had sliced the mini tomatoes in half to expose their insides to a light sprinkling of salt and heaped them with the cucumbers, cut into small chunks, in a small cut-glass bowl. She dressed the salad with olive oil and balsamic vinegar and finished off with another sprinkling of salt and a few grinds of fresh pepper.

Mother and daughter regarded each other in the soft light cast by the antique crystal chandelier that hung over Pamela's dining room table. The meal was finished and only hints of the feast remained on the rose-garlanded plates: a bit of fat trimmed from a slice of pork tenderloin, a streak of cheesy sauce from the scalloped potatoes, a dark green shred of collard glossy with the garlicky olive oil the cooked leaves had been sautéed in as a final step.

Penny had described her busy final weeks on campus, finishing up papers and studying for tests, but despite Pamela's gentle probing she hadn't revealed whether the summer break was interrupting a budding romance.

Pamela rose to her feet, but not to gather up dishes and head for the kitchen. Rather, she made her way through the arch that separated the dining room from the living room. In the living room, she bent down to open a drawer in the large bureau that provided storage for table linens as well as a surface perfectly suited to display many of the thrift-shop treasures she had accumulated over the years.

From the drawer she plucked a carefully folded sweater, a simple crew-neck pullover but brought up to date with random-width stripes in blue, pale green, brown, and three shades of pink. She unfolded it and held it out in front of her as she returned to the dining room.

"I know it's too warm to wear it now," she said smiling, "but Merry Christmas!"

"Oh, Mom!" Penny jumped up from her chair and met her mother under the arch. "It's beautiful!" She reached out for the sweater and tugged it over her head. Pamela may have been prejudiced, but to her eyes her daughter—with her petite frame, bright blue eyes, and dark curls—displayed the sweater to even more advantage than had the model wearing it in the pattern book.

"And now," Pamela said, "what do you want for your birthday?"

The question was apt, because Penny's birthday was coming up in just two days. Pamela actually had a few surprises tucked away, and there would be a cake, of course, and, if Penny didn't have plans with her friends, another special dinner. But now that the striped sweater was finished, she'd need a new Knit and Nibble project and was always happy to take requests from her daughter.

"Be thinking," she added, as they returned to the table and began clearing away. But Penny had had a long day, starting at eight a.m. with the final exam in her Industrial Design class. She struggled to suppress a yawn, looking so much like a young sleepy Penny from years back that Pamela had to swallow hard to ease the catch in her throat.

After Penny went up to bed, trailed by Ginger as she climbed the stairs, Pamela tidied the kitchen. Then she retired to the sofa and opened *The Future of Fashion Is*

Slow at the page where she had left off. Catrina joined her, stretched against her thigh and vibrating with contented purrs.

Something had distracted Catrina and Ginger from their breakfast. Pamela didn't notice at first because her attention was on measuring enough beans into the coffee grinder to provide for two people rather than just one. She tipped the last few beans into the grinding chamber, replaced the top, and pressed down to launch the crunch, clatter, and whir that would transform the beans into fine grounds.

As the noise subsided Penny's voice became audible. Pamela turned toward Penny, who was sitting at the kitchen table, still in her pajamas and with her dark curls uncombed.

"*Mo-om!*" Penny said, as if this wasn't her first attempt to be heard. "What's wrong with Catrina and Ginger?"

"I don't know." Pamela looked from her daughter to the corner where the cats were accustomed to take their meals. A few morsels of chicken-fish blend remained in the communal bowl, but instead of finishing off their breakfast, both were staring toward the kitchen doorway with ears tipped forward on high alert.

As Pamela watched, Catrina abandoned the rest of her breakfast and approached the doorway, advancing warily with her tail held low and flicking back and forth. Ginger remained where she was, but in a crouch as if preparing for action.

Penny stood up and tiptoed after Catrina, remaining in

the doorway as Catrina slipped past her ankles and disappeared around the corner.

"She's sniffing at the basement door," Penny reported, adding, "It's like there's something down there." She stooped, reached out, and murmured, "What is it, girl?" Then she rose back up and stepped around the corner herself. Pamela heard the basement door open and braced herself for . . . what?

A snarl from Catrina? A coo of pleasure followed by a "Here, kitty kitty" from Penny? Instead there was silence, for a moment. Catrina did not return, but Penny appeared in the kitchen doorway with a frown creasing her smooth forehead and her lips in a puzzled knot.

"Something's down there," she said. "Catrina has gone down to investigate, and I think we should—"

She was interrupted by an outraged squeal as a streak of black fur darted across the black and white tiles of the kitchen floor, coming to a halt under the chair Penny had vacated.

"Mo-om?" Penny took a few steps toward Pamela, turned back and leaned through the kitchen doorway to close the basement door firmly, then advanced until she was standing a few feet from Pamela. "Is there something you haven't told me?"

Pamela tried to will away the smile she felt forming. Penny had been a sweet and cooperative child, as if loath to add to her widowed mother's cares after Michael Paterson's death. But there had been occasions, albeit rare, when Pamela had had to summon a stern expression and make inquiries of Penny such as the one Penny was now making of her.

Penny's attempt at sternness was more amusing than

fearsome, given her pretty features and the fact that she was a head shorter than her lanky mother, not to mention that she was still garbed in her pajamas with hair tousled from sleep. But Pamela had tried valiantly in recent years to treat Penny as the young woman she had become.

"There's a cat in the basement now," she explained.

"Why does it have to be down there?"

"It . . . it wants to be," Pamela said. "It's not used to being here yet and it's kind of shy."

"Was it a stray?" Penny asked. "Like Catrina?"

Catrina had been adopted as a forlorn waif on a chilly autumn night a few years previously. She had scurried through the open front door when frightened by a flock of wild turkeys and had then hidden under the washing machine for several days.

"Not exactly." Pamela studied the floor. "It belonged to someone who's . . . no longer with us. And Marlene Pepper suggested I might be willing to adopt."

"'Someone who's no longer with us'?" Penny crossed her arms across her chest and resumed her stern expression. "*Mo-om!* You're not getting involved in that murder, are you?"

"Why would I do that?" Pamela was aware that her attempt at offhandedness was not too convincing.

"*Hello?* The murder weapon was a knitting needle. You belong to a knitting club. The police probably think a knitter did it. So you're probably—"

The doorbell's chime offered a welcome distraction.

"Don't worry," Pamela murmured. She stepped past Penny and through the doorway that led to the entry.

Visible through the lace that curtained the oval window in the front door, a colorful figure stood out against the bright spring green of Pamela's lawn. She opened the door to admit Bettina, wearing a crisp shirtwaist dress in tangerine cotton with white polka dots, accessorized with a necklace of large white beads and earrings to match. The effect with her red sneakers and scarlet hair was striking. She was carrying a white bakery box in one hand and a few envelopes in the other.

"Your mail came already," she said, extending the envelopes toward Pamela.

Penny had ventured into the entry at that point. Pamela glanced at the envelopes and held them out to Penny, noting, "They look like birthday cards, from both sets of grandparents."

"Wilfred went out already." Bettina flourished the bakery box as the three of them headed for the kitchen. "He came back with two dozen of those cookies like Johan served us. They come in lots of flavors and he got some of each—though the raspberry ones Johan had were delicious. But it's too early for cookies now so he got some doughnuts too."

In the kitchen Bettina set the bakery box on the table and then turned to Penny and gave her a hug. "And so, Miss Penny," she said, stepping back for an inspection, "home for the summer, and you're going to be twenty-one, and"—she leaned in again for another hug—"Wilfred and I want to help celebrate."

Catrina had apparently recovered from the shock of her discovery in the basement. As Bettina continued talking, she made her languid way across the tiled floor, aiming no doubt for the sunny spot on the entry carpet where she took her morning naps.

"So I hope"—Bettina glanced toward where Pamela was standing at the counter, slipping a paper filter into her carafe's plastic filter cone—"you'll both join us for dinner tomorrow."

"Oh, I'd love to!" Penny's smile erased the last vestiges of her displeasure with Pamela's likely sleuthing.

Pamela was filling her kettle. Once it was settled on the stove with a burner flickering beneath it, she chimed in with, "That would be wonderful! And I'll make the cake."

Bettina arranged three wedding-china cups and saucers and three small plates around the table while Penny fetched an extra chair from the dining room. The cut-glass sugar bowl was already full of sugar and Penny transferred it to the table, filling the matching cream pitcher with heavy cream and setting it by the sugar bowl's side.

As the kettle began to whistle, Bettina untied the string around the bakery box and folded back its lid to display six plump doughnuts glistening with sugary glaze. Pamela tipped the ground beans into the carafe's filter cone, followed up with the water from the kettle, and soon the rich aroma of fresh-brewed coffee began to fill the little kitchen.

A few moments later Pamela served the coffee and joined Penny and Bettina at the table. Conversation at first focused on the doughnuts: how sweet and yeasty they were and how perfectly the coffee—black and bitter in Pamela's case, and coaxed to a creamy sugary mocha color in Penny's and Bettina's—complemented them.

Pamela was happy to simply listen then, as Bettina caught up with Penny's college adventures and enthused with her about the excitement of another summer working at the fancy home furnishings store in the city.

"There are three doughnuts left," Bettina pointed out as Penny stood up and offered to refill coffee cups.

"One was plenty," mother and daughter said in unison.

Bettina lifted the lid on the bakery box. "I might have another," she said. "They're not as good the next day." She reached inside the box and transferred a doughnut to her plate.

Penny was standing at the stove watching the carafe as the coffee heated up again. In a moment she turned the burner off and used an oven mitt to carry the carafe to the table, where she topped up each cup.

"What are you going to do today?" Pamela asked Penny—casually, she hoped—after the coffee refills were almost gone and nothing remained of Bettina's second doughnut but a few glistening flakes of glaze on the wedding-china plate. It would be best if she and Bettina could carry out their sleuthing errands without Penny wondering where her mother was, especially since Penny now knew about the cat in the basement and how it happened to be there.

"Lorie wants to go to the mall," Penny said, "and then I'm stopping by Aaron's. Wendelstaff's graduation is tomorrow and he's going to Guatemala to help build a school." Lorie was Penny's old friend from high school and Aaron was a more recent local acquaintance. "What are you going to do?"

"Ummm." Pamela shrugged. "Nothing much, but my car is ready, so . . ."

"And Bettina's walking uptown with you to get it." Penny dipped her head to glance pointedly at Bettina's red sneakers. "And then you're going to do *nothing much*." Penny's expression mingled amusement and suspicion.

"A cake!" Pamela said quickly. "I'm going to bake a cake."

Penny raised her brows but she didn't say anything else. She stood up and began clearing away the cups and saucers and plates, after which she excused herself to go upstairs and dress.

"She's turning into a detective," Bettina said with a laugh as they heard Penny's feet on the stairs.

CHAPTER 11

Bettina checked the aisles that offered nails and screws and door hinges, and lightbulbs of all sizes, along with extension cords and light switches and plumbing supplies and sandpaper. Pamela roamed among hoses and garden tools and then past the counter where people could page through books showing all the color combinations that one could explore for painting siding, shingles, shutters, and front doors. In her circuit she passed the front window, where the hardware store cat, plump and luxuriantly furred, was dozing on a sack of potting soil.

They met where they'd started out: at the hardware store's entrance. "Downstairs, maybe," Pamela suggested. "Saturday's a busy day. I can't believe he's not here."

The hardware store's basement was off limits to customers, but jobs like rescreening windows or replacing panes of glass were done there.

Bettina advanced toward the center of the store, where a booth open on all four sides served as a counter, as well as the post from which Dennis or one of his helpers dispensed advice to Arborvillians dealing with issues of house maintenance.

Dennis had not been in the booth when they came in and he wasn't there now. Instead, his second-in-command, a rangy, ponytailed man in his fifties named Rod, was occupied with cutting a duplicate key for a gray-haired woman Pamela recognized as a regular at Hyler's.

"Is Dennis around?" Bettina inquired over the high-pitched buzz of the key-cutting machine.

Without looking up, Rod shook his head no. He completed the key and handed it to its new owner, along with its original. "Not in," he added, glancing toward where Pamela and Bettina stood.

Bettina followed up. "Is he coming in?" she asked.

Rod accepted a few bills from his customer and handed back a coin. "Not today," he said. "What do you need?"

"Nothing. Not a hardware thing, that is." Bettina tilted her head to meet Rod's gaze and offered him a smile that combined friendliness with a touch of flirtation. "Otherwise I'd ask you."

The gray-haired woman had been heading for the entrance with her new key, but she wheeled around, returned to the counter, and addressed Bettina. "You write for the *Advocate*, don't you?" She accompanied the words with an accusing stare.

"Why, yes." Bettina's smile wavered slightly.

"I suppose you're snooping around here looking for an angle on the community garden murder story," the woman said. " 'Murdered Girl's Landlord Talks' or something equally tasteless."

Bettina squared her shoulders and lifted her chin. "If you read the *Advocate*, you would know it is not that kind of newspaper," she responded.

"It isn't at all," Pamela heard herself murmur.

With a skeptical lift of the eyebrows, the woman went on her way.

"Are you Bettina Fraser?" Rod leaned over the counter, suddenly lively.

"Why, yes," Bettina said slowly. Pamela couldn't tell from Rod's manner whether being Bettina Fraser would be a good thing or a bad thing, and apparently neither could Bettina. A small wrinkle had appeared between her carefully shaped brows.

"My wife loves your writing!" Rod exclaimed, and the wrinkle between Bettina's brows vanished. "So do I. That article you did on the county fair last summer—your descriptions of the prize pigs! I could see them as clearly as if they were standing right in front of me."

"Why, thank you!" Bettina was quite herself again, pleasure at this praise lending her complexion a flattering glow.

"I never miss an issue of the *Advocate*," Rod went on, quite oblivious to a customer whose troubled expression and the U-shaped pipe he was clutching suggested that he was in dire need of advice. "In fact . . ." Rod ducked and vanished beneath the counter. When he reemerged, he was waving a copy of the *Advocate*. From the headline, COMMUNITY GARDEN MURDER STUNS TOWN, Pamela recognized it as the issue that had arrived on her driveway the day before.

"Would you autograph this?" He laid the newspaper on the counter and offered a pen when Bettina nodded. "My wife will be thrilled!" he exclaimed as she bent forward to write "All the best from Bettina Fraser" above the masthead of the *Advocate*.

With effusive thanks, Rod folded up the autographed newspaper and tucked it back under the counter. He turned his attention to the customer with the U-shaped pipe, but as Pamela and Bettina approached the door, he called, "Dennis will be here Monday. Come back then."

It was only a short walk from the hardware store to the service station, also on Arborville Avenue but on the other side, where Pamela's car had had its battery replaced. As she and Pamela waited on the curb for a break in the traffic, Bettina studied the screen of her smartphone.

"I know Deb lives in the Farm," she said, "so she's close. I'll just check the address for sure."

Pamela nodded and Bettina's fingers began to dance over the face of her device.

"The Farm" was a recently developed area of Arborville. It featured large and modern houses, in contrast to the old houses like Pamela's and Bettina's that made up most of Arborville's housing stock. It was so called because it had been a real farm, the Van Ripers' farm, for generations, dating back to the Dutch settlement of northern New Jersey—until modern descendants of the Van Ripers sold the land to developers.

"A few blocks from Roland and Melanie," Bettina announced after a moment, and they set out across the street.

The bill paid and her car claimed, Pamela took her place behind the steering wheel as Bettina settled into the passenger seat. She steered her serviceable compact along

Arborville Avenue for a few blocks, turned right and climbed a slight hill for a block, then turned left. After a few more blocks she had left behind the hundred-year-old houses so typical of Arborville, with their broad porches and peaked roofs with little dormer windows, and was cruising past expansive split-levels with two- and even three-car garages.

"It's the last one down here," Bettina said after a bit. "Right at the end of the cul-de-sac. See the van with 'Debbie Does Delicious' on the side?"

Pamela coasted past a few more of the large houses and nosed into the curb.

"Oh, my goodness!" Bettina exclaimed as they climbed out of the car. "Look at this!"

"What?" Pamela peered across the roof of her car toward where Bettina was pointing.

"Down the driveway," Bettina said. "Look past the van and off to the left." She slammed her car door and darted around the front of the car to grab Pamela's arm. "Come on!" She pulled Pamela along as she hurried toward the driveway, surfaced with tan pavers, that led from the street to the double doors of Deb Holt's large garage.

Halfway up the driveway she paused. "Look!" She was whispering now, but urgently. "Deb's yard backs right up to the community gardens. They're what's left of the Van Ripers' farm. I did an article for the *Advocate* once. The developer agreed to deed some of the land to the town in exchange for getting the permits he needed."

Pamela looked where Bettina was pointing. "The fence that separates Deb's yard from whoever's garden that is doesn't look very high either."

It was a chain-link fence, but seemingly intended more

to mark the boundary of the yard than to serve much of a security purpose. Beyond the chain-link fence stretched an expanse of land grooved with deep parallel furrows. The level strips between the furrows were dotted with seedlings. Variations in leaf size, shape, and color suggested a variety of crops.

"Oh, my goodness!" Bettina raised a hand to her mouth. "I think that's—" She closed her eyes and opened them again. "See the tool shed off to the right, and the faucet with the hose attached, and the bucket?" Pamela nodded. "Remember the photo of the murder scene in the *Advocate*?"

"Sort of, with all those tomato seedlings uprooted and scattered around."

"I think the garden plot right on the other side of that fence is the one where Jenny's body was found—and where she was murdered." Bettina hadn't let go of Pamela's arm and now she tightened her grip.

On closer inspection, the neat pattern of furrows and seedlings was interrupted near the chain-link fence by a bare spot.

Pamela shuddered. "And that bare spot must be where . . . where it happened."

"So," Bettina commented as they backtracked to the end of the driveway, "we think she had a motive and now it looks like she had opportunity."

"We need to somehow discover if she knits," Pamela said.

They proceeded a few yards along the sidewalk till they reached the end of Deb Holt's front walk. In a few moments they were standing on her porch pushing the button above the small brass plaque that read WELCOME.

Deb Holt answered the door wrapped in a capacious

white apron. The upper part covered all but the sleeves and collar of a pink linen shirt and the rest covered all but the bottom several inches of pink linen pants. Pink loafers completed the look. The pink flattered her well-cared-for skin, as did the pale blond hair that framed her face and waved gently past her shoulders.

"Hello," she said. Her smile was cordial but her voice was tinged with curiosity.

Pamela had wondered aloud to Bettina whether they should call first, but in her capacity as a reporter Bettina often showed up unannounced and usually came away with what she wanted. In this case, Bettina was purportedly shopping for a caterer. Perhaps, though, catering customers sometimes showed up unannounced too.

"Debbie Does Delicious?" Bettina inquired as Pamela mustered her social smile. She needn't have bothered, however, because Deb had eyes only for Bettina.

"Why, yes," she said. She stepped back and, with a graceful wave, ushered them into her spacious living room. "Are you planning an event?"

"Everyone's graduating," Bettina said. "It's that time of year."

Clever, Pamela thought to herself. *She's not lying. It is that time of year, but Deb doesn't have to know that Bettina doesn't actually have a graduation to celebrate at the moment.*

"I know we're in the right place!" Bettina exclaimed as Deb ushered them around a corner, through a tastefully appointed dining room, and into a gigantic kitchen. "Something smells absolutely heavenly."

It did indeed. The aroma blended buttery pastry with cheese and a hint of onion. A clutter of mixing bowls and utensils on the long granite counter, along with a chef's

knife and a cutting board, testified that whatever was now
baking in the oven had been created from scratch.

"Those are my signature cheesy onion tarts." Deb's
manner suggested that she considered the compliment
absolutely justified. "They'll be out in ten minutes."

Besides the long granite counter, which surrounded a
deep stainless steel sink, the kitchen featured a massive
eight-burner stove, two refrigerators, two dishwashers,
and a kitchen island also topped with granite. Hanging
above the island was a collection of copper pots and pans
in all sizes and shapes. Stools were ranged along the far
side of the island as if to provide seating for cooking
demonstrations.

Huge windows looked out on Deb's backyard and the
community gardens beyond. From this vantage point, it
was even clearer that the garden plot closest to Deb's
chain-link fence was the one in the *Advocate*'s photo of
the crime scene.

"Now," Deb said as she led them toward the kitchen
island, "tell me what you have in mind. How many people? What time of day? Indoor or outdoor? Stand up or sit
down? Punch only? Wine and beer? Full bar with bar-
tender?"

What's Bettina going to say now? Pamela wondered. It
wouldn't be fair to Deb to lead her on in the belief she
was about to land a catering contract, even if Deb was a
murder suspect.

"So many questions!" Bettina in real life was seldom
flustered, but now she summoned her acting skills. "So
many, *many* questions!" she repeated, with a frantic waving of hands and blinking of eyes. "And I just don't know
who's coming from out of town and who isn't, and outside in our backyard would be best, but it might be hot if

we do it during the day, but at night there will be mosqui-toes, and what if it rains?" She paused for breath, inhaled deeply, and looked toward the stove. "Were the cheesy onion tarts part of the menu for the reception after Jenny's funeral?"

"No." Deb shook her head. "That was my stand-up smorgasbord package. All the preparation is done ahead—no hot food, and I leave it to my servers to handle the event on their own. I did a sit-down dinner for twelve in Timberley last night and I was busy here in my kitchen all day yesterday. But Jenny was a lovely young woman, and so I wanted to do something, of course, and the . . ."

Pamela hadn't been looking at Deb as she spoke. Instead she had been staring at the view beyond the kitchen's huge windows, mostly at the bare spot, still a little scuffed, where Jenny's body had been found. But she shifted her gaze to Deb as Deb's voice trailed off.

"Yes." Deb's polished manner had been replaced by irritation. "That is where it happened, and no, I didn't know anything about it until the next morning when I heard sirens and all of a sudden there were police all over the place, and yes, it was a sad coincidence—as that pesky Marcy Brewer from the *Register* pointed out—that Jenny was murdered nearly in the backyard of her employer."

"So lovely of you to cater the reception!" Bettina jumped in. "And now that I think of it, there were no hot hors d'oeuvres—just those amazing, amazing little sandwiches. You're a genius when it comes to delicious combinations . . . the salmon with dill, and was that crab salad with chopped tarragon?"

Deb shifted her attention to Bettina, and her mood lightened. "That one *is* my invention," she said.

"It's a gift," Bettina went on. "Being able to cook like that—such delicious food for all those people at the reception and then a sit-down dinner for twelve that night! Why, I can barely manage dinner for me and my husband." She swiveled her head and nodded toward Pamela, who had been unable to keep her eyes from straying back to the bare spot beyond the chain-link fence.

"Pamela cooks!" she exclaimed. "She's a fabulous cook, and she knits too—we both do actually, but she's better. So talented!" She turned back to Deb. "You probably garden too, and sew, and your house is so beautifully decorated. The creative urge, the artistic urge, is just such an . . . urge . . ."

Bettina was becoming quite breathless and Deb was staring at her as if unsure what was coming next.

"And"—Bettina paused for a deep breath—"you probably knit. Do you?"

"What?" Deb took a step backward. Her eyes narrowed, but her mouth stretched wide in disbelieving amazement. "What are you—"

A buzzer near the stove sounded then and she darted around the kitchen island to jerk the oven door open. She fumbled for a pair of quilted oven mitts on the counter, pulled them on, and stooped to lift a broad baking sheet from the oven rack and set it on the stovetop.

Speaking from her post near the oven, she completed her question. "What on earth are you asking me that for? I thought you were here to arrange a catering job." Her eyes narrowed. "*You!*" She waved a hand, still wearing an oven mitt, at Pamela. "Why do you keep staring at that spot where Jenny was murdered? What's the real reason you both came here?"

Bettina, for once, was speechless.

"Just get out!" Deb advanced toward them, making shooing motions with both oven mitt–clad hands. "Both of you! Out! And no, I don't knit. And I don't garden, or sew, and a decorator from Timberley did my house. Go!"

Back on the sidewalk, Pamela and Bettina looked at each other.

"I was hoping she'd let us taste a few of those cheesy onion tarts," Bettina said at last. "I don't know when I've smelled anything that delicious."

"I guess we answered our question," Pamela said. "She doesn't knit."

CHAPTER 12

There was a route back to Orchard Street from the Farm that didn't involve returning to Arborville Avenue, but that wasn't the route Pamela took. She had two crucial errands that involved stops in Arborville's commercial district.

The first stop was the Co-Op. Once through the automatic door, and with a very curious Bettina at her elbow, she picked up a basket—no need of a cart for so few items. Butter, sour cream, and milk were collected from the dairy section, and a large bag of powdered sugar from the baking aisle.

"For Penny's birthday cake?" Bettina said hopefully. Pamela nodded. "What kind of cake are you making?"

"You'll see." Pamela's words were accompanied by a mysterious smile. "I need one more thing here and then we'll go next door." Next to the Co-Op was one of Arbor-ville's three liquor stores.

Pamela led the way over the Co-Op's creaking wooden floor past the ends of several narrow aisles to the more open area where produce was displayed. She bypassed the bins piled with leafy greens and the colorful array of carrots, beets, and radishes, heading for the fruit, specifically the berries.

Blueberries and raspberries and even gooseberries had been available for ages, and strawberries too—but not the good ones until recently. Strawberries were like tomatoes. They could be plump and red and even juicy, but unless they were really in season they tasted like nothing at all. At this time of year, the Co-Op's came from a local farm.

Pamela chose a plastic basket from the strawberry display. A cellophane cover held on with a rubber band restrained the basket's contents, but the berries were visible through the cellophane and through the mesh of the basket. They were deep red berries and textured with the tiny slubs that Pamela knew were actually their seeds. And they were fragrant with the piquant sweetness, slightly acidic, of strawberries at their peak. She added two baskets to her other grocery selections.

"Strawberry shortcake?" Bettina inquired as Pamela led the way toward a checkout station. "But why the sour cream?"

"Not quite strawberry shortcake," Pamela said. "But it *is* a cake and it does have strawberries. We just have to get the champagne now."

"Champagne, yes! For her twenty-first birthday!" Bettina clapped her hands.

"In a way," Pamela responded. "It goes in the cake, though."

At the liquor store next to the Co-Op, Pamela chose an inexpensive bottle of champagne. Soon she and Bettina were on their way back to Orchard Street.

"Come about six tomorrow," Bettina said as she climbed out of Pamela's car. "I can't wait to see what you're going to do with those strawberries and that champagne."

In her kitchen, Pamela unpacked her groceries and the champagne from the canvas totes in which they'd traveled home. She stowed the butter, sour cream, and milk in the refrigerator but left the powdered sugar and the strawberries out on the counter. The powdered sugar would be used soon enough, and the strawberries didn't need to be chilled. Besides, they were already infusing the kitchen with the aroma that tantalized with its evocation of summer.

After a quick lunch of lentil soup from a can and a piece of toasted whole-grain bread with a slice of cheese, Pamela picked up *The Future of Fashion Is Slow*. She was just one chapter from the end and she'd read it in comfort on the sofa before climbing the stairs to her study to begin the writing part of her reviewing task. So with book in hand, she settled into her accustomed spot.

Across the room Catrina was surveying the world from the top platform of the cat climber and seemed disinclined to join her mistress. Ginger was nowhere in sight, but during Penny's breaks from college the cat often took her naps on Penny's bed—as if the bed only beckoned when Penny's recent habitation had left a welcoming scent.

Pamela had made a few notes as she read, and now she made more. She herself was not Alison McDermott's target audience—since fashion, fast or slow, had never tempted her. Clothes were necessary, of course, but Pamela's summer uniform of jeans and the same few casual blouses could never be accused of destroying the planet. And knitting, which provided her winter wardrobe staples, was an example of slow fashion if there ever was one.

She read the last few pages, closed the book, and climbed the stairs to her study with Catrina at her heels.

She'd checked her email that morning, so there was no need to push the buttons that would bring the computer and monitor to life. She let the mouse wander in a random pattern on the mouse pad until the monitor woke up with a click.

The sight that greeted Pamela when she descended the stairs a few hours later was unexpected, to say the least. For one thing, Penny had returned, sooner than Pamela had expected her, and was sitting in the middle of the living room floor. But most surprising, Penny was not alone. She was engaged in a teasing game, obviously enjoyable to both participants.

She held a wand to which was attached a long string culminating in a feather, and she was flicking the wand here and there, causing the feather to leap about as if it was alive. Chasing the feather, leaping over the stylized flowers and foliage that patterned the dark carpet, was a cat—a lithe and slender cat with a pale coat that darkened to sable on its tail, paws, ears, and elegantly angled muzzle.

"Precious!" Pamela exclaimed.

"Is that her name?" Penny looked up at her mother then dipped her head toward the cat, who was watching in amazement as the feather appeared to levitate of its own accord. "That's a perfect name! She's a real beauty."

Precious turned her attention to Penny, who set the wand down, thus bringing the feather to rest. Penny held out a hand and Precious crept close, nuzzling the hand then creeping into the lap created by Penny's cross-legged pose on the carpet.

"How on earth—?" Pamela ventured farther into the room.

"She was in here when I got home," Penny said. "Sniffing around the cat climber. She must come up from the basement when she thinks nobody's around, cats or people, to be afraid of."

"But you're around now and she's not afraid of you."

"No, you're not, are you, Precious?" Penny addressed the cat and added a head scratch for good measure.

"Are you back for good?" Pamela crossed to the sofa and took a seat.

"A while." Penny continued with the head scratch. Precious's eyes narrowed until only a streak of opalescent blue was visible. "Aaron's roommates are having a farewell party for him tonight and I'm invited, but that's not till seven or so."

"Do you feel like a trip to the yarn shop in Timberley?" Pamela asked. Timberley's commercial district boasted such things as a florist, a cheese merchant, and a shop where a knitter could pay more for yarn than for a sweater from the fanciest store at the mall. "I want to make you a sweater for your birthday," Pamela went on, "but I thought you could pick out the yarn and pattern, like we did at Christmas. And your job starts Monday so we should go today."

Precious opened her eyes to study Pamela, but under the spell of the head scratch apparently decided she was safe on Penny's lap.

"I'd love to, Mom." Penny's enthusiasm brightened her already bright eyes. "But"—she raised her free hand and held up a finger—"I want to be the knitter. Will you teach me?"

"Of course! That will be the present too—knitting lessons, whenever you want to start. But first we need the yarn." Pamela stood up. "Shall we go?"

Penny lifted Precious from her lap and gently set her on the carpet, but as soon as Penny was on her feet Precious slipped around the corner and disappeared.

The trip to the yarn shop had been successful. Penny had been drawn right away to a sweater featured on the cover of a knitting magazine displayed with the other magazines and pattern books. The sweater, a roomy pullover worked in the garter stitch, seemed eminently doable for a first-time knitter, but its wide neckline and the absence of ribbing at cuffs and hem gave it a modern look. She had chosen a rustic yarn from Iceland, exactly the creamy color of the sheep who had been sheared to create it.

Now the magazine and the yarn sat on the coffee table. It would be fun to teach Penny to knit, and Pamela was happy her daughter was about to discover the joy of creating a garment from scratch—a theme that the author of

The Future of Fashion Is Slow had returned to again and again. But as Pamela contemplated the opportunities for mother-daughter bonding that lay ahead, she realized she hadn't solved the problem that had put the idea of a birthday sweater for Penny into her mind in the first place. She needed a new Knit and Nibble project. If Penny was going to be knitting her own sweater, what would Pamela bring to work on when Knit and Nibble met on Tuesday night?

In the kitchen, Pamela took two cans of fish medley from the cupboard and, in a fresh bowl, used a spoon to break one can's worth into smaller morsels for Catrina and Ginger. She put half of the other can in a smaller bowl, filled another bowl with water, and tiptoed down the basement stairs to set both bowls in the open space near the entrance to the shadowy alcove where the furnace lurked.

As she delivered Precious her breakfast the previous morning, that alcove had struck her as appealing to a creature seeking safety and privacy. A few bags destined for the thrift shop were stored elsewhere in the basement, and she had extracted an ancient blanket from one of them and arranged a bed back in the alcove's shadows.

When she returned to the kitchen, the refrigerator door was open and Penny was peering inside.

"There's lots more of the tenderloin," Pamela said. "You have a party to go to and I have a review to finish writing, so why don't I just make some sandwiches?"

The sandwiches, on whole-grain bread with mustard and mayonnaise, were assembled and dispatched, along with a quick tomato and cucumber salad. Penny was on her way then, in a fetching cotton dress from the 1950s that she'd found at her favorite thrift shop the summer before, and Pamela climbed the stairs to her study to finish her review.

On May 16th twenty-one years earlier, Pamela had awakened in this same bedroom, in this same bed, with the sunlight setting the white eyelet curtains aglow just like it was now. But her husband had lain beside her—and the curious twinges that had awakened her told her that this was the day her daughter would be born. Now, instead of her husband, she was sharing the bed with Catrina, and it was Catrina's insistent kneading of the bedcovers in the region of Pamela's breastbone that had caused her to open her eyes.

"Okay, okay," she murmured and began to sit up. Catrina leapt to the floor and waited while Pamela tugged a robe over her pajamas and slid her feet into her slippers. Then she scampered ahead to precede her mistress down the stairs.

Pamela had no sooner stepped through the kitchen doorway than a streak of pale fur grazed her ankles and disappeared around the corner in the direction of the basement door.

"She's getting used to Ginger," Penny announced, her voice overlapping with Pamela's "Happy birthday!" Penny was standing at the counter, spooning cat food into one of the large bowls that Catrina and Ginger shared as Ginger milled about below. "But she took one look at Catrina and that was that," Penny went on. "I'll take her breakfast down to her when I finish this."

Once the cats had been fed, Pamela took over at the

counter and set water boiling for coffee. As she arranged the paper filter in the filter cone atop the carafe and ground the coffee beans, she and Penny talked about their plans for the day. The birthday party the Frasers were hosting wasn't till that evening.

Pamela had a cake to bake, and the pleasant weather demanded a walk. "But what about a knitting lesson?" she asked. "Do you want to start today? It's officially your birthday now."

"Could we?" Penny turned from the refrigerator, where she was retrieving the heavy cream.

"Sure," Pamela said. "And what else will you do?"

"My job starts tomorrow"—Penny's expression combined excitement and nervousness—"and I've barely looked at my work clothes since last August."

Penny didn't approach Bettina's fashionista status, but under the influence of Richard Larkin's daughters Laine and Sybil, she had discovered the delights of prowling thrift stores for one-of-a-kind vintage outfits. Pamela had nodded in agreement as the author of *The Future of Fashion Is Slow* saw signs of hope in the fact that Penny's generation didn't see "secondhand" as a negative.

"I'll bet you're looking forward to more shopping adventures with Laine and Sybil now that you're home," Pamela said. The kettle began to whistle then and she tilted it over the ground beans in the filter cone.

"They're in San Francisco." Penny stretched her pretty lips into grimace. "With their mother," she added, "and Laine might not come back now that she's graduated." She filled the cut-glass cream pitcher and returned the cream to the refrigerator.

Penny would graduate next year, Pamela reflected, watching her daughter. She seemed so small, and so young—but she'd told Pamela more than once that she wasn't going to be one of those children who moved back in with their parents when they finished college. She didn't have a parent in San Francisco to draw her all the way across the country, but she'd go somewhere, even if only to Brooklyn.

Pamela tried to banish this gloomy prospect as she slipped two slices of whole-grain bread into the toaster. Penny was saying something about how much Sybil liked Jocelyn Bidwell, and Pamela tried to keep her expression neutral as she listened and nodded.

When the toast popped up, she buttered it and joined her daughter at the table, jumping up again when she remembered that Penny liked jam with her toast.

The knitting lesson was set for three p.m. After breakfast, Pamela went upstairs to dress. Once she was dressed, she stopped by Penny's room to watch for a few minutes as Penny began to transfer from her closet to her bed the colorful dresses and blouses and skirts that she'd assembled into her work outfits the previous summer. Then Pamela returned to the kitchen and opened *Special Cakes for Special Occasions* to the page she had marked the day before.

The champagne had to be heated, but not boiled, until only a cup remained from a whole bottle. And then it had to cool before anything else could happen. So that step would be the first.

As the champagne cooled in a Pyrex measuring cup, Pamela turned on the oven and set her favorite mixing bowl on the counter, the caramel-colored pottery one with three white stripes circling it near the rim. Near it she set a smaller matching bowl. Into that bowl she sifted flour, salt, and baking powder and then moved it out of the way. She blended butter and sugar in the larger bowl, added sour cream and vanilla, and beat in six egg whites.

She combined the floury mixture in the smaller bowl with the buttery and creamy mixture, frothy with egg whites, in the larger bowl and beat until the two were well combined. Finally she beat in milk and most of the boiled-down champagne and kept beating until the batter was smooth.

The cake would be a grand three layers, with a delicate angel-food texture. The cake pans had to be lined with parchment paper cut to fit, and the parchment paper buttered and the sides of the pans as well. Then she divided the batter among the three pans, using a rubber spatula to capture every last bit, and opened the oven door.

Leaning into the blast of heat, she carefully arranged all three pans on the same shelf, closed the oven door, and checked the clock. In less than half an hour they would be done. That was just enough time to prepare the strawberries.

Pamela freed them from their plastic mesh baskets and rinsed them in a colander. Some would be pureed as an ingredient for the filling that went between the layers, but others would remain whole to serve as decoration for the completed cake, so first she picked out the reddest, plumpest, and most symmetrical from the bounty in the colander and set them aside. She made sure too, that the delicate caps with their circlet of green petals were fresh and intact.

Then she used a sharp paring knife to remove the caps from a few handfuls of the remaining berries, sliced the berries in half, and whirled them briefly in her food processor. The result was a puree, faintly pink, and smooth except for the tiny darker seeds. The recipe said to run the puree through a sieve to make it even smoother, but Pamela never minded evidence that her kitchen creations had been made from real ingredients. She didn't mind tomato seeds and skins in her homemade pasta sauce, or the fiber that remained around the orange segments in a fruit salad.

The cake layers would be done in a few minutes but they would have to cool before the cake could be assembled and iced. Pamela opened the oven door a crack to check on their progress. Their centers still looked soft so she closed the oven door again.

She transferred the puree from the food processor to a plastic container, snapped on the cover, and placed it in the refrigerator. Opening the refrigerator reminded her that the butter needed for the cake's filling and icing would be easier to cream if it was room temperature, so she removed four sticks of butter and set them on the counter.

Stepping through the kitchen door and to the bottom of the stairs, she called, "I'm having a walk."

"Okay," Penny called back.

The cake layers were done now, as tested by a toothpick stuck into the center of each. They smelled fragrant and sugary and they'd risen to the very tops of their pans, smooth and pale but with a faint hint of toasty brown around the edges. Pamela set them on the stove top and turned off the oven, then she was on her way.

CHAPTER 13

May could be hot, too hot to walk just for pleasure, but this day was perfect. Pamela returned an hour later glad she'd made space in her schedule to stroll down Orchard Street instead of up and wander a bit in the nature preserve across County Road, the thoroughfare that marked the western boundary of Arborville.

She returned home to find Penny sitting on the sofa and staring raptly at a magazine open in her lap. She looked up only when Pamela greeted her, and she lifted the magazine to display the cover, which featured the sweater she proposed to make. She had been studying the pattern. But in lifting the magazine from her lap she revealed a surprise beneath it. Precious was curled into a comfortable oval with her eyes closed, her tail lapped neatly around her and tucked under her chin.

Penny raised a finger to her lips to signal *shhh*, but the

damage had been done. The cat stirred, looked up at Penny, then at Pamela, and made up her mind. She slithered to the floor and crept across the carpet to take refuge under the comfortable armchair beside the fireplace.

"Are you ready for your knitting lesson now?" Pamela asked. There was plenty of time to finish the cake before they were due at the Frasers.

Penny nodded.

"How about a bit of lunch first?" The walk had awakened Pamela's appetite and it was past noon already.

When they returned to the living room half an hour later, Precious was crouched beneath the arch that separated the living room from the dining room. She watched them, her blue eyes opalescent in the light reflected from the big windows behind the sofa, as they took their seats.

"Now," Pamela said, "the first thing we have to do is roll the yarn into manageable balls."

Like much natural yarn from small producers, the Icelandic yarn they'd bought for the sweater came in the form of hanks—yarn looped around and around and around and twisted into a coil. The hanks that would become the sweater lay in a heap on the coffee table now, resembling large, fuzzy, cream-colored crullers. A knitter starting with her raw material in hanks had to roll it into balls or risk creating a tangled mess as she tugged it from the coiled hank.

Pamela demonstrated for Penny the pose she was to assume—hands extended, flat and facing each other with about eighteen inches between them. She uncoiled a hank and slipped the thick loop of yarn over Penny's hands so Penny's hands were holding it taut. Then she found the spot where the beginning and end of the long looped strand had been tied in a loose knot, untied the knot, and holding one end began to unloop the yarn.

She started by wrapping the end of the strand around a finger, slipped the tiny coil off, wrapped more yarn around it, and wrapped and wrapped and wrapped until only a few turns of yarn remained draped around Penny's hands and the ball she was creating had grown large.

"We only need one ball to start," she said. "And then we'll—ooops!"

The ball had become so large that it slipped from her hands and bounced onto the floor, where it rolled across the carpet trailing the long strand that led back to Penny's hands. Suddenly Precious struck, lunging from her post under the arch to fling herself on the rolling ball of yarn. Mother and daughter looked at one another, each face mirroring the other's disbelief and merriment.

"She needs a toy," Pamela said. "Of course, then Precious will feel welcome in her new home." She rose from the sofa and tiptoed toward the stairs so as not to alarm Precious. In the attic was a large plastic bin filled with odds and ends of yarn left from years of knitting projects.

In the dusty shadows of the attic, she sorted through balls and partial skeins and little orphan twists of yarn in colors and textures of all sorts. Perhaps some aromatic hint of its natural origins still infused the ball of yarn that had tempted Precious to venture from the edge of the dining room. Several years ago Pamela had bought a batch of Icelandic wool for a project of her own, an Icelandic-style sweater with a snowflake pattern worked in natural brown and white wool. A largish ball of the white wool that had formed the snowflakes still remained.

While she was rummaging in her yarn bin, it occurred

to her that knitting needles would be crucial if Penny was to have a knitting lesson. From the large assortment of needles accumulated over the years, she picked out a pair in the size that she recalled the pattern requiring.

When Pamela reached the bottom of the stairs, Precious was batting the ball of yarn here and there, chasing it and pouncing on it with apparent delight. Penny still held the end of the long strand that was gradually growing longer as the ball unwound.

"Pssst!" Pamela whispered from where she stood. Precious froze and looked up, her large sable-colored ears tilted forward. Pamela lobbed the substitute ball of yarn across the carpet. It bounced a few times, and Precious watched it as it began to roll toward the coffee table, one delicate paw still restraining her other prey.

The new ball of yarn came to rest at Penny's feet. She nudged it back the way it had come, whereupon Precious abandoned the ball of yarn that had first claimed her interest. As the cat threw herself on her new toy, Penny quietly stood up and reclaimed the other ball. Precious was so intent on her new prey that she didn't even notice.

Penny took up the long strand of trailing yarn and wound it neatly around the ball as Pamela reclaimed her seat and set the knitting needles on the coffee table. She picked up the magazine and studied the pattern.

The first step would be to cast on. The needles were quite large and the yarn was quite bulky, but Penny was quite small. So even though the sweater was meant to be loose, only forty stitches needed to be cast on.

With Penny at her elbow watching, Pamela demonstrated the long-tail cast-on process—not the easiest way to cast on, but Pamela thought it made for a nicer edge and Penny might as well learn it now. She fastened the yarn to a needle with a slipknot and then formed a sort of cat's cradle with her left hand, using two fingers and her thumb.

She dipped the needle in, looped a twist of yarn over it, bobbed the needle out, and the first stitch was cast on. She demonstrated a few more times and then Penny took over. After a few tangles and fumbles, she settled into an easy rhythm and soon forty neat stitches were lined up on the long needle.

The garter stitch was a good choice for a beginner because it required only knitting at its most basic: the stitch called "knit," and "knitting" was actually easier than casting on. Pamela demonstrated, thrusting the empty right-hand needle into the first cast-on loop on the left-hand needle, looping a twist of yarn around the needle—and then the graceful motion that knotted the twist of yarn into a stitch and slipped the new stitch onto the right-hand needle.

Soon Penny was eager to take over. After she had finished out the row and Pamela had helped her get started going back the other direction, Pamela left her contentedly knitting and returned to her cake-making project.

The filling was basically a buttercream icing made fruity by the strawberry puree. The butter was plenty soft by now and Pamela creamed it until it was smooth, the beaters clanking against the sides of the deep bowl. She added powdered sugar a few scoops at a time and continued beating. When all the sugar had been beaten in, she retrieved the strawberry puree from the refrigerator, tipped the plastic container over the bowl of butter cream, and blended it in.

To make the cake's icing, Pamela followed the same

procedure, except that in place of the puree she added the rest of the boiled-down champagne.

Assembling a cake was always the most fun. Instead of using a wedding-china plate, Pamela took a large round platter, pale blue and a thrift-store find, from the sideboard in her dining room and set it on the kitchen counter. She ran a knife around the edge of each of the three layers, which were still in their pans on the stove top, and inverted one of them onto the platter. She held her breath as she tapped gently on the bottom of the pan and gave an experimental tug. The pan lifted easily, leaving the cake's first layer centered on the platter, a pale disk glowing against the platter's blue glaze.

Pamela removed the other two layers from their pans and set them aside on a large cutting board. She peeled the parchment paper from all three layers, then she spooned half of the butter cream strawberry filling onto the first and spread it evenly to the edges. Using two spatulas, she positioned a second layer atop the first.

The cake went together nicely. After a few minutes, the structure was complete: three layers of the pale, fine-crumbed cake alternating with narrower layers of the lustrous barely pink filling. Pamela scooped the icing onto the top, using her rubber spatula to coax the last bit from the bowl. With a table knife, she gently sculpted and smoothed until the creamy icing covered every inch of the cake's surface.

To make the point that the cake indeed involved strawberries, Pamela took the whole berries she had set aside and, with their leafy caps still attached, arranged them at random on the cake's top as if they'd just spilled from a berry basket.

When she peeked through the arch that separated the entry from the living room to see how Penny was doing with the knitting, she smiled at the sight. Penny was intent on her task, Precious was cuddled up next to her on the sofa, and Ginger was watching them both from the platform at the top of the cat climber.

It was going to be a barbecue. That much was clear, though Bettina had given no hint of what delights were in store for the evening—but as Pamela and Penny approached the Frasers' driveway, the aroma of charcoal set ablaze wafted toward them. Before they reached the walk that led from the driveway to the Frasers' front door, Bettina called to them from the other direction and they turned to see her standing at the corner of the garage.

"Come around this way," she said. "We're out on the patio." She was wearing one of her jersey wrap dresses, in a festive print that seemed to include every color in the rainbow.

A pink-and-white-checked cloth made the patio table festive, and an array of snacks welcomed guests, as well as an ice bucket with the neck of a wine bottle protruding and four of Bettina's favorite Swedish crystal wineglasses. For the quick trip across the street, Pamela had left the cake uncovered. Bettina's quick inspection of the platter and its freight widened her smile, and she pronounced it "a perfect birthday cake." She reached for the shopping bag containing wrapped gifts that Penny had been deputized to carry.

Wide sliding glass doors opened to the patio from the Frasers' spacious kitchen. Though their house was a classic

Dutch Colonial and very old, they had enlarged and modernized the kitchen when they bought the house long ago. The improved version of the kitchen featured a cooking area separated from an eating area by a high counter—and a view of their pleasant backyard through the sliding doors.

Bettina led the way through one of the sliding glass doors and Pamela followed with the cake, setting it on the high counter at Bettina's direction. Bettina added the shopping bag with the gifts. On a lower counter next to the refrigerator, a package wrapped in white butcher paper had been opened and the wrapping smoothed out. Lying in a neat row on the paper were four steaks, thick ovals like deep red marble veined with white.

Penny had stayed outside to chat with Wilfred, who was watching the progress of the charcoal in the barbecue grill, where small flames still danced here and there among the glowing embers.

"And doesn't Penny look all grown up!" Bettina exclaimed as she and Pamela stepped back out onto the patio. Penny was wearing one of the dresses she had rediscovered in sorting through her clothes that morning. Pamela recognized it as something Penny had brought home in triumph after a thrifting expedition the previous summer with Richard Larkin's daughters.

It was a fifties-style sheath dress in a rich shade of green, sleeveless and with a scooped neck, fashioned from heavy cotton lace with a matching lining underneath. Despite Penny's slenderness, the dress gave her figure a womanly air—and the wineglass she was holding added to the effect.

Penny did look all grown up, Pamela had to agree.

This was probably the last summer her daughter would be home—home in the sense of still living in the house where she had grown up.

"Let's have a glass of wine," Bettina suggested.

"Yes, let's!" That sounded like a very good idea at the moment. Pamela followed Bettina to the table and extended a glass as Bettina lifted the dripping bottle of chardonnay from the ice bucket.

On closer inspection the snacks proved to be a bowl of Bettina's favorite pimento cheese, a bowl of creamy green dip that looked to owe its hue to chopped herbs, a basket of pita chips, and a small tray of carrot strips, celery, and baby tomatoes. Pamela and Bettina sat at the table, Penny and Wilfred joined them, and Pamela relaxed into an evening spent with her best friends in their pleasant yard as Woofus dozed under a tree.

The pimento cheese was a rich blend of mayonnaise and grated cheddar, made colorful by chopped pimentos and enlivened by a bit of cayenne. The neutral flavor of the pita chips didn't distract from its flavor and they were sturdy enough to convey generous scoops of the pimento cheese from bowl to mouth. The creamy green dip hinted at chives, parsley, garlic and an elusive something that Wilfred, who had created it, identified as anchovies.

After they had chatted for a bit and sampled the pitas and pimento cheese and the raw vegetables and creamy dip, as well as permutations like celery with pimento cheese, Wilfred inspected the state of his coals and pronounced them ready for the steaks. He headed for the kitchen and returned bearing the steaks on a metal platter.

"Ten minutes," he announced. "Maybe less."

Bettina sprang to her feet and began to clear away what remained of the snacks. Pamela took up the nearly empty vegetable tray and Penny the chip basket and they followed Bettina through the open doorway into the kitchen.

Four of the plates from Bettina's sage-green pottery set, as well as silverware and napkins, had been staged on the scrubbed pine table. Penny handed over the basket to Bettina and headed back through the doorway with the plates.

Bettina, meanwhile, was plucking four plump baked potatoes from the oven and arranging them in an oval serving dish. "They'll stay hot," she observed, "but just in case . . ." She added a cover to the dish and handed it to Pamela. "Come back for the butter and sour cream," she said, "and I'll follow with the salad."

The table was set, and the potatoes waited in their covered dish with butter and sour cream nearby. Bettina appeared in the doorway with the broad wooden bowl that held the salad—crisp Romaine dressed with olive oil and droplets of balsamic vinegar and garnished with grated Parmesan.

Fragrant smoke rose from the barbecue, teasing with its note of seared meat, as the steaks sizzled on the grill. Wilfred leaned into the plume of smoke, flourishing a two-pronged fork on a long wooden handle. He tapped and poked, and then straightened up.

"Dinner is served," he called. "Come and get it."

Pamela and Penny each took up a plate and stepped across the patio onto the grass. Bettina followed with her plate.

Woofus had risen from his nap and was watching with great interest as Wilfred speared the steaks one by one and set them on the plates extended to him by eager hands. The surface of the steaks, which had been seared to a rich russet brown, glistened with melted fat, and the aroma, with its hint of char, promised mouth-filling meatiness.

"Ladies, dear wife, take your seats," Wilfred urged, beaming with pleasure at his grilling achievement. "I'll join you in an instant." He returned the one remaining steak to the metal platter, picked up a knife, and sliced off a generous strip.

Pamela was halfway back to the table, but she turned at the sound of an eager _yip_ from Woofus. Holding the steak strip between thumb and forefinger, Wilfred bent and extended it toward the shaggy creature. Woofus leaned forward and gently took it from Wilfred's hand.

"That's all for now, boy," Wilfred said in a soothing tone as Woofus chewed happily on his treat. He fetched his own plate and claimed the rest of his own steak.

By the time Wilfred and Pamela reached the table, Penny had replaced the glasses from which they had drunk their Chardonnay with a fresh set and Bettina had brought out a bottle of red wine. Wilfred poured a few inches in each glass as Bettina added a baked potato to each plate.

"Salad with or after as you prefer," she announced. "Help yourselves!"

The steaks more than lived up to their promise. "Rib eye," Wilfred explained, "from a New Jersey farm, according to the Co-Op's butcher."

The meat was juicy and tender and just the right shade of dark pink—so tempting that everyone sampled a few bites of steak before slitting the dusky skins of their baked potatoes to garnish the steaming interior with butter and sour cream.

Conversation focused at first on the meal itself: Wilfred's discernment in choosing exactly the right steaks and his skill in coaxing them to the perfect state of doneness, not to mention Bettina's perception that simple baked potatoes with butter and sour cream would complement the steaks without distracting.

At this point attention turned to the salad. It sat precisely in the center of the table, accessible to all and furnished with wooden servers that matched the bowl. When the portion of her plate taken up by the steak had diminished enough to make space for it, Pamela had helped herself to a generous serving. The others had followed suit and first bites had been followed by general agreement that grated Parmesan was just the touch that romaine needed to make it worthy of accompanying a dinner of barbecued rib eye.

Pamela was happy to let the conversation flow around her then, and enjoy the food and the pleasures of the Frasers' yard with its bountiful shrubbery and patio with its geraniums in colorful ceramic pots. Wilfred and Bettina were eager to hear from Penny about the courses she had just completed and her plans for the summer.

With plates empty and stomachs nearly full—but with room for dessert—everyone leaned back in their chairs. They stared at one another in contented silence until Bettina said, "I think there might be cake."

"Indeed there might." Pamela stood up. Penny did too, but Pamela waved her back into her chair. "It's your birthday cake," she said. "You shouldn't have to serve it. And you"—she smiled at Wilfred and then at Bettina—"did so much work for this lovely meal. Please let me take over now."

In a few quick trips, she cleared away the plates, the silverware, and the serving bowls and deposited them on the counter near the sink. When she stepped back around the high counter to access the cupboard where Bettina kept her sage-green pottery, she happened to glance toward the sliding glass doors. Visible beyond them was the table on the patio, and something was going on.

Wilfred was not in evidence—though a glance to the left indicated he was tending the barbecue. Bettina had moved her chair to the same side of the table where Penny sat, the side that faced away from the glass doors. Head-to-head, they were staring at something in Penny's hands.

CHAPTER 14

Pamela collected four dessert plates from the cupboard and set them on the high counter. She circled back around the counter to take four dessert forks from Bettina's silverware drawer. She would deliver plates and forks and then return for the cake. It would be presented whole, in all its strawberry bedecked glory, and candles would be added and lit. Penny would blow the candles out and Pamela would slice and serve the cake.

She carried the plates and forks to the pine table and set them down for a minute so she could slide the glass door back. As soon as a narrow gap opened between the door and the doorframe, the conversation on the patio became audible.

The first words Pamela heard were "Brian Delano, photography professor at Wendelstaff College." Curiously, they were uttered not by Bettina but by Penny.

Pamela slid the door back farther. Head-to-head, Bettina and Penny were unaware of their eavesdropper, but Pamela could see now that the object in Penny's hands was her daughter's smartphone.

"Yes," Penny went on. "This is him, all right—and there's a picture." She handed the smartphone to Bettina.

"Cute!" Bettina exclaimed. "Your mother didn't tell me that part."

Pamela seized the plates and forks, stepped through the doorway, and reached the table in three long steps. Making no effort at stealth, she dodged around Bettina's chair and set the plates and forks down with a thump and a jangle.

Penny looked up with an expression that reminded Pamela of a much younger Penny caught reading in bed long after lights were supposed to be out.

"I was just looking something up for Bettina," Penny said. "She asked me if I thought Aaron might know anything about . . . about this professor she'd heard you mention. Aaron majored in political science, but Wendelstaff isn't very big . . . and . . . Aaron is interested in art . . . and . . ." Penny's voice faltered to a stop. With a quick swipe of a finger, she returned the smartphone's screen to darkness.

"Bettina." Pamela's voice was severe. "You promised you'd never mention Brian Delano again."

"Mention him to *you*." The doubt in Bettina's eyes suggested that she recognized this hairsplitting would not be well received.

"So it's okay to . . . to . . . I can't even think of the right word." Pamela knew she was frowning in a fearsome manner but she didn't care. "It's okay to enlist *Penny* in your meddling schemes to . . . to"—Pamela's voice rose in a howl—"get me married!"

Wilfred had been contentedly cleaning his barbecue grill by scraping the burnt-on grease into the still-glowing coals. Now he snapped to attention and focused his gaze on the patio. He hadn't heard the whole exchange, but it was quite possible he understood what had led to Pamela's outburst—because Bettina's concern with Pamela's single state had been an ongoing theme.

He carefully fitted the grill back into place and then strolled calmly across the grass. Penny was staring straight ahead but Bettina's head had sagged forward. Even the tendrils of her bright hair seemed dejected.

"Here, here!" Wilfred exclaimed. "We have a birthday to celebrate." He laid a hand on Bettina's shoulder, then he addressed Pamela.

"She only wants the best for you," he said. "We both do." It was hard to remain angry in the face of Wilfred's gentle magnanimity. "Water over the bridge, Pamela?" he inquired.

Pamela nodded.

"All's well that ends well, then. Shall we have the cake?" Wilfred began setting out the plates and forks.

Back in Bettina's kitchen, Pamela took the little box of candles out of the shopping bag that held the presents and arranged them on the cake, placing them here and there among the strawberries. She was happy to have this excuse to be by herself for a bit. It wasn't Penny's fault that Bettina had tried to enlist her as a fellow matchmaker, and Penny's twenty-first birthday certainly shouldn't be marred by an argument between her mother and the friend and neighbor who had been almost a second mother to Penny.

The smile she mustered as she picked up the cake and advanced through the doorway felt more like her social smile than a genuine expression of pleasure, but it would have to do.

Wilfred fetched his matches from the barbecue grill and soon the cake—already impressive with its three-layer height, the white icing that Pamela had smoothed to perfection, and the vivid strawberries complete with their green caps—was enhanced by a flickering halo.

Wilfred led an off-key rendition of "Happy Birthday" and Penny leaned toward the cake and took a deep breath. The sun was far from setting, but the candles added an extra glow to Penny's eager face and made her eyes even brighter.

"Make a wish first," Bettina urged.

Penny took a deeper breath, held it for a second with puffed-up cheeks, then exhaled in a huge gust that left only wisps of smoke where there had been twenty-one flames.

"We'll need a knife and a spatula." Bettina jumped up. Pamela removed the candles one by one, a bit sad that the cake's carefully iced top now resembled a pale version of a yard that had been ravaged by burrowing creatures.

"Who wants to serve?" Bettina had returned. Without waiting for an answer, she offered the knife to Pamela. Bettina had brought the shopping bag containing the gifts too, and set Pamela's large package in the center of the table with the smaller package on top, as well as a third package wrapped in paper different from the roses-and-violets pattern that Pamela had used.

Pamela plotted out the servings carefully, trying to give each slice a few of the whole strawberries she'd arranged on top. One by one, people extended their plates and Pamela slid the fourth slice onto the plate at her seat.

Almost in unison, forks were raised, but slices were attacked from different directions. Pamela teased off a bite of cake from the bottom layer, with a bit of strawberry filling at its edge, while the others started with the top layer, twisting their forks to capture plenty of icing too.

"Ummmm!" Bettina was the first to speak, if her utterance could be called speech. Her lips curved into a smile that resembled nothing so much as the expression of a contented cat, and she opened them to exclaim, "I can taste the champagne!"

Pamela never sampled her creations when she was in the process of creating them, and she had been curious about the flavoring qualities of champagne concentrated into an essence from which all the alcohol had been boiled away.

The cake itself was moist, with a fine white angel food crumb. The champagne lent a depth that balanced the sweetness, rather in the way that wine in a braised dish or stew added a touch of sophistication to humble onions, carrots, and celery. She took her time, enjoying the hint of strawberries in the filling, before carving off a sample that included the icing too and conveying it to her mouth.

Bettina was right: one could taste the champagne—though Pamela suspected that Bettina's presence at the liquor store while that essential ingredient was purchased had allowed her friend to give a name to the elusive tang that calmed the icing's extreme sugariness.

No one rushed, and the conversation turned from the cake to anticipation of the summer to come. The Arborville grandchildren would be taking swimming lessons at the town pool three days a week, and Bettina was to shepherd them there and back and serve them lunch afterward. And the Frasers' other son and his wife and the Boston grandchild would be coming down for a long visit, with cultural events in the city while Wilfred and Bettina babysat.

Bettina set down her fork, regarded her empty plate, and sighed happily—whether at remembered enjoyment of the cake or the prospect of so much family togetherness Pamela wasn't sure.

Wilfred gathered up the plates and forks, and the remains of the candles. Pamela rose and reached for the platter with what was left of the cake.

"I hope you'll take it home with you," Bettina said.

"But it was my contribution to your lovely barbecue," Pamela responded. "I can't take it back."

"It's Penny's birthday cake."

"We'll share it." Penny spoke up. "Half for you and Wilfred, and half for me and Mom. There's plenty."

There was plenty, much more than half left. Three-layers make for a monumental portion, even if the slice is just a few inches wide. In the kitchen, Pamela cut the remainder in half, transferred one of the halves to a plate from Bettina's cupboard, and swathed plate and cake in plastic wrap. She wrapped her own share in plastic too. Wilfred, meanwhile, was on his way back out to the patio, bearing candleholders with tall flickering tapers.

"It's getting dark," he said when Pamela returned, "but candles are nicer than the porch light."

It was time for the presents. Bettina picked up the package she had contributed to the small pile of gifts and handed it to Penny with an enthusiastic "Happy Birthday!" Penny slipped off the ribbon and then peeled back the wrapping to reveal a small ring box in the distinctive shade of blue that indicated the contents were from Tiffany's. She raised the hinged lid.

Before she could say anything, Bettina spoke. "It was mine," she said. "My parents gave it to me when I turned twenty-one. I only had boys, so . . . now it's yours."

"It's beautiful!" Penny reached inside the small box and took something out, a something that glittered golden in the candlelight. Pamela was sitting across the table and half-rose in her chair to get a better look. The something could be slipped on a finger, evidently, and in a moment Penny was extending her right hand to admire and then to display an unusual ring. It was a simple gold band with no stones, but the band swelled into a dome where a stone might be, and the dome was ridged in a way that suggested the texture of a thick rope.

"I've never seen anything like this," Penny exclaimed.

"It was a very modern look thirty-five years ago," Bettina said.

"You should still wear it! It's beautiful—too beautiful to give away. And it means something to you. It was a gift for your twenty-first birthday." Penny's expression was so sweet and earnest that Pamela felt a little pinch in her throat.

"Now it will mean something to you." Bettina reached out to grasp the hand wearing the ring. "And you'll think of Wilfred and me when you wear it."

"I will!" Penny nodded vigorously and her dark curls bounced. "I always will!"

Pamela reached for the other small package atop the large one and handed it to Penny with a fond smile. "From your mother," she said.

Penny untied the bow that anchored the ribbon around

the package and set the ribbon aside. She removed the rose-and-violet patterned paper to reveal a small box with the logo of the fanciest store at the mall.

"It's not really from there," Pamela cautioned. But when Penny opened the box, her sharp intake of breath suggested the contents were as exciting as if that store had been the present's source. From the box she began to lift a silver chain. As the hand holding the chain rose, a gleaming emerald pendant came into view, teardrop shaped and smooth rather than faceted. It was suspended from the chain by a silver mounting that resembled the petals of a half-open flower.

"It's your birthstone," Pamela said.

Penny grasped the necklace in both hands and held it up as if picturing it adorning an invisible neck. In the candlelight the pendant glowed a cool green. Then Penny undid the clasp and fastened the necklace around her own neck. Framed in the neckline of the green lace dress and echoing its color, the pendant lay against Penny's smooth skin.

Pamela had found the necklace online. She'd pondered and pondered—what would be a special gift for a special birthday? Penny had never had any birthstone-themed jewelry, and emeralds were beautiful, if expensive. Old things were almost always better than new things, so she had searched the Internet and been very pleased when the little parcel from a small town in Rhode Island arrived.

The online posting had identified the necklace as "an old family heirloom from an estate" and placed its age at "one hundred years or more." Another young woman had probably worn the necklace too, maybe even a young woman with a May birthday whose parents had recognized her emerging womanhood with the gift of an emerald necklace to enhance her beauty. Maybe that young woman too had sat at a dinner table in flickering candlelight as her mother rejoiced in her daughter's maturity while reflecting with a pang that she would soon embark on her own life.

"It's beautiful, Mom." Penny's tone was almost reverent. She tipped her head to admire it and raised a hand to finger its smooth contours. "Thank you! This is the best twenty-first birthday party a person could ever have." She looked up and her glance and smile took in all three of her fellow diners.

The last gift seemed an anticlimax, but Pamela nudged it across the table saying, "One more to go."

Penny removed ribbon and wrapping to reveal a large coffee-table-type art book.

"Berthe Morisot," Pamela said as Penny bent close to try to read the print on the cover. It had grown too dark for the candles to help very much. "You emailed once about a paper you wrote on female French Impressionists. I saw it at a tag sale and put it away for . . . for now."

It had also become almost chilly. "Shall we go inside for coffee?" Bettina suggested. "And maybe a little more cake. From my share," she added hastily. "Your share is for you and Penny to have for breakfast."

An hour later, coffee had been drunk by all and cake had been eaten by some in the cozy comfort of the Frasers' living room. While Penny and Wilfred were clearing away cups and plates and forks, Pamela and Bettina set a time the next morning for their return visit to the hardware store to talk to Dennis Cummings. Then Pamela and Penny crossed the street to their own house as Wilfred and Bettina waved them on their way.

It was late, and Penny had to get up early to catch the bus into the city for her first day back at work. But she came downstairs in her pajamas, looking more like the Penny of old than the young woman ready to embark on her own life.

"Mom?" she said as Pamela looked up from the BBC mystery she was watching. "I'm sorry."

What could Penny mean? Pamela reviewed the evening in her mind—the coffee, the gift opening, the cake, the barbecue . . . it had all been so pleasant, except—

Penny articulated the thought just then taking shape in Pamela's mind.

"Brian Delano." Penny's head sagged forward and her pretty lips twisted into a rueful smile. "I shouldn't have gone along with Bettina."

Pamela climbed to her feet. As a calm British voice announced that a suspect had been arrested, she gathered Penny up in a hug and assured her that all was forgiven.

Monday morning, Penny was the first one stirring. By the time Pamela and Catrina arrived in the kitchen, Ginger was already nibbling at the cat food Penny had set out, the *Register* had been fetched, and the kettle was whistling.

Penny was standing at the counter pouring ground beans from the coffee grinder into the filter cone atop the carafe. She was dressed for her first day back at work in a dress that Pamela recognized as another thrift-store find. The fabric was crisp white cotton with black polka dots, and the style—a full skirt gathered onto a fitted bodice—evoked the 1950s.

"You look summery," Pamela said. "Are you nervous?"

Penny laughed. "It's not a very hard job, Mom. I just mostly sit at a desk and make sure things get delivered to the people who bought them." She turned off the burner under the kettle and tipped the kettle over the filter cone. With a sizzle, the boiling water surged through the kettle's spout and the aroma of brewing coffee rose from the carafe. "It's fun being in the city, though, and going outside at lunchtime and walking around . . . like I *belong* there."

As the boiling water dripped through the grounds, Pamela slipped two slices of whole-grain bread into the toaster and set the butter on the kitchen table. Catrina had joined her daughter at the communal food bowl.

"No sign of Precious this morning?" Pamela asked.

"No." Penny shook her head. "I took some food down, and I made sure to leave the basement door ajar in case she wants to come up later."

Penny just had time for a quick piece of toast and a quick cup of coffee, and then she was off to catch her bus on Arborville Avenue. Pamela refilled her own cup and opened the *Register*. With—apparently—no new developments to report from Detective Clayborn, the *Register* made no mention at all of what it had previously styled the "Arborville Community Garden Murder," not even in the "Local" section, where local stories migrated after the initial excitement wore off. Pamela set that section aside and returned to Part 1 and an article about the governor's push for expanded preschool.

An hour later, dressed in jeans and a fresh blouse, Pamela sat at her computer reading over her review of *The Future of Fashion Is Slow* one last time. She closed the file, attached it to an email, and sent both off to her boss at *Fiber Craft*. No sooner had she done that than the doorbell's chime summoned her downstairs.

CHAPTER 15

Pamela would not have been that uncomfortable sitting on the sack of sand she had been offered. But Bettina, in her white linen pants and matching shirt, asked to remain standing, so Dennis Cummings remained on his feet also. He had led them down a narrow set of steps into the hardware store's basement storeroom and workshop, usually off limits to customers. He was a burly man in his mid-forties, with thick salt-and-pepper hair and a permanent five o'clock shadow.

His offer of the bag of sand had been wordless, because from the moment he beckoned them to follow him down the stairs, he had been snuffling into a large handkerchief, and the sounds emerging from his mouth had been barely controlled gasps and gulps.

Bettina's line of questioning had been gentle. After they entered the store and located him in the booth at the store's center, she had introduced herself as "Bettina Fraser from the *Advocate*" and asked if he thought lax security at the community gardens was responsible for the murder of his late tenant, Jenny Miller.

"Why are you asking me?" he had asked.

"I'm asking lots of people." Seeming to realize that her flirtatious approach to interviewing wasn't appropriate given the topic, Bettina had adopted a look of concern that Pamela associated with female anchor persons on the television news—an intent gaze coupled with a slight frown that detracted not one bit from the effect of their flawless makeup. "Lots of people," Bettina repeated, "but since you were her landlord—"

The goal in talking to Dennis had been to figure out if he had an alibi for the night Jenny was killed. How on earth was Bettina going to work her way around to that? Pamela had been wondering.

But Bettina had paused, then continued. "People who knew her might have stronger opinions. They've lost a . . . friend, after all." Was it Pamela's imagination, or had Bettina stressed "knew her" in a suggestive way, and then inserted an even more suggestive pause before "friend"?

At that point, Dennis's face had seemed to collapse. He had pulled out a handkerchief to hide the ruin and now here they were standing awkwardly in a windowless room surrounded by out-of-season supplies like snow shovels and ice scrapers.

"I guess you knew her pretty well," Bettina suggested delicately as the snuffling abated.

"I . . ." Dennis looked around as if seeking inspiration. "I . . . of course I knew her . . ." he said, in a voice squeezed by a tight throat.

"She was such an attractive young woman . . ." Bettina let the thought hang unfinished in the air. "You've had a hard time keeping your mind on your work, I suspect. Saturday is a busy day for a hardware store, especially this time of year, but—"

"I wasn't here. Yes, yes. Rod told me you were looking for me." The words were muffled by the handkerchief with which Dennis was mopping his face. "I was fishing, trying to work things out."

"Things?" Her sympathetic gaze and gentle tone reminded Pamela of Bettina's interactions with Woofus.

"Ohhh!" Dennis sank down onto a pile of sacks labeled ICE MELT—FIRST CHOICE FOR SIDEWALKS AND DRIVEWAYS. His head sagged and he lifted both hands to his face.

Ignoring the possible effect on her white linen pants, Bettina joined him on a neighboring Ice Melt sack. She reached an arm around his muscular shoulders. "You were in love with her, weren't you?" she murmured. He nodded vigorously, though his face was still buried in his hands. "And your wife . . . ?"

"She didn't know," he moaned. "I didn't know what to do. Sometimes you just can't help . . . I didn't mean for it to happen . . ." Great choking sobs took the place of words then, and Bettina stroked his quivering back.

"I won't tell anyone," Bettina whispered. "Don't worry. I won't put you in the article."

"Oh, that poor man!" Bettina exclaimed when they were back out on the sidewalk. With a few more whispered words of comfort, Bettina had nodded at Pamela and they had left Dennis Cummings to compose himself and emerge from the store's basement on his own.

"It was wrong, of course," Bettina went on, as they walked toward the corner to cross Arborville Avenue at the light.

"*Of course*," Pamela said. "He's married. And besides, I don't see how Jenny could—" She stopped walking but continued talking. "He's so much older than she was, at least fifteen years."

Bettina turned. "Wilfred is older than me," she said with raised brows that implied this was a fact Pamela should have remembered.

"Yes, but that's—"

"Neither here nor there," Bettina interrupted. "When you're swept off your feet."

"Oh, Bettina!" Pamela heard more amazement in her voice than she'd intended, and Bettina took a step backward. "You don't mean you think what he did was okay!"

The light had turned green. Bettina grabbed Pamela's hand and tugged her the remaining several yards to the corner.

"It's eleven-thirty," Bettina said after consulting her pretty gold watch when they reached the other side of the street. "Just the right time for lunch at Hyler's. It won't be crowded yet." Bettina turned away and gestured at the back of her white linen pants. "Do I have dirt back here now?" she asked. "From when I sat on that bag of salt?"

"Maybe a little," Pamela said. "Just a little smudge. I don't think anyone will notice, and we'll be sitting down anyway."

Once they were settled in one of the capacious booths, upholstered in burgundy Naugahyde, that gave Hyler's Luncheonette its character, there was no need to worry that the smudge on Bettina's pants, actually quite large, would be remarked.

They acknowledged their server's welcome and accepted the oversize menus that were a Hyler's institution. For a few minutes, Bettina was silent, and invisible behind the huge menu except for a few tendrils of scarlet hair peeking over the top.

When she spoke, it was to ask, "Can you remember if we had the tuna melts lately?"

From behind her own menu, Pamela responded, "Not for a while, and they are awfully good here."

"We don't always have to have the same thing." Bettina lowered her menu.

"I want a tuna melt," Pamela said, "and a vanilla shake."

"Ready to order, ladies?" The server, a middle-aged woman who had worked at Hyler's the whole time Pamela had lived in Arborville, it seemed, had appeared at the end of the booth.

"Two tuna melts." Bettina handed her menu back. "And two vanilla shakes."

"You don't really think it was okay for him to be having an affair with Jenny, do you?" Pamela asked after the server had noted their orders and turned away.

"No." Bettina shook her head. "But I believe he really loved her—too much to kill her, for whatever reason. And I can't believe that, like we discussed, she could have been holding the affair over him and threatening to tell his wife. She wasn't that kind of person and he's a nice man. He special-ordered a replacement for a valve in our kitchen faucet last year when the sprayer wouldn't work and the plumber couldn't figure out what was wrong."

"So we don't care if he has an alibi for the night Jenny

was killed—because he's so nice?" Pamela hoped she didn't sound scornful.

"We have other suspects," Bettina said. "Lots of other suspects." She raised a carefully manicured hand and began to count off on her fingers, beginning with her pinkie. "Calliope, Danielle—and remember she made sure to tell us she was home with her husband all Monday night, but then Wilfred said he was at the historical society. Why would she volunteer an alibi unless she was guilty? And—" Bettina moved on to the next finger, but Pamela interrupted her.

"Apparently Detective Clayborn doesn't think any of the gardeners are guilty, including Johan Friendly." Pamela tapped the finger Bettina had moved on to. "The murder weapon—"

It was Bettina's turn to interrupt. "—was a knitting needle, and a rather specialized knitting needle at that, and I think we'd know if Dennis Cummings was a knitter. The Arborville knitters are kind of a tight-knit community." Seemingly unaware of her pun, Bettina concluded with an emphatic headshake.

"His wife is a knitter, though." Pamela offered a sympathetic half smile. It was obvious that Dennis's distress had touched Bettina's tender heart.

"Well, you're not going to convince me that he used one of Claire's knitting needles."

Pamela reached across the table, tapped Bettina's index finger, and said, "Claire Cummings."

Bettina sighed and retracted her hand, burying both hands in her lap. At that moment the server delivered the milkshakes with a cheery "Tuna melts coming right up," and Pamela was just as glad to set the topic of who killed Jenny Miller aside for the time being.

The milkshakes were a tempting sight, in their tall frosted glasses beaded with driblets of condensation. Bettina's hands reappeared. With one she coaxed her milkshake closer and with the other she tilted the straw protruding from its crown of bubbly froth toward her lips.

Pamela hadn't had a chance to sample her milkshake before her tuna melt arrived. It shared an oval platter with a small heap of fries and a portion of coleslaw in a fluted paper cup. The bread had been grilled to a perfect shade of golden brown, and between top and bottom slice layers of molten cheese framed a mayonnaise-y streak of tuna salad.

"Mmmm" was Bettina's wordless report on her milkshake. She set the tall glass aside to focus on the contents of her own platter.

Following Bettina's lead, Pamela took a sip of her milkshake. Hyler's milkshakes were legendary, made with real ice cream that had been made with real cream, sweet but not so sweet as to overpower the flavors of vanilla, chocolate, or strawberry that were the only three choices. She savored the creamy coolness with its hint of vanilla for a moment before swallowing, then picked up her fork and tackled the first half of her tuna melt.

They ate in silence for a bit. It was pleasant to disengage the mind, and not that difficult a task when assisted by the distraction of the meal. The grilled bread that enclosed the cheese and tuna salad was toasty and buttery, and the cheese retained its cheddar-y sharpness. The tuna salad, with its liberal admixture of mayonnaise, soothed the sharpness of the cheese, with the pickle relish in the tuna salad adding a sweet and sour note.

The fries and slaw were almost more than was needed,

but the fries were irresistible, their crisp and salty exterior yielding to the tender mealiness of the interior.

"Will you come on an errand with me tomorrow?" Pamela asked after a time, looking up from a plate that still contained half a tuna melt, several fries, and the fluted paper cup of coleslaw.

"Have you thought of another suspect to interview?" Bettina's fork, bearing a generous portion of coleslaw, paused halfway to her mouth.

"It's not that kind of errand," Pamela said. "It's a trip to the yarn shop in Timberley."

"I know Knit and Nibble is tomorrow night." Bettina's fork hovered in the air. "But I already have a project." She raised the fork to her mouth and in a moment she was chewing.

"I know." Pamela nodded. "But I don't. I finished the striped sweater for Penny, and I was going to make her another one for her birthday. She picked out yarn and a pattern—but she wants to do the knitting herself. So I . . ." She displayed both hands, empty and with fingers spread, to dramatize the lack of a project to busy them.

"The coleslaw is very good," Bettina announced after swallowing. "Aren't you going to eat yours?"

"You can have it." Pamela picked up the fluted paper cup and reached across the table to deposit it on Bettina's platter. "So, about the yarn shop," she went on. "What I'm thinking is that I'd like to make something for you."

"Ohhh!" Bettina's expression—mouth open, raised brows puckering her forehead—suggested that she was both delighted and touched. "That would be too too nice!" The open mouth formed a smile instead. "I would love that—and I'll buy the yarn, of course."

"No, no!" Pamela waved a hand. "I'll buy the yarn. I get to have the fun of doing the project."

"But I get to have the fun of wearing it." Bettina leaned across the table. Her voice rose and a pair of women at a nearby table paused their conversation to stare.

After quite a bit more back and forth, with voices lowered, it was agreed that Pamela could buy the yarn if she really insisted, but that Bettina would definitely pay for lunch, as well as several lunches to come.

Pamela returned to her meal then, carving a bite from the second half of her tuna melt and following it with a sip of milkshake. Bettina had finished her own tuna melt, but she tackled Pamela's cup of coleslaw, remarking again how good it was.

They chatted about Memorial Day, which was coming up in less than two weeks and which would be a very busy day for Bettina. Arborville marked the day with a parade down Arborville Avenue, followed by a ceremony in the parking lot behind the library, and she would be reporting on both events for the *Advocate*. Back at home, she and Wilfred would be hosting a barbecue for friends, including Pamela and Penny, and relatives.

Soon all that was left on their plates were a few fries and the fluted cups that had held the coleslaw. Pamela slurped up the last quarter inch of her shake, now thoroughly melted but still delicious.

Hyler's had filled up with the usual lunchtime crowd while they were eating. It was the go-to lunch spot for people from the banks, Borough Hall, the library, the hair and nail salons, the real estate agency, the shops, and the various small businesses operated from the offices above the storefronts. Tables and booths were soon in short supply, and their server, who had been vigilant without seeming to hover, appeared the instant Pamela set her milkshake glass down.

"Check, ladies?" she asked as she stacked one oval platter atop the other.

Five minutes later they were proceeding single file down the narrow passageway that led from Arborville Avenue to the parking lot, shared by the library and police department, where Bettina's faithful Toyota waited. En route back to Orchard Street, they agreed that ten a.m. would be just the right time for their trip to the Timberley yarn shop.

At home, Pamela brought her mail in and filed a few bills, then she climbed the stairs to her office. The computer came alive with beeps and chirps and soon she was watching her email arrive. The only significant message was one from her boss at *Fiber Craft*, and the stylized paperclip that marked its appearance in her inbox indicated that it was delivering work.

Yes, the message brought with it three attachments. The email itself simply read "I agree that 'Paisley Power' deserves publication. Please copy-edit it and the other two and get them back to me by 5 p.m. Thursday." Ranged across the top of the email, each with stylized paperclip and Word logo, were "Adam Delved," "Laundry Basket," and "Paisley Power."

Pamela opened the first one, whose full title turned out to be "When Adam Delved and Eve Span: Gendering Labor." Soon she was immersed in a discussion of the English peasant revolt of 1381, whose rallying cry was

"When Adam delved and Eve span, who was then the gentleman?"

A logical question, she reflected, posed in an era when people pictured Adam and Eve busy after their expulsion from the Garden of Eden with lives that paralleled their own: Adam with his shovel and Eve with her spindle or spinning wheel, and the division of labor between the sexes already firmly established. Never mind that cloth-making would have had a long way to go, given that their garb when they left Eden consisted of fig leaves.

The author focused, however, on what the rhyme revealed about medieval attitudes, and the illustrations, drawn from period texts, were fascinating in their depiction of spinning techniques of the time.

So caught up had she been in the text that Pamela felt obliged to go through the article a second and then a third time to make sure she had caught every deviation from *Fiber Craft*'s style and every British usage, like *colour* for *color*, that needed to be changed. (The author was a British academic.)

She was surprised, then, to hear the front door open and realize that it had gotten to be six p.m. She quickly saved her work and stepped out into the hall. Apparently she had been so absorbed that she'd been oblivious to mild reminders from Catrina and Ginger that dinnertime was nigh. Both were sitting just outside her office door looking at her reproachfully. Preceded by the cats, she hurried downstairs to greet Penny.

"Mom!" Penny was standing in the entry, looking as fresh as if she hadn't ridden the bus to and from the city and put in a full day's work since morning. In fact, she was positively glowing. "Guess what!" Penny exclaimed.

With hungry cats weaving about her ankles, Pamela beckoned Penny to follow her into the kitchen. There she opened a can of seafood medley as Penny revealed the source of her excitement.

"An internship! In the decorating department!" she gushed. "Not yet, because they have somebody for this summer. But they want me for next summer, and then after the summer it could turn into a real job, and"—she paused, eyes bright, to take a breath—"it would be so much fun, decorating people's houses with beautiful, beautiful things. I would just love it!"

After receiving a congratulatory hug, Penny left the kitchen and headed for the stairs. She was back in an instant, however.

"Precious," she said. "We have to give Precious her dinner."

Pamela would have remembered, but with Penny there to do the chore, she could busy herself staging the leftover pork tenderloin and scalloped potatoes to warm in the oven.

Once the salad was made and the leftovers heating, she stepped into the living room to find Penny knitting, with Precious curled up at her side. The Icelandic yarn she was working with was nearly the same color as the parts of Precious that weren't affected by the enzymes that accounted for the sable tint of her face, feet, and tail.

CHAPTER 16

"He's trying to evade me," Bettina announced from the porch.

"Who?" Pamela pulled the door back as Bettina swept in, dressed for the summery day in bright yellow pants and a print shirt featuring sunflowers.

"Clayborn!" Bettina's lips, sporting deep orange lipstick today, twisted into a disgusted knot. "I was supposed to meet with him first thing this morning for an update on the case—though I doubt he has more to report, and that's why he's evading me. Now he's scheduled me for tomorrow at ten-thirty. But I'll believe it when I see it."

"By the way," she added as Pamela reached for her purse and keys, "that was more than 'just a little smudge' on the back of my pants yesterday. I want to drop them at the cleaners on our way through town, and I hope they

can get it out. That bag of salt wasn't very comfortable either."

"Nobody at Hyler's noticed," Pamela said comfortingly. "I'm sure."

Once the white linen pants were dropped off along
Arborville Avenue, Pamela cut over to County Road. For
two centuries or more, County Road had served the in-
habitants of northern New Jersey, connecting farmers
with their markets in the small towns along its route, even
when it was little more than a dirt trail and its traffic consisted of carts drawn by horses. Now it connected Arborville and towns to the south with Timberley and towns to
the north, the per capita income rising the farther north
one traveled.

The stylish blond woman who was the yarn shop's
proprietress nodded in greeting as they entered, but she
was busy with another customer, a middle-aged man.
Pamela and Bettina were happy to browse, enjoying the
experience of being in a room whose walls consisted of
shelves and cubbies piled with yarn of all colors and textures.

"Pick anything you like," Pamela urged as Bettina
paused near a display of yarn identified as NEW—FROM
AUSTRALIA. The texture was delicate and the colors were
muted tones that suggested natural dyes. Bettina fingered
a skein in a shade of blue that evoked the pale but intense
blue of a periwinkle.

"This is just beautiful." She sighed. "Do you think . . . ?"

"Of course." Pamela smiled, picked up the skein, and
counted all the others in that shade. "Plenty for almost
anything, I think," she said. "Now, to find a pattern."

A rack near the counter held knitting magazines and pattern books. As Bettina paged through an issue of a magazine that featured the most avant-garde designs, Pamela absentmindedly watched as the shop's proprietress slipped five skeins of dark green yarn into a bag, along with two sets of knitting needles, and handed it to the middle-aged man, along with a page apparently torn from a magazine.

"This should be all you need for your project," she said, "and if you have an unused skein you can return it. Dye lots don't always match if you have to buy more later. So it's better to buy too much at the start."

With thanks, the man was on his way. As the door closed behind him, the woman smiled. "They always say it's for their wives," she commented. "I don't know why they should be embarrassed. Sailors used to knit."

Pamela nodded. She had once read an article on that very topic for *Fiber Craft*. And of course there was Roland.

From the direction of the magazine and book rack Bettina's voice claimed her attention then. "What would you think of this?" she asked, holding the magazine open to a page that showed a lissome fair-haired model wearing a wide-necked sweater that dipped off one slender shoulder. It had been worked in a shade of blue similar to the yarn that had caught Bettina's eye.

The sleeves tapered, from wide at the shoulders to narrow at the wrists, and the sweater tapered too, fitting snugly but without ribbing around the model's slender hips. The stitch the pattern used created an interesting pucker texture.

Bettina handed the magazine to Pamela, who took it and studied the pattern's description. "Seersucker stitch," she murmured, then said to Bettina, "Sure! It will keep me busy for many Knit and Nibbles, it should be finished by the time the weather gets chilly again, and it will be a chance to learn a new stitch. The sweater will look great on you besides."

Bettina certainly didn't resemble the lissome model, but she wore her clothes with great flair. Pamela was sure her friend would show the sweater to fine advantage.

Pamela's afternoon had been busy. Bettina had stopped in for a bit when they returned to Orchard Street and they had rolled one of the skeins, a hank really, of the Australian yarn into a manageable ball so Pamela could launch the new project that evening.

When Bettina left, Pamela had walked to the Co-Op to stock up on food for the week. With Penny home and providing an audience for her cooking, Pamela looked forward to revisiting recipes that she never made just for herself.

She had spent an hour at her computer working on "Paisley Power," and then braised chicken thighs with tomatoes and green olives, to be served with brown rice. The brown rice was ready just as Penny arrived home from the city and they'd had a pleasant meal and chatted about Penny's day and Pamela's new knitting project.

Now she was standing in her entry with knitting bag in hand, watching through the open door as Bettina backed her Toyota out of the Frasers' driveway. In a minute Pamela had joined her friend at the curb and they were on their way to the Farm, since that evening's meeting of Knit and Nibble was to take place at Roland's.

* * *

Melanie DeCamp opened the front door before they rang. She was accompanied by the DeCamps' dachshund, Ramona, who was squirming with delight. The fact that Melanie held a leash that was tethered to Ramona's collar suggested the reason for the animal's excitement: a walk was in the offing.

Though the occasion was only a walk around the neighborhood, Melanie DeCamp was groomed with her usual fastidiousness, her blond hair pulled into a smooth twist and a long silky blouse in a flattering shade of cream lending elegance to her smooth black leggings.

"Please come in!" she welcomed them, stepping back and leading Ramona to a spot where she wasn't underfoot. "You're the first ones and Roland is still in the kitchen." She smiled. "He's very excited about the dessert he's going to be serving."

Bettina stepped over the threshold and Pamela followed her into the DeCamps' living room. Bettina looked longingly at the comfortable armchair, but they knew that was always reserved for Nell. The room's other seating possibilities were sleekly modern, a low-slung turquoise sofa and a matching low-slung chair.

"You're going to have to help me up," Bettina cautioned as she lowered herself onto the sofa.

Through the open door, they could hear Melanie greeting Holly and Karen and then Nell.

"I guess Holly isn't bringing Claire tonight," Bettina said as Pamela joined her on the sofa. "So we don't have to think about whether the whole group should get a say about new members."

But no sooner had she spoken than Holly stepped into

the room saying, "Claire told me she wanted to come, but nobody was home when I stopped to pick her up."

Noticing the look Pamela and Bettina gave each other, and interpreting it correctly, she raised a hand to her mouth and said, "I did a bad thing, didn't I? I shouldn't have just assumed I could add a new member on my own." She glanced from one to the other.

"All the Knit and Nibblers should weigh in." Nell had followed Karen, who had entered on the heels of Holly. "But no harm done. And it seems Claire isn't that committed to joining anyway."

She crossed the room to the comfortable armchair and Bettina spoke up, saying, "Go ahead, Nell. It's yours."

"Where's Roland?" Holly nodded toward where Roland's briefcase waited next to the low-slung turquoise chair that was usually his seat.

As if in answer, an electric mixer whirred into action in the kitchen.

Holly was looking very summery tonight, in shorts and a tie-dye T-shirt. The shirt echoed the orange streaks in her hair with bursts of orange against a dark background. She and Karen, who looked summery too in a cotton sundress that flattered her fair prettiness, took seats next to Pamela and Bettina on the sofa.

Once settled in the armchair, Nell had immediately reached into her knitting bag to pull out an in-progress elephant and the skein of yarn to which it was tethered. On the sofa, Pamela was studying once again the directions for the periwinkle blue sweater that would be her new project, and Bettina was pondering a length of knitting, taupe-colored, that had been set aside in mid-row. She contemplated first one side and then the other as if trying to decide which direction she had been going when she left off. Holly and Karen, with knitting bags on laps, were chatting.

Everyone, however, looked up when Roland strode into the room, preceded by Cuddles, the cat he had adopted from the litter of six that Catrina had produced nearly two years ago. Cuddles, the tiniest of the bunch, had grown into a splendid creature, glossy and black and devoted to Roland.

Roland pushed back his faultlessly starched shirt cuff to consult his impressive watch. "Ten minutes late," he announced. "I apologize."

With that, he lowered himself onto the turquoise chair, lifted his briefcase to his lap, and extracted a long swath of charcoal-gray knitting. Cuddles jumped up beside him.

"A new project?" Holly inquired as Pamela set aside the directions she had been studying and pulled from her knitting bag the ball of Australian yarn.

Pamela opened the magazine to the page with the photo of the sweater being modeled and offered it to Holly.

"Ohhh!" Holly glanced from the photo to Pamela and back to the photo. "This will look *amazing* on you," she said. "You're so tall and thin and—"

Bettina burst out laughing. "She's not going to be the one wearing it," she said, and she explained how Pamela came to be knitting a sweater destined to be worn not by her but by her friend.

"That is *awesome*!" Holly exclaimed when she had finished. "That is just so nice." She leaned across Pamela to inspect the project in Bettina's lap. "And what's yours? I didn't get a chance to ask you about it last week."

Bettina picked it up and displayed a piece of knitting about twelve inches wide, several rows of ribbing followed by a few rows worked in the stockinette stitch.

"Taupe?" Holly asked. "Would you call that color taupe?" With her taste for the colors that enhanced her vivid beauty, Holly could be forgiven for puzzlement when confronted by a shade that evoked a carpet color chosen in the hope that it wouldn't show dirt.

Bettina nodded.

"And you're making something quite small," Holly observed.

Bettina nodded again, mournfully this time, and said, "It's a sweater for my little grand . . . grand*child*."

When there was no response, Bettina went on. "You're thinking it should be pink. Or blue. Or apricot, like Karen's lovely project." She tipped her head toward Karen, who was sitting at the far end of the sofa. "I do too, for my beautiful little Morgan, but . . ."

And Bettina was off. Pamela had heard the lament many times before. She understood Bettina's grief, though she herself would have faced more stoically the pronouncement by Morgan's parents, academics both, that they were raising "an ungendered *child*," in her mother's words. "Not a *girl*."

Bettina's Arborville grandchildren were little boys, delighted with their grandfather's basement workshop projects, but Bettina was not to have the pleasure of mall visits with a granddaughter. And "girly" clothes and toys had been proscribed.

With Bettina, voluble in her distress, sitting right next to her, Pamela had no choice but to echo Holly's comforting murmurs. Across the room, Nell was listening too. Her lips were curved into a small knowing smile but her eyes, in their nests of wrinkles, were melancholy. When Bettina at last was silent, Nell spoke up.

"When I was a girl, girls had to be girly," she said. "Some of us—maybe even most of us—were fine with that. I loved my dolls, and playing house. But girls who don't want to be girly shouldn't feel they don't have a choice."

At that moment, the front door opened and Ramona stepped in, her toenails clicking against the wooden floor. She was followed by Melanie, and in the pleasant hubbub of greeting, as well as Holly cooing over Ramona, any thoughts of refuting Nell's point or agreeing with it were forgotten.

Melanie unleashed Ramona, who trotted down the hallway toward the back of the house. Then Melanie made a circuit of the room, exclaiming over each knitter's work in progress. She especially lingered in front of Holly, stooping to get a better look. Holly's project since she finished a sweater for her husband at Christmas had been a hand-knit dress in a bright tangerine yarn.

Holly rummaged in her knitting bag for the pattern book to display a photo of the finished product. It resembled a miniskirted pinafore knit in a stitch that created the effect of horizontal ripples. The model's back was bare to the waist except for six narrow knitted straps connecting the skirt to a band at the neck.

"That is fantastic," Melanie enthused. "And the tangerine will be perfect with your skin and hair. If I was younger . . . and maybe in blue . . ." She bobbed to her feet.

For his part, Roland was just casting off. He dispatched the last few stitches, folded the piece of knitting—a sweater back or a front by the looks of it—and nestled it into his briefcase. After clicking the briefcase closed and replacing it beside his chair, he pushed back his shirt cuff to check his watch. With a nod and a brisk "Back on schedule," he rose and headed for the kitchen with Cuddles scampering along at his heels.

Melanie perched on the edge of the chair that Roland had just vacated and joined the conversation, which centered on the town's proposal to host a farmers' market in the library parking lot on Sundays during the summer. The topic was uncontroversial, though Pamela wondered what objections Roland might have raised had he not been in the kitchen.

A cry of "Melanie!" from that direction was followed by "Never mind, I found it" and shortly afterward the aroma of brewing coffee announced that refreshments would soon be arriving.

In a few minutes Roland entered bearing a pewter tray holding five cups of steaming coffee, as well as two empty cup and saucer sets. The cups and saucers were pale porcelain, elegant but simple in their design. He set the tray on the coffee table and waved Melanie back in her seat when she rose to help as he headed back the way he had come.

On his return, he set a second tray beside the first, taking care to align the trays so they were perfectly parallel. The second tray was also pewter, and it held a porcelain teapot and cream and sugar set that matched the cups and saucers, a pile of small napkins, and forks and spoons.

As he turned toward the hallway that led to the kitchen once again, Bettina struggled to rise from the low-slung sofa. "Roland, please," she said. "Let me help carry things."

"No, no, no!" he called over his shoulder. "Just a few more trips."

It took four more trips in fact, Cuddles making the circuit each time as well, as Melanie served the coffee and tea. Finally Roland fetched a wooden chair from the dining room, pulled it up next to Melanie, who occupied his knitting chair, and tried unsuccessfully to hide his pleasure as people exclaimed over his creation.

To begin with, it was impressive to look at: a wedge of pie containing sliced fresh strawberries suspended in a shimmering jelly that was itself a deep red strawberry color. Each slice was topped with a cloud of whipped cream.

The jelly was Jell-O, Roland confessed, but with an admixture of cornstarch and extra sugar that made it linger in the mouth like a dense fruit syrup. The syrup was chilled, he explained, and then the raw strawberries folded in. The mixture was poured into a prebaked crust and chilled again, so the result was a refreshing summery pie, topped with the whipped cream that offered a contrast to the acidic note of the fresh strawberries.

From Bettina, on Pamela's left, came moans of pleasure as she lifted forkfuls of pie topped with dabs of whipped cream to her mouth. Not until her plate was empty did she turn her attention to sugaring and creaming her coffee to her preferred sweetness and hue. Holly, however, put her reaction into words, pronouncing the pie just "too, too amazing."

Bettina took a sip of coffee and lowered her cup to its saucer. "I can't decide, Pamela, whether your cake or Roland's pie is a better thing to do with fresh strawberries."

"Fresh strawberry *cake*!" Holly swiveled toward Pamela. "That is *awesome*! What do you do?" A dimple-inducing smile underscored her enthusiasm.

Not wanting to rob Roland of his moment in the limelight, Pamela said, "It's a little hard to describe, but I'll email you the recipe first thing tomorrow."

"Strawberries are at their peak now, that's for sure." Nell joined the conversation. "Did you know the Native Americans right here in northern New Jersey used to harvest the wild ones?"

"Wild strawberries?" Holly exclaimed. "Like that Swedish movie?"

"They're around," Nell said. "I come across them every once in a while in my yard. They're little and sour, though. We get spoiled with our Co-Op strawberries."

Heads nodded in agreement, and with the topic seemingly exhausted, people focused on their coffee.

But Nell spoke up again. "My rhubarb is ready, though, and there's plenty if anyone wants to claim some now. Just let me know when you're coming."

Pamela did want to claim some, and she gave Nell a smile and a nod.

With a glance at his watch, Roland rose and began clearing away plates and silverware. Melanie replaced the dining room chair and excused herself. Soon fingers were busy once again looping and twisting yarn as needles clicked and crisscrossed, and Roland had resumed his usual seat with Cuddles at his side.

Pamela was finding concentration crucial to the launch of her new project. The seersucker stitch involved sequences of knitting one stitch, two, or three, before switching to purl or purling one stitch, two, or three before switching to knit. Wandering attention meant purls or knits popping up where they didn't belong. It was a pleasure, though, to finger the delicate yarn and observe how the muted blue color enhanced the textured seersucker effect.

She looked up from her work, however, when she heard Bettina say, "What are you doing, Roland?"

He was evidently casting on for the next part of his project. That much seemed clear, because he was using the same charcoal-gray yarn that he had used for the section completed right before the break.

He glanced up with a frown, raised a finger, and intoned, "Twenty-one and counting."

"Sorry," Bettina whispered, ducking her head in self-effacement.

The next section of Roland's project apparently required a large circular needle and two skeins of yarn deployed at once. He murmured more numbers, checked the count of cast-on stitches by fingering them two at a time, then started the cast-on process again, but with the second skein of yarn.

Pamela returned to the row she had been in the middle of and checked back over what she'd done, to verify that the next step in the sequence was to be three purls. Bettina, however, continued to watch Roland.

After a bit, Pamela heard her repeat her original query. "Casting on," Roland replied. Without looking up, Pamela could picture his expression: a look he probably lobbed across a conference table when forced to explain a legal argument that he considered self-evident.

"Why the circular needle and two skeins of yarn?" Bettina inquired.

Pamela did look up then—conveniently, she had reached the end of a row. Holly and Karen, and even Nell, had gotten interested. "What's it going to be?" Holly asked.

"Sleeves, of course." Pamela had been correct about his expression, and now it intensified. But faced with a gallery of puzzled knitters, he explained.

"It's a technique for making sure the sleeves turn out exactly the same length. Both sleeves are in progress at once and you knit a row on each one and then another row on each one and so on. You just keep switching from one skein of yarn to the other."

Once the explanation launched, he warmed to the subject, seemingly as proud of his expertise as if he had been called to elucidate a difficult point of law.

"My neighbor told me about it," Roland went on. "We got to comparing notes about our hobbies and it turns out he's a knitter too. Ed Holt, just over in the next block."

Pamela felt the sofa tremble, then Bettina seized her arm. "Ed Holt?" Bettina nearly shrieked it. Roland drew back in alarm and laid a soothing hand on Cuddles's head.

"Is Ed Holt related to Deb Holt?" Pamela asked the question, trying to sound matter-of-fact. "She's that local caterer. Bettina and I are great fans of her food."

"I believe he is," Roland said. "Related by marriage, that is. He's her husband."

"Such a coincidence," Pamela murmured. Next to her Bettina had turned rather pink, and her expression suggested she was barely containing her eagerness to discuss this interesting new development. Deb had been so adamant about not knitting, but if her husband knit . . .

Roland had begun knitting now, deploying one skein of yarn while the other rested next to it in his lap. A strand of yarn from each skein led to the circular needle on which the sleeves would gradually take shape.

Pamela studied the narrow strip of knitting hanging from her needle and consulted her directions before launching another row. Soon she was caught up in the rhythmic dance of needles, fingers, and yarn, enjoying the conversation that ebbed and flowed around her without feeling a need to contribute. Roland's voice chimed in occasionally, and even little Karen's, but mainly Holly, Bettina, and Nell were comparing notes on the pleasures and perils (mosquitos!) of outdoor entertaining in the summer, though they were all largely in favor.

Uncharacteristically, Bettina was the first to pack up her work. As she tucked away the skein of taupe yarn and the needles with project attached, she whispered, "I can't wait to talk. Hurry and finish that row."

Across the room, Roland hurriedly checked his watch. "Not quite nine," he commented. "Only ten to."

But the others apparently felt they had done enough for one night, and soon Roland was on his feet, nodding at the compliments and thanks echoing around him.

"Really," Bettina assured him as she and Pamela stepped onto the DeCamps' porch, "it was one of the best strawberry recipes that I've ever tasted."

They made their way down the walk that bisected the DeCamps' artfully landscaped yard, followed by Holly, Karen, and Nell. The evening was clear, summery with the fragrance of flowery yards and cool with the moisture exhaled by the sweeping lawns that characterized the Farm. When they all reached the curb, Holly and Karen veered off toward Holly's orange VW Beetle, but Nell lingered behind, though Holly was giving her a ride up the hill to her house in the Palisades.

"Do come for some rhubarb soon," she told Pamela. "I have so much more than I can use—though I do freeze a lot. Not everyone knows what to do with it, but I suspect you have lots of good ideas."

Pamela assured her that she'd be stopping by and squeezed her hand in thanks.

CHAPTER 17

"Can you believe it?" The moment Bettina was settled behind the steering wheel of the Toyota, she turned to Pamela. "Deb Holt's husband knits! And not only that, but he knits with circular knitting needles!"

"Motive." Pamela held up a finger. "Deb believed Jenny was stealing her recipes and was going to steal her catering clients." She held up a second finger. "Opportunity. Deb's yard backs right up against the garden plot shared by Jenny and Janice and where Jenny was killed."

"With just a low fence in between." It was dark in the car but Bettina's nodding head was silhouetted against the lights on the DeCamps' porch.

"And now we have," Pamela went on, "means!"

Bettina nodded again, so vigorously that the silhouetted tendrils of her hair quivered. "She borrows a circular knitting needle from her husband's knitting bag, and that's that. I'm seeing Clayborn tomorrow right after lunch. I'll hint around to see who he's interviewed from Debbie Does Delicious—if anyone. And I'll mention that Deb's husband knits with needles resembling the murder weapon."

"And if he's not interested in following up?" Pamela paused and answered her own question. "We'll figure out a way to find out what Deb was doing the night Jenny was killed."

"We can't just come out and ask her," Bettina said. "But Clayborn can. So let's hope . . ."

"What do you think about Claire not coming?" Pamela asked as Bettina turned her key in the ignition and the Toyota's engine growled to life. "And not even being home—after she arranged with Holly to pick her up?"

Bettina shrugged and began to pull away from the curb. Once the car was in motion, she said, "You aren't thinking something happened to her, are you?"

"I'm not sure." Pamela stared straight ahead, into the darkness beyond the range of the Toyota's headlights. "Can a husband and wife be each other's alibi if either one of them might have committed a murder?"

"What?" Bettina's hands twitched on the steering wheel and the car lurched. "You think Claire is the killer?"

"We talked about that," Pamela said. "Maybe she found out about Dennis's affair with Jenny and decided to remove the competition."

"Why would she disappear, though?"

"Lots of reasons. She's the killer and she's hiding out. Or"—Pamela shuddered—"she's the killer and Dennis found out and killed *her*. Or Dennis is the killer and she was his alibi, but she found out about the affair and threatened to retract what she told the police. Or—"

"Stop!" Bettina exclaimed, and suddenly the Toyota lurched to the curb. "Take your phone out right now and call her. I won't be able to sleep unless we make sure she's okay."

"She won't be in my contacts," Pamela said. "I barely know her, and she's probably not in your phone either. But I could look up the Cummingses' landline." She retrieved her phone from her purse and launched a search for "Dennis Claire Cummings Arborville NJ." Bettina leaned over and studied the little screen as Pamela scrolled down.

"The hardware store is here," Pamela said at last, "but I guess the Cummingses don't have a landline, and I don't think there's a way to look up a cell phone number online."

"Lots of people don't have landlines anymore." Bettina edged away from the curb. "We'll just have to go to the hardware store tomorrow morning and ask Dennis if she's okay."

"The hardware store opens really early," Bettina said as she pulled into Pamela's driveway. "Contractors, you know. So I'll pick you up at eight—and we're not walking."

Penny was up and out by eight, though just barely. As soon as the door closed behind her, Pamela picked up the phone and keyed in Bettina's number.

"Stay at home," she said as soon as Bettina answered, and she quickly added, "Don't pick me up. I'll be right over, but I don't want Penny asking questions about what you and I were up to so early. She's just on her way to the bus stop now."

The route they took to the hardware store was there-
fore roundabout: down Orchard Street instead of up, and
north on County Road, and then a right turn onto the
cross street that led past the library and police station.
Bettina parked in the lot behind the library, and they
walked single file through the narrow passageway that
connected the parking lot to Arborville Avenue.

Despite the early hour, Bettina's ensemble reflected
her fashionista instincts. A crisp cotton shirt with wide
fuchsia and white stripes had been paired with cropped
fuchsia pants. White wedge-heeled espadrilles and her
jade pendant earrings completed the look.

A small crowd blocked their way to the booth that
served the hardware store as a counter, a crowd composed of men, mostly fit and young, wearing T-shirts
emblazoned with names and logos of companies like
TradeMark General Contracting or Plumbers R Us. Pamela caught a glimpse of Dennis hard at work processing
charge slips and bagging purchases.

Eventually the crush subsided. Dennis had apparently
been so busy that he hadn't noticed Pamela and Bettina
waiting off to the side, and now he was bent to the task of
filling out a form. He looked up with a start when Bettina
greeted him, and glanced around as if to make sure no
one else was nearby. The recollection of his tearful confession must have been very fresh. Did he fear a conversation that would launch more tears?

"We're just trying to get in touch with Claire," Bettina
said, with a smile that implied no ulterior motive at all.
"She was so interested in our knitting club and was going
to ride with one of our members, but she wasn't home
when Holly stopped by to pick her up last night."

"Odd." Dennis shrugged. "We were both there from a little after six. Just eating dinner like always."

Pamela and Bettina looked at each other, Pamela hoping her disbelief wasn't reflected in her expression. Bettina continued to smile. "Do you have her cell number?" she asked.

"Sure." Dennis nodded, wrote the number on a scrap of paper, and handed it over. "She won't answer now, though. She's at her job, children's librarian in Meadowside. She always loved kids, and we didn't . . ." He laughed, but not like anything was really funny. "Too much information," he said. "I already went there once."

The route to Meadowside led south on Arborville Avenue, past some of Arborville's oldest and grandest houses, situated on expansive lots and evoking in their classic architecture what passed for old money in Arborville.

Meadowside was not old money. It was new money—the new money of young people happy to find an affordable house in a town with good schools and lots of activities for children to get involved in, like the programs at the Meadowside Library.

The library was on a cross street just before the commercial district. It was larger and newer than Arborville's library, with a lot that offered plenty of parking. Soon Pamela and Bettina were standing side by side in the elevator transporting them to the children's library, which was on the building's lower level.

Claire Cummings seemed ideally suited to her role, that of a gentle ambassador from the world of books. Nothing about her, from her soft brown hair to her utilitarian sandals, was distinctive. She was just finishing a story hour when Pamela and Bettina entered her domain.

Ten children, no older than kindergarten or first grade by the look of them, sat on a rug at Claire's feet. Claire herself was perched on a child-sized chair, holding an open picture book with the pages facing outward. The children, who were white, black, and various shades of brown, were watching and listening as if entranced to a story featuring a duck, a fox, and an angry farmer.

"'And so,'" the story concluded, "'Farmer Wilson learned that there was more than one way to fool a fox.'"

Claire closed the book. Sitting with it on her knees she chatted for a few minutes with the children about what parts of the story they had liked the best. Then an older woman who had been sitting off to the side rose and the children began to scramble to their feet.

"I'll see you in a week," Claire sang after them as, holding hands in pairs, they were led from the room by the older woman.

The children's library was now empty except for Pamela, Bettina, and Claire, who turned to her visitors with the rueful smile of a person whose secret has been found out. Before she could say anything, Bettina spoke up.

"We were just in the neighborhood," she said, "and we thought we'd—"

"You don't have to lie." Claire closed her eyes and bowed her head. "I know you write for the *Advocate*. The big story is Jenny's murder and you know Detective Clayborn interviewed me and Dennis and pretty soon everybody in town will know. And they'll know why Dennis was a suspect, and why I could be a suspect too."

"You didn't answer the door when Holly came to pick you up for Knit and Nibble last night," Bettina said. Sympathy had driven away the cheer that usually rosied her skin and plumped her cheeks. "We thought something might have—"

"Happened to me? Can you die of embarrassment?" Claire's voice caught in her throat and she fumbled in the pocket of her slacks for a tissue.

"Oh, dear!" Bettina reached out and pulled Claire into a hug.

"I knew about the affair." Claire moaned the words with her face buried against Bettina's shoulder. "We've been married fifteen years. Men get restless." She pulled away, leaving a damp spot on the fuchsia-and-white fabric of Bettina's blouse, and dabbed at her eyes with the tissue.

"Otherwise he's been a good husband." Claire sniffed and transferred the dabbing to her nose. "I thought he'd get over it. And now, anyway, she's gone, so . . ."

Pamela directed a furtive glance at Bettina, wondering if her friend's reaction to this last statement was the same as hers, but Bettina's expression was inscrutable.

Claire noticed Pamela's glance, however. "You don't think—?" Her eyes widened and she took a step back. "Oh, no no no no no!"

She shook an admonitory finger at them. "I'm in the clear. He's in the clear. We were both home all night the night . . . it happened. That's what we told Detective Clayborn, so we have alibis and there hasn't been anything about either of us in that vile *Register* despite that pesky reporter coming around."

The door opened and a head appeared. "Is it too early?" a young woman asked.

Claire looked startled for a minute, then she glanced up at the clock. It was eleven a.m. on the dot.

"Come right in," Claire said, transforming right before their eyes into the gentle ambassador from the world of books. The door opened wider and a small parade of children entered, holding hands two by two.

"Can a husband and wife each be the other one's alibi?" Pamela asked as she settled into the passenger seat of Bettina's Toyota. She had asked before, but the question hadn't been answered.

"It sounds like Clayborn doesn't think they're guilty." Bettina shrugged. "Based on that or based on something else, I don't know."

"Maybe he doesn't know she's a knitter," Pamela said.

Fifteen minutes later, Bettina pulled into Pamela's driveway. Pamela started to climb out of the car but Bettina stopped her. "Wilfred is making his five-alarm chili for lunch," she said. "Why don't you come over? I've got a meeting with Clayborn but not till one."

"I'd love to"—Pamela smiled—"but I've got work for the magazine. Let me know what he says, though. I'll have coffee waiting—and maybe a treat."

Pamela collected her mail on the porch and, once inside, dropped obvious junk mail into the paper-recycling basket. She'd promised Bettina a treat, so before doing anything about her lunch, she set the oven to 350 degrees and took from the freezer a small roll of sugar-cookie dough. It was the remains of a huge batch she'd made way back at Christmas.

After a quick grilled cheese sandwich, she cut the still-frozen dough into slices and arranged them on a greased cookie sheet. She set the cookie sheet on the stove top so the heat rising from the oven could thaw the dough a bit.

The cookies could be baked frozen, of course, but she had an idea to make them a little more special—since at Christmas the dough had been glazed with bright icing and garnished with colored sugar.

She rummaged in the refrigerator for a jar of jam. Any kind would do, and what she found was strawberry. Once the cookie rounds had thawed, she pressed each one into a ball and returned it to the cookie sheet. Then she used her thumb to flatten each ball slightly, leaving it with a thumbprint depression in the center. The final step was to spoon a dollop of jam into each thumbprint.

She looked over the mail that wasn't junk while the cookies baked, a matter of ten minutes, and left them cooling on the stove top as she ascended the stairs to copy-edit the article whose title had been abbreviated as "Laundry Basket."

The full title turned out to be "What Was in Nausicaa's Laundry Basket?" and it was a fascinating attempt to determine exactly what, based on inventories of noble Bronze Age households, Nausicaa and her handmaidens would have been laundering when the shipwrecked Odysseus washed ashore.

Pamela had barely started her editing work at her computer when the phone rang. She swiveled her chair around, startling Catrina, who had just settled into her lap.

The voice on the phone was Bettina's, and she was clearly irritated. "I can't get in to see him," she reported. "I can't even get into the parking lot now, so I don't know when I'll be over. I'm still in my car. The parking lot is full of reporters and that van from the TV, and I just saw Marcy Brewer run by, and something's going on—just a minute—"

Bettina was silent, but on the other end of the line

Pamela could hear a muffled hubbub of excited voices and then Bettina's voice, also muffled, asking, "What happened?"

Pamela heard the words "body," "gardens," and "murder," surrounded by unintelligible sounds, then Bettina spoke into the phone again.

"Pamela," she gasped. "Janice Miller is dead!"

"Oh, no!" Pamela stared blankly ahead without focusing on anything, feeling as if time had just stopped.

"I'm going to park on a side street and see what I can find out," Bettina said, shifting into reporter mode. "I'll be over, but I'll get there when I get there."

CHAPTER 18

Pamela stood up, forgetting about Catrina, who jumped to the floor, magically landed on all four feet, and then reclaimed the chair as its sole occupant. Pamela, meanwhile, stepped over to the window that faced her backyard. She pushed the curtain aside and stared at the lawn and the shrubs. What did this latest murder mean? First the daughter and then the mother, both killed in the community garden plot they shared.

Bettina would come and they would have coffee and eat the cookies and talk about this latest development. But until she arrived? Pamela had always found that the routines of normal life were the best response to shocking events. She gently lifted Catrina from the chair, sat back down, replaced Catrina on her lap, and reread the sentence that she had been pondering when the phone rang. Definitely too long, she decided, and set about re-punctuating.

"Oh, Pamela!" Bettina swept in from the porch look-ing uncharacteristically disheveled. "I had to walk and walk"—she plopped into the chair that, along with the mail table, furnished Pamela's entry—"and these shoes just aren't . . ."

She untied the laces that, wrapped around her ankles, secured her espadrilles to her feet and slipped the shoes off with a sigh. Ginger appeared from the living room to inspect these curious objects and sample their smells.

"It's just"—Bettina stood up—"just too sad. I talked to Marcy Brewer—one reporter to another, you know—and she had almost the whole story. Is there coffee?"

"There will be," Pamela said. "Follow me."

Bettina hobbled after her, took her accustomed seat at the kitchen table, and accepted a glass of water as Pamela quickly ground beans and got the kettle started. The now-cool cookies waited in neat rows on the cookie sheet. Pamela took a wedding-china plate from the cupboard, freed the cookies from the cookie sheet with a spatula, and arranged them on the plate.

"Go ahead." She slid the plate in front of Bettina.

"These are delicious!" Pamela turned away from the counter to see Bettina holding the remains of a cookie, just a fragment. She'd already eaten the thumbprint, with its dab of strawberry jam. "They're like the Co-Op ones, except they're sugar cookies instead of that oatmealy tex-ture."

"I said there might be a treat." Pamela smiled.

When the coffee had finished dripping through the filter into the carafe, Pamela poured a cup for each of them and joined Bettina at the table, after first making sure the sugar bowl and freshly filled cream pitcher were at hand.

Bettina took her time sugaring and creaming her coffee. When it was the pale mocha color of melted coffee ice cream, she took a sip, closed her eyes, and sighed.

"I feel better now," she said. "So . . ."

And she described what she had learned from Marcy Brewer, who was the *Register* reporter usually assigned to events in Arborville, about Arborville's latest murder. The body of Janice Miller, who had shared a garden plot with her daughter Jenny, had been found that morning by a fellow gardener. The police had been called, and they had summoned Detective Clayborn, who had noted that the murder weapon was a circular knitting needle.

"Same killer," Pamela said. "Don't you think?"

Bettina nodded.

"You know what this means, don't you?"

Bettina, in the midst of biting into a cookie, shook her head no.

"Think for a minute." Pamela hadn't meant to sound so stern, but she went on. It was obvious. "Some of our suspects aren't suspects anymore." As Bettina chewed, Pamela explained, holding up one finger, then two. "Dennis . . . and Claire. If either of them killed Jenny because of the affair, why kill Jenny's mother too?"

"I didn't think he was guilty anyway," Bettina ventured. "And she's such a nice person, and a knitter." She reached for another cookie. "Who else isn't a suspect anymore?"

"Debbie Does Delicious." Pamela held up a third finger.

"You're right." Bettina nodded slowly. "Speaking of

delicious," she said, "have a cookie before I eat them all up."

"If Deb killed Jenny because Jenny was stealing her recipes and likely to steal her catering clients, why would she kill Jenny's mother?"

"She wouldn't." Bettina nodded decisively and the jade pendants at her ears swayed.

"So that leaves . . ." Pamela smiled expectantly and Bettina recognized her cue.

"The gardeners!"

"Johan, Calliope, and Danielle." Pamela took a sip of coffee, her first, and reached for a cookie. "The choice of murder weapon is so odd, though, for a person who isn't a knitter. How would a non-knitter even know that such a thing existed?"

"I don't know," Bettina said. "But the motives hold up: resentments about the tomatoes, and the genetically modified corn, and . . ." She paused and a pucker appeared between her brows. "Calliope—what was it she didn't like?"

"She thought they were hogging the land she needed to grow her flax."

Several hours later, Pamela was standing at the kitchen counter turning the last of her lettuce, cucumber, and cherry tomatoes into a salad. A trip to the Co-Op was planned for later in the week, but the nearly bare refrigerator shelves had yielded up the salad ingredients, as well as eggs, bacon, and Parmesan for a simple spaghetti carbonara.

Catrina and Ginger were already at dinner in the corner of the kitchen that constituted their dining room, feasting on a can of crab and salmon medley. Pamela had carried a serving of crab and salmon medley down the basement stairs too, and set it with a bowl of water near the shadowy alcove that Precious had claimed for her home.

When she heard the front door open, Pamela sang out a cheerful "Hello," but the "Hello" that came in response was anything but cheerful. And when Penny appeared in the kitchen doorway, her glum expression contradicted the festive effect of her colorful circle skirt and polka-dot blouse.

"I know about it, Mom." Her matter-of-fact tone implied resignation. "Lorie texted me."

"Oh, Penny!" Pamela set her knife down and reached her daughter in two large steps. She gathered Penny into a hug, resting her chin atop Penny's curly head.

"You and Bettina won't—" Penny's voice, muffled against Pamela's breast, faltered.

Pamela stepped back, gripping Penny by the shoulders. "Why would we?" she asked. "We're not gardeners, at least not *community* gardeners."

Asking a question like that wasn't the same thing as lying, was it? And besides the second part was true.

"I wish I could believe you," Penny said, and started for the stairs.

The next morning, Pamela extracted the *Register* from its flimsy plastic sleeve even before she fed the cats. As they prowled around her slippered feet, she spread the newspaper out on the table. Janice's murder was, unsurprisingly, the day's biggest story. In its largest, boldest typeface, the *Register* declared SECOND COMMUNITY

GARDEN MURDER SHOCKS ARBORVILLE. Slightly smaller letters below added WHOLE TOWN ON EDGE. The byline credited Marcy Brewer.

Pamela read the story quickly and noted that it contained nothing she didn't already know from Bettina's report. Marcy Brewer had been generous in sharing the details she had gleaned by the time Bettina approached her.

She folded the paper up and tucked it in an out-of-the-way spot on the counter. There was no point in giving Penny cause to raise once again her concerns about her mother's amateur sleuthing. But Penny, in fact, had something entirely different on her mind when she appeared in the kitchen ten minutes later and accepted a cup of freshly made coffee.

"I've decided something, Mom," she said to Pamela's back. Pamela was at the counter slipping two slices of whole-grain bread into the toaster.

"Ummm?" Pamela turned. Penny looked as bright and rested as ever, not like a person whose sleep had been troubled by worry about her mother's sleuthing. In fact, Penny was glowing with anticipation, as if entertaining an idea she couldn't wait to share.

"I'm never going to move out," she announced. "I mean, I'll finish school in Boston, but then I'll have that internship and they'll offer me a job, and I'll work in the city and that way I can live here forever with you and you won't be alone."

Pamela felt as if an intrusive hand had just reached between her ribs, grabbed her heart, and squeezed.

"Mom?" Penny tilted her head and squinted. "You don't look happy," she said in a small voice.

"Oh, dear!" Pamela sank into the chair nearest her.

"Penny," she wailed, "you have to have your own life. Take that job in the city, but live in the city, with room-mates—young women like you. You'll want to go to clubs, and shows, and bars, and parties, and you won't want to be taking the bus back to New Jersey afterward." She rested her arms on the table and lowered her head onto them.

"I don't want you to be alone." Penny sounded hurt. Pamela didn't want to see her face so she didn't lift her head. For good measure, she closed her eyes.

"I won't be alone," she said. "I promise."

The doorbell summoned Pamela away from her desk. Once she reached the landing, she knew her visitor was Bettina. Visible through the lace that curtained the oval window in the front door was a scarlet-haired figure garbed in bright chartreuse that stood out even against the fresh May green of lawns and shrubs.

"Nothing much that we didn't already know, or sus-pect." Bettina began talking the moment Pamela opened the door, and then bustled into the entry. "I smell coffee," she added. "Are there any more thumbprint cookies?"

"What you smell is the remains of coffee," Pamela said. "But I can make more." She stood aside and waved Bettina toward the kitchen doorway.

As Pamela set water boiling and arranged the paper filter in the plastic filter cone atop the carafe, Bettina de-scribed her meeting with Detective Clayborn.

The details of Janice's murder were exactly the same as Jenny's: she was garroted with a circular knitting needle in the garden plot the two had shared. The murder hap-pened sometime between dark and nine a.m., when a fellow gardener—thankfully not poor Marlene Pepper this time—found her. No detailed interviews with the other gardeners had taken place yet, but it had been determined that no one else had worked beyond dark and no one heard or saw anything before leaving.

"Hold on a minute. I've got to do this." Pamela raised the hand holding the coffee grinder and then pressed down on its lid. Violent rattling smoothed to a whir, then there was silence and Pamela poured the aromatic ground beans into the filter.

"Does he suspect any of the gardeners?" Pamela asked.

"I couldn't tell," Bettina said. "He can be cagey. But so far Clayborn seems to have satisfied himself that none of the gardeners are knitters."

"They could lie," Pamela said. "I can't see who besides a gardener could have a motive now that Janice has been killed too."

The kettle whistled, and Pamela added the boiling water to the grounds in the filter. Then the bustle of setting out cups and saucers, and making sure cream and sugar were at hand, temporarily took precedence over the mystery of the garden murders.

"Cookies?" Bettina asked hopefully as Pamela finished pouring coffee and took her seat. "I'll get them," Bettina added. "Just tell me where to look."

Only a few were left, but once the need for cookies and coffee was satisfied, Bettina circled back around to the topic they had been discussing. "Maybe Clayborn didn't go about it the right way."

"Ummm?" Pamela was chewing, enjoying the way the oven's heat had rendered the strawberry jam almost candy-like.

"If you knew that a murder weapon was a knitting needle and a police detective asked you point blank whether you were a knitter, what would you say?" Bettina fixed Pamela with a gaze that had doubtless convinced many a reluctant interview subject to cooperate.

About to take another bite of cookie, Pamela paused and responded, "I, personally, would say yes."

"But what if you hadn't knit in ten years, but you knew that in your attic there was a bin full of incriminating knitting equipment?"

Pamela smiled to herself. The question reminded her of those that had been raised in the logic class she took long ago in college. What did it mean to call oneself a knitter? How recently did one have to have knit? It was usually she, or Wilfred, who ventured into territory that might be considered philosophical.

She nodded and said, "That's a good point. If a person hadn't knit in ten years, it wouldn't really be lying to say, 'I'm not a knitter.'"

"I think we should talk to all those garden people again," Bettina said, "if only to establish that they didn't do it. Just a chat, you know. Try to work knitting into the conversation."

"That didn't work so well with Deb Holt," Pamela reminded her.

"We'll try to be more subtle." Bettina winked. "We have to try. Marlene Pepper would be so relieved. She's terribly worried that the town is going to terminate the community garden program—especially now that there's been a second murder."

Pamela started to stand up. The cookies were gone and the coffee cups were almost empty. "I'll get my purse," she said.

Bettina waved her hands as if to push Pamela back

into her chair. "I have to rush home and write up my meeting with Clayborn first—I've only got an hour before this week's *Advocate* goes to press. I'll do that and grab a bite of lunch and I'll pick you up at one."

"First stop, Johan Friendly," Bettina announced as she leaned over to open the passenger-side door for Pamela.

"Do we think he might knit?"

"Roland knits, and now we know that Ed Holt knits. And there was that man in the Timberley yarn shop." Bettina backed out of Pamela's driveway and they were off.

Five minutes later, she was turning into the parking lot that served the hardware store and the other shops on the east side of Arborville Avenue.

As Pamela and Bettina climbed out of the Toyota, Johan Friendly emerged from a door near the back entrance of the nail salon. He was wearing a summer-weight suit in the same pinstripe that Roland favored, tailored to flatter as best it could his portly frame, and he bore a capacious leather satchel.

"Ladies!" he greeted them. "Bettina! Pamela!" It seemed he had forgotten the awkward conclusion to their last meeting, when he had seemed to welcome the fact that Jenny Miller was dead. "Do you have an errand at the hardware store, or appointments at the nail salon?"

"Actually," Bettina said, "I was hoping you'd be in. Our conversation about your garden was so interesting, and I have plenty of time to do the article, especially since—"

He nodded and finished the sentence. "—the community gardens are once again in the news, and not in a good way." He dipped his head and murmured, "So sad." But when he looked up, he was all rosy-cheeked geniality again. "You were right about the crumb cake," he said, "and yes, I'd be flattered to tell you more about my garden for your article, but just now"—he hefted the satchel—"I'm off to Haversack for court. Today, and who knows how much longer?"

CHAPTER 19

"Up to the gardens to look for the other gardeners?" Bettina asked as they climbed back into the Toyota. "Clayborn said the crime-scene tape is gone."

Pamela nodded. "If we're going to try for casual chats with subtle probing, a seemingly chance encounter will be less suspicious than tracking them down at home."

The route to the gardens led north on Arborville Avenue for a few blocks, then to the right up a gentle incline that eventually became the steep backside of the cliffs overlooking the Hudson River. But before that happened, the route turned left and meandered through a hilly patch of woods.

Beyond the woods, the actual road ended and the Toyota bounced ahead on a rutted path covered with gravel. The path widened into the gravel-covered lot where the gardeners parked.

Pamela was of two minds about whether she wanted the visit to the gardens to include a look at the garden plot where Jenny and Janice had been killed. Glimpsing the spot from Deb Holt's kitchen window had been troubling enough. She had been silent on the short journey, pondering the question and so lost in thought that she jumped when Bettina said, "We're here."

She was saved having to decide just then by the fact that right before them, in the garden plot that bordered the parking lot, she recognized Calliope Drew. Gray hair bound into a careless bundle that overflowed onto her muscular back, Calliope was stepping gingerly among a stand of spiky plants that reached the hem of her long, gauzy skirt.

Calliope looked up as they crunched across the gravel, Bettina walking carefully given that she was wearing a delicate pair of multi-strapped sandals. "Bettina!" Calliope cried. "Coming to inspect the scene of the crime?"

Bettina waited until they reached the edge of the garden plot, which was marked off with stakes at the corners but no fencing, to respond.

"Oh, no," she said. "I met with Clayborn this morning and learned all I wanted to know—too much, really—about the . . . crime, and I already filed my article for this week's *Advocate*. Such a shock! Two murders in our little town—and so close together!"

Calliope's angular face, free of makeup but rather handsome, already showed the beginnings of a tan. She listened expectantly, as if Bettina somehow owed some explanation for her visit to the gardens. Bettina was a mistress of deflection, however. Bending over to examine one of the spiky plants, she commented, "How lovely—and you have so many of them."

"Flax," Calliope intoned. "Quite lovely indeed! You should see this plot when they're all in flower—it's like a sea, a small sea, of blue. But that's not why I grow flax!"

"Linen," Pamela suggested.

"Of course!" Calliope nodded at Pamela as if commending a clever student. "One of humanity's oldest fibers—thousands of years old. And flax was probably grown right here in Arborville, before it was Arborville and before the US was the US. Linen was such a crucial part of people's wardrobes in the Revolutionary era that up to a quarter acre of farmland would be devoted to growing flax for each member of the household." Her expression dared them to contradict her.

But Pamela had no wish to contradict. "So interesting," she murmured. "*Fiber Craft* magazine had an article on growing flax and all the steps you have to do to turn it into linen. The process sounds very complicated, but it must be so satisfying—to make your own clothes starting with seeds!"

"It is." Calliope beamed at Pamela.

"And then," Pamela went on, "after you've done all those steps and you've got the fibers, and you've spun it or however that works, do you weave it? Or can it be knit?"

Pamela was quite aware that linen could be knit. She herself had made more than one garment from yarns that were at least partly linen.

Was it Pamela's imagination, or had Calliope's eyes suddenly darted from Pamela's face to Bettina's and back to Pamela's? And had suspicion narrowed her eyes or was she just squinting into the sun?

"Both," she said quickly. "Both, of course. Why not?

But linen isn't the only natural fiber I've thought about producing."

"Is it hard to knit?" Pamela asked. "Wool is a little stretchy and that helps, but a flax fiber—"

"Silkworms!" Calliope exclaimed. "Of course you have to feed them the mulberry leaves—that's all they'll eat. But mulberry trees grow in Arborville. There's a big one right down the street from me. Huge, in fact. It's been there forever, I'm sure." Calliope paused. She was panting a bit. "I was all set to order some silkworms and get started. Then I realized that they are living things and you have to kill them to harvest the silk from their cocoons. Many people don't know this! I couldn't do that—murder a silkworm. Could you?" She bobbed forward and fixed Pamela with a wide-eyed stare.

"Of course not." Pamela backed away.

"I'm glad to hear that." Calliope turned away and stooped to pull up a small broad-leaved shoot that was an obvious intruder in her flax field.

Only a few other people were at work in their garden plots, though all the plots, which stretched off into the distance with the backyards of houses that were part of the Farm on the left side and a woodsy hill on the right, appeared to be under cultivation.

Some were grooved into neat furrows and ridges, the ridges streaked with the pale green of emerging seedlings. Some were divided into quadrants or simply sown at random. Clusters of larger plants suggested transplants already rooted on windowsills, or the reappearance of perennials like asparagus. In a few plots, wire cages surrounded small tomato plants not yet in need of their support, and narrow stakes formed tripods in anticipation of climbing beans and peas. Here and there were trees and shrubs, or peonies and other perennials already fully sprung from the earth.

There was no sign of Danielle Hardy, so Pamela and Bettina bade Calliope happy weeding and went on their way. But when they reached Bettina's Toyota a small figure came into view. A woman was approaching along the gravel path that ended in the parking lot, head erect and arms swinging in a rhythm that matched her energetic stride.

They lingered near the Toyota until Danielle reached the parking lot. Then, as if she had just noticed Danielle's presence, Bettina waved and greeted her.

"What brings you up here?" Danielle inquired. "You don't have a garden plot." She studied Bettina with the large, pale eyes that dominated her features, then her mouth opened with a sharp intake of breath, and her eyes opened wider, as if she'd just realized something. "The *Advocate*," she breathed. "Coming to inspect the scene of the crime?"

"Well, I—"

What would Bettina's strategy be this time? Pamela wondered. The goal was to find out if the gardeners were or had ever been knitters. But Bettina had no chance to employ any strategy at all. Danielle lunged forward and grabbed her arm.

"Why hasn't Johan Friendly been arrested yet?" she demanded. "He should have been arrested *long ago* and now another person is dead, because *he* wants to protect *his* supposed right to *grow* his *unnatural* corn." Her pitch rose to operatic heights and then receded, only to rise again.

"I *know* you talk to Clayborn," she went on, fairly vibrating with indignation. "Why hasn't he *done* something? It's *crystal clear* who the killer is. Clayborn *interviewed* Johan, I know, because he interviewed *me* and I told him I was *home* all Tuesday evening and night and I think he believed me even though I'm *sure* Calliope told him all about the *tomatoes*, again. But I *really liked* Janice and she *wasn't* the one growing the prize tomatoes and it's just a shame what happened."

Then she was off, marching toward the narrow path that divided Calliope's flax field from the plot to its left, which featured a tangle of berry bushes and a small, blossoming tree.

Pamela and Bettina looked at each other. Bettina took a deep breath, as if she, and not her conversational partner, had been the one talking nonstop.

"The historical society doesn't meet on Tuesday nights," Bettina said, after they had both taken their seats in the Toyota. "So this time the alibi that she was home with her husband could hold up. Police might be talking to Danielle's husband right now."

Pamela nodded. "Calliope, on the other hand . . ." She stopped nodding and shook her head. "She got so nervous when I brought up knitting, as if she had something to hide."

"She *was* nervous." Bettina steered the Toyota out of the gravel lot. "We're talking about linen—and then all of a sudden we're talking about silkworms." She swiveled her head toward Pamela. "*Hello?* Where did that come from?"

"Of course maybe she was just nervous because she thinks Detective Clayborn has a reason to suspect her," Pamela said. "She brought that up the day she latched onto me at the Co-Op after Jenny was killed."

"I'd be nervous if I thought Clayborn suspected me of something," Bettina agreed. She drove in silence for a few minutes, over the wide gravel path and past the hilly stand of woods. After she made the turn that would take them back to Arborville Avenue, Bettina spoke again.

"I don't think Calliope is the murderer," she said, "even if she did think Jenny and Janice were trying to encroach on her flax-growing territory." She pulled over to the curb and turned to face Pamela. "She seems like such a tenderhearted person. She said she wouldn't even kill a silkworm. How could a person who wouldn't kill a silkworm kill a human?"

"That's exactly what she told me when she accosted me at the Co-Op," Pamela said, "and in just about the same words." Pamela chuckled. "It was like something she had rehearsed."

Pamela looked at her watch. It had gotten to be three p.m. already. The articles she had copy-edited were due back by five and she wanted to check over them once again before sending them off.

The shopping expedition to the Co-Op would have to be put off till the next morning, and tonight's dinner would have to be pizza delivered from When in Rome. But Penny wouldn't mind at all.

Bettina dropped Pamela in front of her own house, and Pamela hurried inside and up the stairs to her office. On the stroke of five p.m. she clicked on SEND, and "Adam Delved," "Paisley Power," and "Laundry Basket" were on their way.

When the phone rang, Pamela had just reached the landing. She continued on down the stairs and picked it up in the kitchen. Half expecting Bettina on the other end, perhaps with a new argument in favor of Calliope's innocence, she was startled when the voice that responded to her "hello" was deep and masculine.

"Brian Delano here," the voice said. "Is this the Pamela Paterson who was waiting for Triple A in the Wendelstaff parking lot last week?"

"Oh . . . uh, yes." Pamela frowned. Brian Delano was calling her. Could Bettina have possibly put him up to this?

"I took a chance," he said. "Everything is on the Internet now."

That was true. Maybe the call wasn't Bettina's doing. Brian's voice had been pleasant in the parking lot and it was pleasant now. Pamela suddenly felt wobbly. She sat down.

"I hope you don't think I'm stalking you." He waited as if for an answer. When no answer came, he went on. "I enjoyed our conversation. Maybe we could continue it . . . I think you said you weren't too far from the campus."

"No," Pamela said, "or yes, I mean. I'm not too far away. You mentioned coffee." What did it mean that she remembered his words so clearly?

"Or lunch? I've got an errand at the college Saturday—organizing some stuff for the summer school class I'm going to teach."

She imagined Bettina sitting across from her at the table and made an encouraging sound.

"How about Saturday? We could meet in the Wendelstaff parking lot at noon and take it from there."

"Oh, um . . ." Across from her the imaginary Bettina scowled and whispered, *Do it!* "Okay," Pamela said. "Saturday at noon, in the Wendelstaff parking lot."

Her hand was shaking as she returned the handset to its cradle. What had she done? But it was just lunch, not a big deal. She wouldn't tell Bettina, though, or Penny, until after the lunch—and anyway, after the lunch there might not be anything to tell. There was no point in getting them excited for no reason.

She sat there for a few minutes breathing deeply. Then from the counter she took one of the notepads that appeared so frequently in the mail. The sheets of this one had a seasonally themed border of rippling surf, sand buckets, and crabs.

"Lettuce," she wrote, and proceeded to list the items she would buy on the next morning's trip to the Co-Op. As she wound up with "whole-grain bread," the sound of a key in the front door lock announced Penny's arrival.

She stood up and stepped toward the doorway that led to the entry, but she stopped at the threshold. Sitting on the carpet and watching as the door swung open was Precious. Penny entered and stooped down, and in a moment Penny was cuddling a limber stretch of pale fur. A sable tail flicked in contentment.

The Co-Op wasn't Pamela's only errand on Friday morning. Knit and Nibble was meeting at Pamela's house the following Tuesday and she had promised that the goody would involve rhubarb.

Nell had rhubarb on offer and had spoken highly of rhubarb's possibilities as a pie filling. But Pamela had something else in mind. She consulted a few cookbooks and added the necessary ingredients to her list.

After a quick phone call to alert Nell that she was

coming, Pamela drove up the steep hill to the Palisades, where Nell and her husband, Harold, lived in a splendid old house constructed of randomly shaped gray stones. She climbed the steps that wove through a small forest of azaleas and rhododendrons and rang Nell's doorbell. In a moment Nell was escorting her down the long hall, decorated with souvenirs from the Bascoms' many travel adventures, that led to the kitchen.

With avocado-green appliances and pink Formica countertops, the kitchen too dated from an earlier era. A previous owner had modernized it in the 1950s and the Bascombs had bought the house as newlyweds and lived there ever since. Spread over the kitchen table in colorful profusion were stalks and stalks of rhubarb, like giant celery but glowing richly red with a slight pinkish cast.

"I cut the leaves off and put them in the compost pile," Nell explained. "They're poisonous, but the stalks aren't—and a good thing too. I have such fond memories of the rhubarb pies my mother used to make. Of course, people didn't eat so much sugar back then. An occasional pie was a real treat."

Pamela had come prepared with her own bag, though it actually was one she owed to Nell, who had given canvas grocery totes to all her friends in an effort to convert them away from paper and plastic.

"Help yourself." Nell waved at the bounteous display. "Four or five make a good pie, but take more if you like. You can slice some up and freeze it for later."

"That's very sad news about Janice," Nell commented as Pamela slipped rhubarb stalks into her tote. Pamela looked up to find Nell gazing intently at her, faded blue eyes grave in their nests of wrinkles. "Especially since it happened in the community gardens. To have a place as full of life as a garden become a place of death is just . . ." She shook her head.

"I'm sure Detective Clayborn will figure things out," Pamela said. Nell looked quite forlorn, still in her ancient bathrobe and with her white hair not yet combed.

"Are you really?" Nell's gaze could be quite penetrating. "Since knitting needles are involved, I wouldn't be surprised to hear that you and Bettina had been nosing about—on the basis that knitters might be able to identify a killer who is also a knitter better than the police could."

"Ummm?" Pamela tried to sound unconcerned.

"Are you?" Nell was holding a rhubarb stalk in a way that evoked an old-time schoolmarm brandishing a ruler.

Pamela hefted the tote, which had gotten quite heavy. She peered inside. "This looks like enough," she said. "I think you'll like my rhubarb creation." She squeezed Nell's free hand. "Thank you so much!"

CHAPTER 20

Sometime later, Pamela steered her shopping cart through the Co-Op's automatic door and toward the spot where her serviceable compact was parked at the curb. Normally she walked to the Co-Op and limited her purchases to a number that could be comfortably transported home in two of Nell's canvas gift totes. But choosing to drive rather than walk up the hill to Nell's and to combine fetching the rhubarb with her grocery shopping trip had provided an opportunity to stock up on staples and cat food, as well as ingredients for the Knit and Nibble goody and several nights' meals.

The space next to where she had parked was occupied by a BMW. Its passenger-side door, which faced Pamela's driver's side door, was open and a woman was leaning into the BMW, none too thin or limber, but managing to bend nearly double. She was muttering to herself. With a thud, Pamela's cart cleared the curb and she steered it into the empty parking space on the other side of her car. From there, she proceeded to stow her many canvas bags of groceries in the trunk.

She wheeled the empty cart up onto the sidewalk and added it to the ranks of carts waiting off to the side of the Co-Op's entrance. When she turned back, the BMW's door was still wide open, impeding her access to her own car. She stepped into the empty parking space and circled around to approach the BMW from the rear.

From this vantage point, she could see that the door was open because the woman was still leaning into the interior. She was probing under and behind the passenger seat, bobbing this way and that. Then she stretched farther to probe around the driver's side seat as well. A few bags of groceries sat on the back seat.

"Well, doesn't that just beat all!" the woman exclaimed at last. "Completely disappeared." Straightening up, she slammed the door and turned. At that moment Pamela recognized her—the portly girth, the rosy cheeks, and the tidy brown hair—and she in turn recognized Pamela.

"You were in my son's office," Frederica Friendly said, almost accusingly, "with that woman who writes for the *Advocate*." Her cheeks were even rosier at the moment, and her expression even less cordial. "You'll want to be getting into your car."

"No great rush." Pamela mustered her social smile, despite Frederica's grim expression. "I know what it's like when things go missing. Especially in a car. There are so many nooks and crannies."

Perhaps she hadn't expected to encounter sympathy. With a little *hmmm* and a surprised frown, she nodded. "I know I had the bag in my hand when I came out of the hobby shop," she said. "I didn't leave it on the counter."

Pamela nodded in recognition.

"Just a small bag." Frederica held up both hands and mimed a bag less than a foot wide. "It's not in the trunk—why would I put a small bag there?—but I checked. And it's not under the seat—either seat—or on the seat in the back or on the floor." She sighed. "I suppose I shall just have to drive back to Meadowside once again. And it's all the more annoying in that this is the third knitting needle I've had to replace in the last few weeks. They vanish! Like socks in the wash."

"Just one needle?" Pamela asked. The skin on the back of her neck contracted as if being swept by an icy finger. "Not a pair? Just one?"

"One of those circular needles, you know?" Frederica raised a pudgy hand to sketch a circle in the air. "This is the third one that's gone missing."

There were groceries to put away, some things that had to stay cold. Without even unpacking the canvas tote that held the meat and other perishables, Pamela wedged it into the refrigerator. The other bags could wait on the kitchen table. The cats weren't likely to be interested in fruit and vegetables and they weren't capable of opening cans of cat food themselves.

Bettina opened the door, took one look at Pamela, and wrapped an arm around her waist to sweep her inside. "What on earth has happened?" she exclaimed. "Have you seen a ghost?"

"Motive and means," Pamela chanted. "Motive and means, and plenty of opportunity, I'm sure."

."Come back in here." With her arm still around Pamela's waist, Bettina led her to the kitchen, which was fragrant with cinnamon. "And sit right down here," Bettina continued, offering one of the chairs that surrounded the scrubbed pine table.

In a moment, a mug of coffee appeared, followed by a platter containing twirls of yeasty dough glistening with a syrupy glaze. Bettina joined Pamela at the table then, with her own mug of coffee, forks, and two small sage-green plates. "You've found something out," she observed, somewhat unnecessarily, since Pamela was still chanting "motive and means."

"Spill!"

"Johan Friendly may not be a knitter, but his mother is," Pamela said, re-experiencing the quiver she'd felt as the import of Frederica Friendly's words sank in. "So he would have had access to knitting equipment. And from what we saw at his office, he spends a lot of time at his mother's house—coming for dinner, maybe even every night."

Bettina nodded.

"And not only is she a knitter, but . . ." Pamela described Frederica's search for her recent hobby shop purchase and her irritation at the fact that this was the *third circular knitting needle* that had vanished in two weeks.

Bettina listened with such rapt attention that her coffee went undrunk.

"And so," Pamela concluded, "circular needle number one vanishes, and Jenny is killed. Circular needle number two vanishes, and Janice is killed."

"Oh, my," Bettina murmured. "And now another circular needle has disappeared." Her eyes grew wide. "Do you think Johan is going to kill someone else? Another gardener?"

Pamela sampled her coffee then. She was quite convinced that Johan had used his mother's circular knitting needles to eliminate the two gardeners who were crusading against his genetically modified corn. But had he set his sights on a third victim? A jolt of caffeine might help puzzle out the answer to that question.

She took one, two, three sips, savoring the rich bitterness.

"Well," she said after a bit. "Needle number three vanished before Frederica even got home. She had grocery bags on the back seat of her car, as if she'd stopped off at the Co-Op en route from Meadowside."

Bettina smiled a tiny hopeful smile. "So maybe she really just lost the knitting needle and there won't be any more murders?" She tugged the platter toward her and used the forks to guide a yeasty swirl onto each plate. "Cinnamon rolls," she explained. "Homemade. Wilfred wanted to see if he could duplicate the Co-Op's recipe."

Pamela held up a finger and continued talking. She wasn't quite ready yet to turn her attention to cinnamon rolls. "Johan's office is right in the next block," she said. "Maybe he knew what his mother's errand in Meadowside was, and while she was in the Co-Op . . ."

Bettina had been about to apply her fork to her cinnamon roll, but she paused. "She could even have stopped by his office to ask him what he wanted for dinner, and so he knew the knitting needle would be in her car but she would be in the Co-Op . . ."

"Motive, means . . . and *opportunity*, I'm sure," Pamela said. "As a gardener, he certainly knew his way around the gardens, and who came when and who stayed late."

"He was on his way to court, though." Bettina spoke slowly, as if loathe to dampen Pamela's excitement.

"But that was yesterday. This is today." Pamela lifted her own fork and tackled the cinnamon roll, whose construction soon became clear. Yeasty, buttery dough had been twirled into a plump spiral, each circuit marked with a dusting of cinnamon, and the whole had been bathed in a rich syrup that hinted at brown sugar.

"I'll have to tell Clayborn," Bettina said. "He should stake someone out at the gardens tonight. And even if there isn't to be another murder, he'll be glad to have such a promising suspect for the other two—and it will be a great relief for our little town to have these murders finally solved."

Back at home, Pamela did a proper job of storing her groceries, leaving out one can of soup for lunch—though thanks to the cinnamon roll, that meal was likely to happen later than usual. She climbed the stairs to her office and awakened her monitor from its nap by letting the mouse roam at random on its mouse pad.

The morning's email had been sparse, but her boss at *Fiber Craft* had evidently been busy while Pamela was out. Three more articles had arrived for editing. Strung across the top of the email message that accompanied them were their abbreviated titles: "Quipus," "Shibori," and "Mourning Attire."

"Quipus" proved to be about the ancient Inca record-keeping system involving bundles of knotted string. She was soon totally absorbed, with Catrina's contented purr as a concentration-enhancing white noise—until the telephone interrupted her internal debate about whether "further" or "farther" would be the better form, given a context in which distance was only metaphorical.

"It's me," said an annoyed voice on the other end of the line. "He obviously doesn't care if there's another murder in the gardens tonight, and he told me he gets paid so I don't have to solve crimes myself."

"I guess you talked to Detective Clayborn?" Pamela clicked to save her work and swiveled around so the computer screen was behind her, the better to focus on Bettina. "He didn't think Johan's access to knitting supplies and the disappearance of the first two circular knitting needles meant anything?"

"He said Johan *and* his mother, who provided his alibis, were interviewed and thoroughly investigated. And then he thanked me for my interest." Bettina snorted. "Honestly! Sometimes I think Roland has a point. What do we actually get in return for all the taxes we pay?"

After a break for lunch, Pamela returned to her editing work until Catrina leapt to the floor and began pacing back and forth between Pamela's desk and the doorway, pausing occasionally to direct a meaningful look at her mistress. Even before Pamela checked the clock, the stiffness in her back and shoulders told her that it was time to click on SAVE and think about dinner, for both humans and cats.

An hour later, she and Penny feasted on pasta with red sauce, enhanced by the addition of basil leaves from the pot on the back porch. As Penny cleaned up the kitchen, Pamela repaired to the living room, looking forward to a pleasant evening involving mother-daughter knitting projects and BBC mysteries. But she paused in the arch between the entry and the living room, then tiptoed back to the kitchen to summon Penny.

Together they watched as Precious cavorted with the ball of yarn that had been designated her special toy.

"She's getting much braver," Pamela whispered. "She came in here all by herself."

Catrina and Ginger, however, were not so pleased. They had retreated to the cat climber, Catrina on the upper platform and Ginger on the next lower, each cat in a tense crouch with her tail flicking back and forth to signal her irritation.

After her first week back at work, Penny had earned the right to laze in bed on Saturday morning, and Ginger had resumed her habit of sharing Penny's bed and sleeping late when Penny did. But Catrina was ready for breakfast. Urged by a set of paws insistently kneading her upper chest, Pamela opened her eyes and checked her bedside clock.

It was only seven a.m., but the white eyelet curtains at her windows were bright with sun on this May morning. She'd fallen asleep rehearsing the—to her, though not to Detective Clayborn—momentous discovery of the previous day, and the fact that if the vanishing circular knitting needles were related to the community garden murders, one circular knitting needle remained unaccounted for.

Or at least it had been as of yesterday. She sat up with a start, dislodging Catrina, who admonished her with a squeal.

Normally Catrina dashed down the stairs ahead of Pamela, but today Pamela slid her feet into slippers and grabbed her robe from the hook on the back of the door before Catrina had even hopped off the bed. And Catrina watched in dismay as Pamela headed not for the kitchen but for the front door when they reached the entry.

When Pamela stepped out onto the porch, Bettina was already halfway across the street, her summery robe billowing out behind her as she scurried across the asphalt in her pink satin mules. She was waving that morning's copy of the *Register*, unfolded to display its front page. As she got closer, Pamela could read the main headline: GOVERNOR TO APPOINT NEW SCHOOLS CHIEF.

"It didn't happen," Bettina announced when she reached Pamela's side. Pamela was holding her own copy of the *Register*, still encased in its plastic sleeve. "No murder in the community gardens last night."

Bettina's glance strayed toward the driveway of the house next to Pamela's. She raised a hand and waved. Pamela turned in the direction of the glance and wave to see Richard Larkin loping back to his porch with his copy of the *Register*. Unlike his neighbors, he had not ventured out in his robe but was wearing worn jeans and a denim shirt that suited his lanky body. She closed her eyes. She'd had her chance and passed it up and there was no point in thinking about what might have been.

"He *is* a neighbor," Bettina said defensively. "Wilfred and I still talk to him."

Pamela extracted her own copy of the *Register* from its plastic sleeve and studied the front page. Then she flipped through the sections to find the "Local" section. "Usually something like a murder would be on the front page of Part 1," she observed. "And it's not." She displayed the front page of the "Local" section. "And it's not here either."

"It could still happen." Bettina nodded glumly. "I didn't sleep last night thinking about it." Faint purple smudges beneath her hazel eyes attested to that, and she'd rushed outside without combing hair, whose tousled state reflected a restless night on the pillow.

"It could still happen," Pamela agreed. "Frederica might have had an inkling where those knitting needles disappeared to, at the same time not wanting to admit to herself that her son could be guilty of murder. So when Detective Clayborn asked about Johan's whereabouts the nights the murders took place . . ."

"She'd want to protect him."

"Of course," Pamela said. "Any mother would."

"Well . . ." Bettina sighed and folded her copy of the *Register* into a more manageable bundle. "We'll see what happens tonight." Suddenly she brightened. "I know! I'll call Marlene Pepper and tell her to get the word out that the gardeners should all be sure to leave their plots well before sundown." She managed a smile. "I feel better now."

Pamela reassembled her copy of the *Register* and started to fold it.

"It looks like it's going to be another beautiful day," Bettina said, obviously much cheered.

It was indeed beautiful. Overhead the feathery leaves of Pamela's black walnut tree stroked the gentle breeze, and all up and down Orchard Street pastel drifts of azalea interrupted the fresh green of lawns.

"What are you and Penny going to do?"

"Oh . . . uh . . ." Pamela didn't want Bettina to become any more interested in the Brian Delano theme than she was already. And if the lunch didn't go well, she certainly didn't want to have to answer Bettina's eager questions about what Bettina would insist on calling her *date*. So she shrugged and said, "I'm sure Penny will want to do something with her Arborville friends, and I've got work . . . the magazine, you know."

Bettina shook her head and her unruly scarlet tendrils bounced. "All work and no play makes Jill a dull girl, as Wilfred would point out. I hope you at least take a walk."

And with that, Bettina set out across the street.

CHAPTER 21

Pamela pulled into the Wendelstaff parking lot at five minutes after twelve. She hated to be late for appointments and the drive to the campus wasn't long. And after Penny announced that she and Lorie Hopkins were going to a newly discovered thrift shop in Meadowside that morning, Pamela had been sure that Penny would be gone and she could leave the house without having to explain where she was going.

But Lorie had come and Penny had sat her down on the sofa to show off her in-progress knitting project and then Penny had suggested they make sandwiches to eat before going out and finally Pamela had departed on what she described vaguely as "a few errands."

The parking lot was nearly deserted. She hadn't noticed what kind of car Brian Delano drove, but as she circled to a spot near the edge of the campus, the door of an aged but well-cared-for Saab opened and a familiar-looking dark-haired man stepped out. He waved, then leaned back into the car and emerged with a large shopping bag.

Pamela stepped out of her own car. It had been so long since she had been on a date with a new person, with anyone really. She couldn't remember if she had always felt nervous. But now she definitely was nervous, aware of her quick shallow breaths and the dampness of her palms.

"I hope you like pulled pork," Brian said, hefting the bag.

She remembered his voice more than his face, though his face went with his voice somehow—wolfish, but attractive in a good-natured way, with strong brows offset by a gentle mouth.

Pamela summoned up a smile that she hoped was a notch or two more genuine than her social smile, thought for a minute, and said, "Just what I was in the mood for."

"We're all set, then!" He took a few steps toward the grassy bank that led down to the river, but in a moment he turned back. "That is, if you don't mind walking a bit." He glanced down at her feet.

Pamela had dressed that morning as if for a regular day—in jeans, a casual blouse, and the sandals that Bettina described as "not as bad as your Birkenstocks but not much better."

"Oh, no. Not at all." Pamela caught up with him. "I like to walk. I walk all the time."

"The tide is high just now," Brian observed as he led the way along the riverbank. "It's a nicer view than when the water is low and you get a look at all the things that have ended up in the river. I counted five shopping carts one day."

The back of one of the noble brick buildings that faced

the quadrangle came into view. They continued on over the grass, past the back of the student union with its floor-to-ceiling windows gazing out at the river and Haversack beyond.

"Almost there," Brian announced as they reached a cluster of dorms designed like garden apartments at the other edge of the campus.

On a grassy plot under a tree behind the dorm building closest to the river were a few picnic tables.

"The kids are all gone until summer school starts," Brian said as he set the shopping bag on one of the tables. "So we have this spot all to ourselves." He gestured toward one of the benches. "Make yourself comfortable."

Humming a pleasant tune and smiling to himself, he delved into the shopping bag and came up with a table-cloth, which he spread out on the picnic table. Still humming, he removed more things from the bag—china plates and cloth napkins and metal forks and real glass glasses—and he set two places, one across from the other.

The food came out next, the sandwiches wrapped in foil, a small vat of coleslaw, pickles in a ziplock bag, and a large sweat-beaded bottle filled with some amber-colored liquid.

"Sweet tea," he explained. "The guy who runs Barbecue Sam's says unless you're drinking beer, you have to drink sweet tea with pulled pork."

Pamela had been on the Wendelstaff campus more times than she could count. And the Haversack River had never struck her as anything other than something that one crossed to get to Haversack, unless it was in the news when heavy rains made it flood the park on its Haversack shore.

But under the influence of the picnic table on the

river's bank and the interesting menu presented so artfully, Pamela felt quite transported—as if on vacation, though she was only fifteen minutes from Arborville.

Once unwrapped, the sandwiches were revealed in all their glory—plump buns filled to overflowing with mounds of shredded pork bathed in a thick sauce. Pamela sampled hers and recognized the sweet tang of brown sugar, paprika, and cayenne, a perfect complement to the tender pork. The coleslaw was different from Hyler's, with more vinegar and less mayonnaise, like a relish designed to balance the rich intensity of the pulled pork.

"Sweet tea?" Brian unscrewed the cap and tilted the bottle over Pamela's glass. "It's still pretty cold, I hope."

It *was* cold, and sweeter than Hyler's version—or at least sweeter than Pamela's one packet of sugar rendered hers when she ordered it there.

He talked, but not at too great length, and he listened—with an attentive head tilt, a slightly raised brow, and a half smile. The conversation flowed easily, from the food, to the basics—her job and his, to a mutual fondness for BBC mysteries and the Nature Channel, thence to the importance of creative pursuits, be they knitting, cooking, or photography, and finally back to the food.

"Barbecue Sam's is my go-to for this kind of food," Brian said in response to Pamela's compliments. "I got to love it when I lived in Alabama."

"Are you from there?" Pamela asked. He had no trace of an accent.

"My first teaching job." He shrugged. "And I learned a lot too. We can be a little insulated up here."

"You always taught photography?" Pamela folded her napkin and set it beside her plate, wondering if he'd realized that cloth napkins are brave when one is serving juicy food to be eaten with the fingers. Hers had acquired several streaks that combined grease with barbecue sauce.

"Always." He wiped his fingers on his own napkin and produced a smartphone from a pants pocket. "It's a way to support myself so I can do my own work—and it's great to see students realize they have talents they didn't know they had."

He poked at the phone's screen for a moment, and Pamela found herself revising the positive impression she'd formed. Was he one of those people who couldn't focus for too long on a face-to-face meeting without checking on his cyberspace contacts?

No sooner had she thought this thought than he handed her the phone. "This is what I've been doing lately," he said.

The photo she was looking at evoked a centuries-old still life. Flowers and foliage spilled from a vase that was itself a work of art, their rich colors enhanced by some digital magic. But the composition held surprises. Looking more closely, Pamela recognized the foliage as poison ivy, and a cutworm lurked on the stem of a peony.

"There are more," Brian said. "Just scroll sideways."

Still lives with poison ivy and garden pests composed one series. Another group of photos resembled those found on food bloggers' websites, except it seemed the ingredients had been chosen more because they looked good together than that they would realistically be used in the same recipe. In one, dried chiles, cherries, a head of radicchio, strawberries, and a giant tomato were grouped in an apparent exploration of the color red.

"I like them," Pamela said as she handed the phone back. She really did. They were slyly funny, as well as beautiful. "Is the poison ivy from your own yard?"

"My parents' house in Kringlekamack." Brian pocketed the phone. "I live in a condo." He began to gather up the food wrappings and the dirty dishes.

"This was . . . really nice," Pamela said. "Nicer than just coffee."

Brian smiled. He had an easy, confident smile and Pamela smiled back. "Shall we do it again sometime?"

"I'd like that." Pamela nodded.

"Not here, though." Brian's gesture took in the picnic table, the grassy bank, and the river. "Once summer school starts, the kids will take over."

Pamela had enjoyed the lunch. Being with Brian hadn't felt magical, not like the jolt she'd experienced the first time she met Michael Paterson. But maybe you didn't feel that jolt—about anyone—as you got older. Bettina would say to give it time and see what happened. She wasn't going to tell Bettina, though, at least not yet.

Penny was still out when Pamela got home. Feeling at loose ends, she wandered from room to room. She was hosting Knit and Nibble that coming Tuesday, and the house would have to be cleaned and the rhubarb goody baked. But it was only Saturday. Work for the magazine awaited too, but it wasn't pressing. All work and no play, Bettina had said—though certainly the lunch with Brian had counted as play.

She decided to take a walk.

Penny returned while she was gone, and Pamela entered the living room to find Penny's thrift-shop finds displayed on sofa and chairs: a 1960s-style minidress in nubby red tweed, a brown leather jacket worn to a soft luster, a silky robe styled like a kimono, and a huge straw purse decorated with fish shaped from wooden beads.

"Lorie found some good things too," Penny said, "and she was here for a while, but she had to go home and babysit for her nephew. I'm going there after dinner."

By the time the thrift-store finds had been admired—and modeled in the case of the jacket and the robe—and Penny had described the wonders of her new shopping discovery, it was time to start dinner.

Penny opened a large can of cat food, scooped Catrina- and Ginger-sized portions into a fresh bowl, and scooped a Precious-sized portion into a separate bowl to be delivered to the basement.

"Did she come up at all today?" Penny asked as she broke the chunk of salmon-chicken medley into manageable nibbles.

"I didn't see her," Pamela said, "But I don't know what they all do when we're not here."

Penny returned from the basement to report that Precious had greeted her at the bottom of the steps.

"She's getting braver," Pamela observed. "But Catrina and Ginger haven't been very welcoming. Maybe I'll have to find her another home."

"I hope not," Penny said. "She's the most beautiful cat I've ever seen."

"Maybe they're jealous." Pamela opened the refrigerator and took out the pork cutlets that were going to be served with mushroom-caper sauce and orzo.

As she worked on breading the cutlets and slicing the mushrooms, Penny stood at her side rinsing lettuce for salad and tearing it into bite-sized pieces.

* * *

Dinner was over and Penny had gone upstairs to put her thrift-store finds away before leaving for her friend Lorie's house. Pamela was sitting at her end of the sofa hard at work on the periwinkle blue sweater for Bettina, glancing back and forth between the pattern in the magazine open at her side and the swath of knitting that hung from her needles. It was easy to lose track of how many knits to do before switching to purl, or vice versa, while creating the peaks and valleys that gave the seersucker stitch its name.

She was interrupted by Penny's whispered *"Mom!"* She looked up. Penny was standing in the arch between the entry and the living room, pointing. Precious had crept upstairs without Pamela noticing, and the elegant Siamese had just batted her ball of yarn. It rolled over the richly patterned carpet toward Ginger, who—amazingly—batted it back.

"They've been playing," Penny whispered. "I don't know about Catrina, but I think Ginger is getting used to her."

The ball of yarn continued to roll, back and forth, like a cat version of volleyball. Each time Precious took her volley, Pamela felt a curious mental twinge, like déjà vu. Yes, she'd watched Precious play with her ball of yarn on this carpet, but there had been another ball of yarn and another carpet too . . .

"Siamese cats always produce more Siamese cats, don't they?" Penny said. "As long as they mate with other Siamese cats?"

"I think so." Pamela nodded. "That's the whole point of being a specific breed. People try to keep the bloodlines pure so the result is predictable."

Not like the case with Ginger, the product of Catrina's fling with a dashing ginger tomcat. But the result hadn't been completely random. All three of Catrina's female offspring had turned out to be ginger and all three of the males black. Reading up on cat genes after the fact, Pamela had learned that ginger females were a possible result of such a pairing, though three in one litter, all ginger like their father, was unusual. *The sisters all looked like their father*, she murmured to herself.

Penny was saying something, but Pamela's attention was elsewhere—on the commotion in her brain, as scattered puzzle pieces came together. There was an empty space, though, before the puzzle could be declared complete.

"*Mom?*" Penny had advanced to the sofa and stooped down to study Pamela's face. "Are you okay?"

"Fine." Pamela blinked and gave her head a quick shake, as if to settle her thoughts. "I was just thinking . . . about my knitting pattern." She lifted the needles to display her progress.

Penny stood up. "What I *said* was, I'm leaving for Lorie's in a few minutes." Pamela knew exasperation had occasionally crept into her voice when she was raising Penny, and she suspected she had sounded exactly the way Penny did now.

"Yes, yes." Pamela nodded. "I'll be here. Have fun."

But she wouldn't be here—at least not the whole time—if she could reach the person she suddenly needed to call. Penny stepped back into the entry and Pamela started to stand up. She quickly sat down again when, instead of opening the front door, Penny headed up the stairs.

Pamela picked up her knitting and studied it, trying to figure out where she had been in the *knit three, purl one* sequence when Penny had interrupted her to point out Precious and Ginger playing. She launched herself back into the project, but instead of counting stitches she was rehearsing in her mind what she planned to say on the phone. And what instructions she would give Bettina about her role in the evening's adventure.

She finished the row, switched the full needle to her left hand and the empty one to her right, and started in again, this time on a *knit one, purl two* sequence. The cats continued to play with the ball of yarn and she continued to knit until, finally, she heard Penny's feet on the stairs again.

Penny popped around the corner to say that she was off. Pamela waited a moment, then she went to the door to watch through the lace that curtained the oval window as Penny made her way down the front walk and turned right to head up Orchard Street.

Satisfied that she was really gone, Pamela went to the kitchen and picked up the phone. She suspected the swath of periwinkle blue she left behind on the sofa was going to need to have more than one row ripped out and redone, so distracted had she been as she waited for Penny to leave.

Helen Lindquist answered right away—but that didn't mean she was home. She could be at her mall job or on a date. Pamela crossed her fingers.

"It's Pamela Paterson." Pamela tried to sound ordinary, though her heart had migrated to a spot near her collarbone and seemed to be ticking instead of beating. "I hate to bother you, and this might not be a good time—but

Precious has finally gotten brave enough to join us upstairs and we've realized she's missing her own toys. I'm sure the crime-scene tape is down at Jenny's by now. Or maybe you have the toys."

"I have them," Helen said. "You can take them—and when the crime-scene tape came down I helped myself to all the cat food in Jenny's cupboards too. You can have that."

Precious had been happy with the various . . . Pamela thought of them as "flavors" that Catrina and Ginger liked. But Helen's offer of the cat food suggested she had no suspicion that Pamela's request for the toys was anything other than what Pamela had claimed—and not a ruse to get inside Helen's apartment.

"Would now be an okay time?" Pamela asked, leaving her fingers crossed.

"Sure," Helen said. "I worked all day at the mall and don't have plans to do anything but lie on the sofa and binge on Netflix."

The next call was to Bettina. "I'm going to pick up cat toys from Helen," Pamela announced as soon as Bettina answered. "You need to come along."

"I do?" Bettina sounded puzzled. "Will there be a lot to carry?"

"Cat food too," Pamela said. "I'll pick you up in five minutes. And bring your smartphone."

"I always have my smartphone with me," Bettina responded with a laugh. "You're the one who forgets."

"It's not really about cat toys and cat food," Pamela explained as she steered her serviceable compact up Orchard Street. "I have to check something to see if I'm re-membering right, but I'm pretty sure I am. And if so . . ."

She would nod, she said, and she described what Bettina was to do next, and it would be better if her phone was in a pocket rather than her purse.

CHAPTER 22

Helen buzzed them in and they climbed the narrow stairs to the apartments above the storefronts, Pamela carrying a few canvas totes. Helen was standing in the open door of her apartment when they reached the hallway, dressed in leggings and a loose button-up shirt, with her dark hair tamed into a long braid. With it drawn back away from her face, her lovely features were all the more striking.

"I've got them in a box for you," she said. "I'm glad I didn't get rid of them after you adopted Precious."

She stood aside and gestured for them to come in. Music was coming from somewhere, the soothing music a person might put on after a long day at work, and the apartment smelled of recently cooked food. A small box sat on the sofa. Helen pointed at it.

Pamela scanned the living room quickly. Part of the

coffee table's surface was taken up with papers, magazine clippings, bills, and other odds and ends, as it had
been on their first visit to Helen's apartment. The same
items had littered the carpet when they returned for Precious after their visit to Johan Friendly—the result, Helen
had indicated, of a struggle to convince Precious that she
wanted to enter the cat carrier.

The item Pamela had been hoping to see wasn't visible. She caught Bettina's eye and frowned slightly.

"You'll be wanting the cat food too," Helen said, and
she stepped toward the kitchen.

Mind reader that she was, Bettina scurried after her,
carrying a canvas tote. As soon as Helen disappeared
through the kitchen doorway, Pamela bent over the coffee
table and began to rummage through the piles of random
things. Bettina's voice drifted in from the kitchen.

"What a nice job you've done in here!" she exclaimed.
"I love the curtains!"

Pamela could picture Bettina's expression—probably
the same admiring gaze she focused on her interview sub-
jects. Bettina could be hard to resist when she was determined to catch and hold someone's attention.

"They were already here," Helen replied. "I really
haven't done much to the kitchen at all."

"I can see you like to cook, though—the spice rack,
the cookbooks . . ."

"The last renter left them behind," Helen said. "She
was moving to Florida and didn't want to bother shipping
them."

Pamela heard a cupboard open. "I'll just put these cans
in your tote," Helen said. "It won't take a minute."

"No hurry."

But hurry there was, on Pamela's end. She tried to re-

assemble the heap of magazine clippings she'd dis-
arranged and moved on to the disorderly pile next to it,
lifting the edge of each item to peer at the one beneath.
And at last, there it was: the photo. She slid it out to study
it for a moment. It was just as she had remembered.

"So, I guess we're all set," Bettina announced in a
voice designed to carry beyond her immediate audience.
"And Precious will have much more use for Kitty
Seafood Treats than you will, I'm sure." She paused and
added, "Here, let me take that."

The next moment Bettina stepped through the kitchen
doorway carrying the tote. Pamela slipped the photo back
into place and stood up, tipping her head toward Bettina
in a subtle nod just as Helen appeared.

Then she circled the coffee table and reached for the
box of cat toys. "Thank you so much," she said.

Bettina, meanwhile, reached into her pocket and extracted her phone. "I thought I felt it vibrate," she explained as she poked it with a manicured finger and
studied the screen. "Could be important. Excuse me."
She stepped toward a corner of the room and lifted the
phone to her ear.

Her amazement was so convincing that Pamela wondered if perhaps the call was real. "Oh, my goodness!"
Bettina breathed. Her mobile face assumed the expression of a tragic mask, but wearing bright lipstick and vio-
let eye shadow. "Yes, yes," she added. "That was the best
thing to do. Of course." She pretended to listen for a moment. "You should stay there, for sure. They'll want to
talk to you, but what . . . ? Just stay calm. I'll call you
later."

Bettina tucked the phone away.

The performance had definitely caught Helen's interest. "Has something happened?" she asked, her amber eyes wide.

"Marlene Pepper." Bettina's eyes were wide too. She shook her head and her lips formed a puzzled zigzag. "She's up at the community gardens and she's just called the police. She saw something, or she found something, like a clue. Or *someone*, like a body. I couldn't tell. She was kind of frantic, but she said the murders all make sense now."

"Oh . . ." Helen's face was serious. "That would be such a relief."

"I'll call Marlene in a bit to follow up," Bettina said, "and I'll check in with Clayborn tomorrow. The *Register* will have the whole story and then some by the time the next *Advocate* comes out, but people like to read about things in their town newspaper."

Pamela and Bettina returned to the lot behind the hardware store where Pamela had parked. The sky above the row of storefronts still glowed faintly with the pink of sunset, but night was falling fast and the lot itself was in that shadowy state when colors are muted to tones of gray.

They put the cat toys and the cat food on the back seat and settled into their own seats, but Pamela made no motion to actually drive. Instead they both watched a door near the back entrance of the hardware store, trusting the increasing darkness and the fact that they were parked at the far end of the lot to hide the fact that the car was occupied.

The door opened and Helen stepped into the cone of light cast by a fixture mounted on the back of the building. Leaving the cone of light behind but silhouetted against it, she made her way across the asphalt toward a nondescript sedan.

"We'll wait a minute," Pamela whispered. There was no need at this distance, but whispering seemed appropriate to the mission.

Across the parking lot, headlights carved tunnels through the darkness, taillights flashed, and Helen was in motion, cruising toward the exit with her left turn signal blinking. Pamela watched her make the turn, then she twisted her key in the ignition and, with a low rumble, they were on their way.

Helen drove north on Arborville Avenue and turned right after a few blocks. Pamela followed, making the same turn. Helen continued, up a gentle incline, but Pamela veered to the curb after she'd gone a short distance and switched off her headlights. It was clear now where Helen was headed, and it wouldn't do to make her abandon her journey by arousing her suspicions.

Pamela waited until Helen made another turn and her taillights vanished. At Pamela's side, Bettina leaned toward the windshield, rapt and motionless but for her rapid breathing.

"Okay," Pamela whispered. She started the car again and resumed her pursuit. It was dark up here at night, with residential streets left behind. The road—just a wide gravel path at this point—skirted hilly woods untouched by development. The gravel lot that served the community gardens lay ahead, beyond the shadowy woods and thus marginally brighter given the moon and a cloudless night.

The outline of a car could be made out, headlights and tail lights off, but the slender beam of a flashlight danced here and there, skittering over the gravel in the direction of the gardens. Then the figure carrying the flashlight whirled around, and Helen advanced into the glare of Pamela's headlights. Pamela switched off the headlights and stopped the car.

"Stay here," she instructed Bettina, "and duck down. And get your phone ready."

She climbed out of the car and was immediately dazzled by the beam of Helen's flashlight. "I thought Bettina said the police were coming," Helen said, her voice reaching Pamela out of the darkness as Pamela blinked.

"They're on their way." Pamela spoke into the darkness. "You're here for a reason, aren't you? You thought what Marlene supposedly found would either prove you were guilty or make it seem that you weren't."

"Wh-what?" Helen stuttered. "I don't know what you're talking about. I just . . ."

"Thought you might audition for a reporter's job with the *Advocate* by covering a breaking story?" Pamela laughed.

There was no answer.

Pamela tipped her head this way and that, trying to escape the blaze of the flashlight beam and get a glimpse of Helen's face. But all she could see was a slender dark form.

"A clue would be terrifying, wouldn't it? You thought you'd been careful, but maybe you hadn't. And the prospect of holding your breath until Detective Clayborn came knocking on your door was unbearable. Better to know the truth, then get in your car and drive and drive."

"No, I . . ."

"But you were hoping there was actually another body, weren't you?" Pamela said. "The police were already at loose ends trying to figure out who killed Jenny and Janice, but looking for someone with a reason to kill *three* people, Jenny and Janice and some random person who had no connection with either of them, would almost guarantee they'd never suspect you."

"Why would . . ." Helen's voice trailed off, as if she realized arguing was hopeless.

"You had a reason to kill *two* people, though, didn't you?"

Pamela was not a person who craved the spotlight, but at the moment she understood the thrill a performer might feel. The script was compelling, all the more so in that it was her own creation. She had observed and questioned and thought—and finally reconstructed what had happened and why. And with that flashlight in her eyes, it was as if she was standing in a spotlight on a stage, unable to see her audience but sure nonetheless that her audience was rapt.

"Jenny was your sister," she said. "Your *half* sister. And her mother, Janice, stole your father, the handsome man in the photo on your coffee table. You both took after him."

From the darkness came a howl. "You sneak!" Helen screamed. "And your fat, sneaky friend! The cat toys were just a ploy!"

The flashlight beam wobbled and shifted to the ground, and Pamela found herself staring into a darkness more extreme for the sudden contrast.

Helen's tone modulated from anger to resignation. "Yes, I killed them," she moaned. "Janice deserved to die. But she also deserved to learn what it feels like to lose the person you care about most in the world, the way my mother felt when Janice stole the man she loved. So I killed Jenny first."

Now the flashlight's beam was aimed at the sky. Pamela's eyes had adjusted to the darkness, and the moon was bright enough that she could make out Helen's form advancing toward her with right arm raised. Helen was wielding the flashlight as if it were a weapon, a weapon that dipped and bobbed as its beam traced zigzags in the darkness.

"Maybe the police *will* find a third victim here tonight," Helen muttered as she got closer. Pamela backed away, lifting her arms to shield her face, but Helen lunged. Pamela felt herself teeter, then she landed hard, sitting on the gravel. Helen bent over her, landing blows with the flashlight as Pamela struggled to fend her off.

Bettina's voice, coming closer and closer, intruded on the inarticulate sounds coming from both Pamela and her attacker.

"They're on their way!" Bettina shouted. "And you— Helen! Stop that right now."

Pamela felt a breeze as something swung by, something large and bulky. Helen grunted, the flashlight fell to the ground with a thunk, and Helen toppled over.

"A tote bag full of cat food makes a good weapon," Bettina commented. She stooped for the flashlight and focused it on Helen, who had been knocked onto her side but otherwise looked fine. "I am not fat," she said.

Sirens pierced the quiet then, faint but coming closer. Soon the sirens were upon them, rising and falling, so loud the sound seemed felt as well as heard. The flashlight's beam was augmented by headlights that swept across the gravel lot, illuminating Helen as if in the glare of a searchlight. She closed her eyes and moaned. The lights atop the police car blazed and dimmed, round and round, as if a photographer was taking flash shots of random things: the trees at the edge of the woods, Calliope's flax field, the sign that welcomed people to the Arborville Community Gardens, a disheveled Bettina holding fast to the flashlight and the tote bag full of cat food.

The officers who climbed out of the patrol car were familiar: Officer Sanchez, the woman police officer with the sweet heart-shaped face, and the boyish and rosy-cheeked Officer Anders.

"I think she wants to tell you something," Bettina said as they approached. She aimed the flashlight at Helen's face.

Despite spending an hour at the police station, Pamela had gotten home in plenty of time to take a soothing shower and settle down with her knitting, all three cats, and a BBC mystery before Penny returned.

"You look contented, Mom," Penny had observed before going up to her room.

It was not until Sunday morning that Penny had an inkling her mother's Saturday night had involved more than knitting, cats, and television.

CHAPTER 23

Pamela awoke with a sense of relief, but without immediately recalling the events responsible for that sense of relief. It was only when she lifted Catrina from her chest and sat up to push the bedclothes aside that the twinges in her back and shoulders reminded her of the previous night's adventure.

She slid her feet into her slippers and tugged on her robe, and a few minutes later she was serving chicken-liver blend in separate bowls to Catrina and Precious. She set water boiling for coffee and, adhering to her unvarying morning ritual, headed for the door to retrieve the *Register*.

Even before she stepped out onto the porch, however, she realized that her morning ritual was about to be disrupted. Through the lace that curtained the oval window she could see the truck from the local TV channel. It was parked on Bettina's side of the street and several people were clustered around Bettina's open front door. Pamela knew it would be only a matter of time before those same people came knocking at her own door.

Talking to them would be unavoidable and it would be better to be dressed. She snatched the *Register* up—it was the bulky Sunday edition—and turned back toward her house. But an eager voice behind her called, "Wait! Wait! Ms. Paterson!"

Let them *wait*, she thought. *I refuse to be on television in my robe and slippers.*

But Marcy Brewer caught up with her just as she reached her front steps. Pamela had dealt with Marcy before. She made up for her small stature—even in her stiletto heels, she barely reached Pamela's chin—with an abundance of determination, and a lipstick-enhanced smile that persisted even in the face of rebuffs.

"Ms. Paterson," Marcy exclaimed as Pamela faced her and sighed. "You were attacked last night in the community gardens by the woman who has now been arrested in connection with the murders of Jenny and Janice Miller. How did you happen to be there? And did your presence have anything to do with her subsequent arrest?"

"Helen was returning to the scene of the crime, I suspect." Pamela smiled sadly.

"And you and Ms. Fraser were there because . . ." Marcy fixed Pamela with a look that dared her to avert her eyes.

"Bettina had been researching an article on the community garden program—nothing to do with the murders, of course. We were out on an errand together and she wanted to stop up there and double-check a few details about the way the plots are laid out. Before we knew it, the sun had set. And—"

"*Mo-om!*" Pamela swung around to see Penny standing on the porch barefoot and wearing only her summer nightgown. "*What* is going on? I heard the kettle whistling and whistling and you're out here and it's just lucky it didn't boil dry and who are you talking to and why is that TV truck parked in front of Bettina's?" Penny's voice trailed off and she gasped for breath.

"I have to go." Pamela said over her shoulder as she sped toward the porch. "My daughter needs me."

"I suspect I'll find the answer to my questions in here," Penny said as she grabbed the *Register* from Pamela's hand.

As Pamela refilled the kettle and set it back on the stove, Penny tore the plastic sleeve from the *Register* and spread the newspaper out on the kitchen table.

"They caught that killer," she murmured as she read. "And she confessed. But *somehow* this happened because"—she raised her head to direct a meaningful look at her mother—"'Arborville residents Pamela Paterson and Bettina Fraser were present when the accused returned to the scene of the crime,' and for *some* reason—those are my words, Mom—'the accused attacked Ms. Paterson with a flashlight, causing Ms. Fraser to summon the police.'"

"Yes," Pamela said brightly. "That is what happened. Toast?"

"I'll make it myself," Penny said, "after I feed Ginger."

Pamela had no sooner poured two cups of coffee than the doorbell chimed. An attractive young woman who she recognized from the TV news stood on the porch, accompanied by another young woman bearing a video camera on a tripod. Gesturing at her robe and slippers, she pointed out that she was in no state to appear on television, but she agreed to answer a few questions off-camera.

With that out of the way, she returned to her coffee, toast, and newspaper, happy to cede Part 1 to Penny and distract herself with "Lifestyle."

By the time Bettina arrived, Penny had gone back upstairs and Pamela had read the *Register*'s report on Helen's arrest.

"I just threw on any old thing when I saw that TV truck pulling up outside," Bettina announced as she stepped over the threshold. Indeed, she didn't look nearly as put together as usual, despite her cropped pants and shirt ensemble in a summery aqua. Her only makeup was lipstick, and her ears, neck, and wrists were bare of the statement jewelry that was such a part of her style.

"I made extra coffee," Pamela said after she accepted her friend's hug. "I knew you'd be over." She led the way to the kitchen.

"What did you tell Marcy Brewer and the TV people?" Bettina asked as she lowered herself into her usual chair.

"What we agreed on." Pamela set a steaming cup of coffee in front of Bettina and moved the sugar and cream closer. "You were checking the layout of the garden plots, and Helen was revisiting the scene of the crime. We just happened to be there at the same time."

Bettina nodded and scooped a heaping teaspoon of sugar from the cut-glass bowl. "At some point Clayborn will realize what really happened," she said. "Helen is bound to tell him that we lured her up there."

"But he might not say anything." Pamela joined Bettina at the table with her own fresh cup of coffee. "Why give people like Roland more reason to think their tax dollars aren't well spent?"

Bettina looked up from stirring her coffee. "Let the police take the credit. The main thing is that the murders have been solved." She added a large dollop of heavy cream. "It's a sad story, though."

"I had figured out part of why she did it," Pamela said, "but not all those details she told the police."

"Her father walked out while Helen's mother was pregnant with Helen." Bettina sounded properly indignant.

"He didn't exactly walk out," Pamela said. "His job transferred him to Manhattan from Minnesota, where he and Helen's mother were living. Helen's mother was going to finish the term at the school where she taught and then join him and they were going to get married. Neither of them knew she was pregnant. Then he met Janice in Manhattan and fell head over heels."

"He should have controlled himself!" Bettina slapped the table.

Pamela laughed. "Weren't you defending Dennis Cummings the other day for falling in love with Helen? You said something about people being swept off their feet, as if that makes it okay to be unfaithful."

"I didn't say that at all," Bettina said. "I just felt sorry for the poor man—he was so sad. And Helen's parents weren't married yet, and Helen's father never knew he was a father."

Pamela nodded. Apparently, Helen had been more than happy—eager even—to explain her motive for killing Jenny and Janice, and that backstory had made it into the *Register*—not that newspapers had any objection to the reader appeal of family dramas. "According to Helen," Pamela summarized what she had read, "her mother never told him. She raised Helen herself, too bitter to trust a man again, and Helen never knew what her origins were until just before her mother died last year."

They sipped their coffee in silence. After a bit, Bettina said, "Nell gave Wilfred a big batch of rhubarb a few days ago. He wants to know if you have a good pie recipe."

"I do," Pamela said, "but that's not what I'm going to make for Knit and Nibble. Wait and see."

Monday morning's *Register* did not add much to the previous day's "Arrest in Community Garden Murders" story except for a photo of Helen Lindquist being escorted into the Haversack courthouse by police. It mentioned Pamela Paterson and Bettina Fraser by name, but only to say they had confirmed preliminary reports about what had brought them to the community gardens Saturday night and what had transpired there.

Pamela tipped her wedding-china cup for the last few sips of coffee and folded up the newspaper. Work for the magazine awaited her upstairs, and she welcomed the chance to return to her normal routines—though, given recent somber events, she planned to immerse herself in "Shibori Kimonos in the Windermere Collection" before tackling "Grief Made Visible: Victorian Mourning Attire."

On her way to the stairs, she paused in the entry to smile at Catrina and Precious. Friends now, both were luxuriating in the patch of sun where Catrina had long been accustomed to take her morning nap. Before she turned away, the phone rang and she hurried back to the kitchen to answer it.

"Hello," said a pleasant male voice. It was familiar but not too familiar, certainly not Wilfred, or Roland—or, thankfully, Detective Clayborn. "Brian Delano here," the voice added before Pamela could respond.

"Oh." Pamela sat down. "Hello. How are you?"

"More like, how are *you*?" Brian said. "I've been reading the *Register*."

"Oh." (Why did she keep saying *oh*?) Pamela was feeling a bit breathless but she managed a laugh. "Quite a story isn't it? Such a coincidence that my friend and I were up there when Helen Lindquist decided to return to the scene of the crime."

"A frightening coincidence, I'd say. I'm glad you're okay."

"I'm fine," Pamela said. "It's a great relief for Arborville that those murders have been solved. And it's thoughtful of you to call."

"I had something else in mind too." There was something Wilfred-like about Brian, Pamela realized—a cheerful confidence that made him seem approachable. As she had relaxed in his presence during the lunch by the river, she felt herself relaxing now.

"Hmm?" Had she injected the slightest bit of flirtation into that wordless monosyllable?

"Dinner next weekend? Or sooner?"

"I'd like that," Pamela said. "I'm busy tomorrow night, but after that . . ."

"Wednesday, then?"

"Wednesday." She smiled into the phone.

CHAPTER 24

Tuesday morning, Pamela waved Penny good-bye as she headed out to the bus stop, rinsed the cups and saucers and plates from breakfast, and went upstairs to dress. Back in the kitchen, she took out the cookbook that contained the inspiration for the creation she planned to serve that evening. It was to be a cheesecake, but a cheesecake in the shape of a pie.

The cookbook didn't contain a recipe for rhubarb cheesecake in the shape of a pie, but Pamela had made cheesecakes that involved sugary compotes of cherries or pineapple, and she had also once made a pumpkin cheese-cake for which the graham-cracker crust was pressed into a pie pan instead of a spring-form mold. She planned to combine elements of both, and the first step was to turn Nell's rhubarb stalks into a compote.

She took them from the refrigerator and washed them,

admiring again the reddish-pink glow of the shiny stalks. Making the compote would be rather like making cranberry sauce from scratch, except that the stalks would have to be cut into narrow crosswise slices to begin. She plied her sharpest knife methodically, revealing the rosy pink interior of the stalks as a small pile of slices accumulated on her cutting board. Two cups of sliced rhubarb would be plenty for the recipe she planned, and as Nell had foretold, she had several stalks left over. They would be sliced too, and frozen, to be brought out later for a more traditional rhubarb pie—or another experiment.

She transferred the sliced rhubarb to a small saucepan, added sugar and a tiny bit of water, covered the saucepan, and set it boiling over a low flame. As the rhubarb slices softened, quickly turning into compote, Pamela gathered the rest of the ingredients for her cheesecake pie: graham crackers, butter, cream cheese, sugar, and eggs. It would be easier to blend the sugar and eggs into the cream cheese if the cream cheese was soft, so she opened the packages of cream cheese and peeled off the inner foil wrappers. Then she set her big pottery mixing bowl with the caramel-colored glaze and three white stripes on the counter and added the cream cheese, cutting the rectangular blocks into smaller chunks.

By this time, the rhubarb slices had softened into a thin soup the color of cranberry sauce. Setting the saucepan lid aside, she turned up the heat and stirred and stirred. After a few minutes the soup thickened to the point that it was just right. She turned off the flame and left the compote to cool.

The next step, while the cream cheese was softening and the compote was cooling, was to tidy the parts of the house that the Knit and Nibblers would see. She tackled the living room with enthusiasm, first running the vacuum over the ancient Persian carpet with its stylized vegetation rendered in dark blues, greens, and burgundys.

It was a pleasure to lose herself in the mundane. She organized the magazines on the coffee table, dusted her thrift-store knickknacks, and realigned the pillows ranged along the back of the sofa, making sure the needlepoint cat was right-side up.

The work wasn't as cerebral as sifting through clues to recognize the pattern that solved the mystery, but the process of cleaning and putting things to rights was deeply satisfying in the same way.

Once the house was in a fit state to receive that evening's guests, Pamela returned to the kitchen. The graham crackers had to be reduced to crumbs, which she accomplished by slipping them several at a time into a large ziplock bag and rolling over them with a rolling pin. Then they were mixed with sugar and melted butter and pressed onto the bottom and sides of a pie pan. From her collection of vintage pie pans, Pamela chose a rustic one made of brown and cream speckle ware that looked like it would be at home in a Revolutionary-era kitchen.

The cream cheese had softened to the point that the electric mixer easily converted it from chunks to smoothness, and as the beaters continued to whir, the sugar vanished into it. Then Pamela cracked the eggs into the bowl, and for a moment the bright yolks perched on the pale creamy mixture beneath them. The beaters started up again and the eggs, yolks and all, were spun about and twirled into the batter, imparting a slight golden tint as the only sign of their presence. A bit of vanilla was the last ingredient. With her rubber spatula, she coaxed the batter onto the graham-cracker crust, smoothing it to the edges.

Now it was time for the special touch that would mark the cheesecake pie as Pamela's unique creation: adding the rhubarb compote. In the pumpkin cheesecake pie that had been her inspiration, pumpkin puree had been blended into the cream cheese batter along with the sugar and eggs. The pie's filling had ended up a pretty pastel orange, and it had tasted faintly—and deliciously—of pumpkin throughout.

But Pamela didn't want the filling of her rhubarb cheesecake pie to be pink, and she wanted a contrast between the richness and smoothness of the cheesecake and the jammy piquancy of the rhubarb.

She spooned the rhubarb compote onto the top of the cheesecake filling, big spoonfuls placed at random here and there. Then she took a table knife and pulled it through the puddles of compote, distributing it in streaks through the filling but not trying to mix it in.

She carefully slid the pie into the oven, which had been heating while she worked, and occupied herself cleaning up the counter and scrubbing the kitchen floor while it baked. Forty-five minutes later, the cheesecake pie was sitting on the stovetop cooling.

The cheesecake filling had turned from creamy to golden in the baking, shading to toasty brown at the edges. Streaks and dabs of brilliant crimson, like the abstract brushstrokes of an inspired artist, enlivened the smooth surface. The cheesecake pie would cool to room temperature and then go into the refrigerator to be served chilled at eight p.m.

Satisfied with her work, Pamela checked her email. No new *Fiber Craft* chores presented themselves, and the three articles weren't due back yet. The May day was lovely, preparations for the evening were nearly complete, and it had been a while since she had walked simply for the pleasure of walking.

When she returned, Pamela put the cheesecake pie in the refrigerator.

Three hours later, Penny had retreated to her bedroom after sharing a quick dinner with her mother, and Pamela was beating heavy cream, sour cream, and sugar together for her cheesecake pie's topping. She had modeled the idea on the sour cream topping that's a feature of classic cheesecake, spread on the cake when the cake is nearly done, then baked for five minutes when the cake is returned to the oven. But she planned instead to top each piece with a drift of whipped cream plus sour cream in the same way a slice of pie might be served.

She turned the beater off to hear voices in the entry—Bettina's saying, "I rang and rang" and Penny's responding, "I know she's home."

"Mom?" Penny stuck her head through the kitchen doorway. "Didn't you hear the bell?"

Pamela turned away from the counter and lifted the mixer, its beaters coated with white fluff, to demonstrate the cause of her inattention.

The next moment, Penny retreated and Bettina entered the kitchen. "That looks promising!" she exclaimed as she joined Pamela at the counter to inspect the contents of the mixing bowl.

She had dressed for the meeting in a fit and flare dress that hugged her ample waist and flared to a knee-skimming hem. The fabric evoked the season with a print of red roses climbing on trellises. She had accessorized it with a triple strand of oversized pearls, pearl earrings, and red kitten heels.

"I'm early, I know," she said, "but I thought I could help. It looks like we need cups and saucers and plates."

"Silverware and napkins too." Pamela nodded. "Get those lacy white ones. They're in the top drawer in the laundry room."

While Bettina fetched the napkins, Pamela used her rubber spatula to coax the topping that had clung to the beaters back into the bowl. She covered the bowl with plastic wrap and put it in the refrigerator next to the cheesecake pie, rinsed off the beaters, and put the mixer away.

Bettina returned with the napkins and opened the cupboard where Pamela kept her wedding china. She put six saucers on the kitchen table, nestled six rose-garlanded cups in them, and added six dessert plates to the arrangement. Pamela contributed six forks and six teaspoons.

"Too soon to fill the cream pitcher," she commented as she spooned additional sugar into the cut-glass sugar bowl.

From the entry came the chime of the doorbell.

"I'll get it," Bettina sang out, and she hurried through the kitchen doorway.

Pamela recognized Holly's cheerful greeting and Karen's timid echo. She put the sugar bowl on the table next to the cream pitcher and joined the others in the entry.

"Bettina and I are through in the kitchen." Pamela gestured toward the living room. "So let's all sit down."

"The big chair is always for Nell," Holly said, heading for the sofa. She sat down and Karen joined her. "I never get tired of looking at your amazing things." Holly glanced around the room and smiled her dimply smile. "Your rugs, the art, everything is just perfect. So cozy and homey."

The doorbell chimed again. Holly checked her watch. "Roland, I'll bet. It's exactly seven."

Indeed, the figure visible through the lace that curtained the oval window was tall, slender, and wearing a dark suit. Pamela opened the door and Roland stepped across the threshold, impeccably turned out in summerweight pinstripe accented with a sedate but lustrous tie, its flawless knot nestled between the wings of his aggressively starched shirt collar.

"Good evening," he said. "I don't believe I'm late." He directed a glance through the arch that separated the entry from the living room.

"No, and we're still waiting for Nell."

"She's coming." Roland allowed himself a small smile. "I passed her, walking. I offered a ride but she said she likes the exercise."

Just then, Precious strolled into the entry.

"Who's this?" Roland bent down and offered a hand for nuzzling.

"She's still a little shy," Pamela said, and she began to explain how the elegant Siamese had come to be a part of the household.

Nell arrived then. Apparently noticing people just within, she tapped rather than ringing. Pamela opened the door and greeted her, and soon all six Knit and Nibblers had taken their accustomed places in Pamela's living room.

A disturbing topic had been introduced, however, while Pamela was detailing Precious's origins for Roland and describing the slow process by which Catrina and Ginger had come to accept her.

"I do not blame that poor woman one bit," Bettina was exclaiming. "To not be able to trust your husband! I can't imagine!"

Pamela, sitting in the rummage-sale chair with the needlepoint seat and the carved wooden back, looked up from probing in her knitting bag for her other knitting needle. Who on earth was Bettina talking about? But the answer came clear the next moment.

"I never would have thought that of Dennis Cummings," Holly said. Indignation didn't detract from her dramatic good looks, enhanced by the blue streak in her dark hair and her sparkly chandelier earrings. "He's always been so helpful, in a gentlemanly way, when I need something at the hardware store."

"Well, Claire is better off without him," Bettina declared. "No children to worry about, and she's got a good job. She'll be—"

A sound like a cross between a moan and growl issued from the direction of the armchair next to the fireplace. "This is a sad story," Nell said. She glanced from person to person, her faded blue eyes mournful. "And it is none of our business. I suggest we all tend to our knitting and leave our neighbors to look after themselves."

She seized up the knitting that she had lowered to her lap, and in a moment her needles were busy once again. It was apparent that she had recently begun a new elephant, this one an almost realistic pale gray.

Pamela had expected that the first topic of conversation would be the arrest of the community gardens killer, and she had expected that Holly would raise the topic with an enthusiastic commendation of Pamela's and Bettina's roles. But Holly seemed chastened by Nell's scolding. Uncharacteristically quiet, she plied her knitting needles methodically, looping and twisting her bright tangerine yarn as her daring dress took shape.

It fell to Bettina to break the silence. "That is amazing," she exclaimed, leaning toward the hassock where Roland had perched. "They are both exactly the same length."

The sleeves Roland had been casting on the previous week had grown considerably, and dangled from his circular knitting needle in matching swaths.

"Of course they're the same length." Roland looked up with a frown. "This is a very scientific way to knit sleeves. I don't understand why everyone doesn't do it."

"It's that circular knitting needle." Holly shuddered. "After what happened . . ."

"I wouldn't even want to touch one," Karen piped up in her timid voice.

From Nell's armchair came another moaning growl, and silence descended once again.

Pamela was just as happy to concentrate on her knitting, given the challenge of keeping track of knits and purls. After a time, she noticed that a quiet conversation about plans for the Memorial Day weekend had sprung up between Holly and Karen. Bettina was still silent, however, laboring away on the taupe sweater for Morgan, with pauses to consult the booklet that contained her pattern.

Pamela had reached the end of a row, put her knitting down, and closed her eyes for a moment when Roland's voice intruded.

"Eight o'clock," he intoned.

She opened her eyes to see him tugging his shirt cuff back over his watch and transferring his knitting from his lap to the hearth.

"At last," Bettina breathed. "I can hardly wait to see what that whipped cream goes on top of."

"It's not just whipped cream," Pamela said with a smile. "You'll see."

She headed for the kitchen with Bettina following. In the kitchen she removed the cheesecake pie and the bowl of topping from the refrigerator and set them on the table. As she was staring into her utensil drawer in quest of the perfect knife and server, she became aware that she and Bettina were not alone.

She turned to find Holly, with Karen at her elbow, standing with Bettina at the table. They were not there to admire the cheesecake pie, however, though Bettina had already made it clear that based on looks at least the Knit and Nibble dessert would be a hit.

"Okay," Holly whispered. "Anyone who knows you two amazing women knows perfectly well that your presence at the gardens when Helen Lindquist 'returned to the scene of the crime' wasn't just a coincidence."

"It wasn't," Bettina whispered back. "Pamela figured out that Helen was the killer, but we had to get her to do something to give herself away."

Pamela began to slice the cheesecake pie as Bettina talked—whispered really—detailing the ruse by which Helen had been lured to the gardens. The graham-cracker crust held up fine as the slices were transferred to the plates, and the rhubarb streaks in the pale filling gave the cut surfaces on the sides of the slices just the marbled look she had hoped for.

Her pleasure in the success—so far—of her creation was short-lived: Nell appeared in the kitchen doorway, arriving just in time to hear Bettina say, "So it turned out

just the way we had planned, and she confessed everything."

"I suspected as much from you two," Nell said, her expression grim.

"But Nell"—Holly stepped forward and laid a hand on
Nell's shoulder—"wouldn't you admit that it's a relief to
know the killer has been caught and that there won't be
any more murders to spoil the gardeners' enjoyment of
their plots this summer?"

Roland's head came into view, bobbing over Nell's
shoulder. "Has something gone wrong?" he asked. "I
don't smell coffee."

"You will," Pamela assured him. "You will."

She handed the bowl of topping to Bettina with a large
spoon and hurried to the counter, where she filled the kettle and set it boiling on the stove. The next moment a clatter and whir, and a dark, spicy aroma announced that beans
were being ground.

Bettina spooned a drift of the whipped cream-sour
cream topping onto each slice, handing plates in turn to
Nell, Karen, Holly, and Roland. She followed them to the
living room with napkins, forks and spoons, and cream
and sugar. When she returned to the kitchen, boiling
water was dripping through the ground beans in the filter
cone and water was boiling afresh for the tea.

After a quick bustle of brewing tea, pouring coffee,
and delivering steaming cups, Pamela and Bettina took
their places and, almost as if their movements had been
synchronized, the Knit and Nibblers lifted their forks and
tasted the rhubarb cheesecake pie.

"Mmmm," was the verdict.

Pamela herself was very pleased. Just as she'd anticipated, the streaks of compote in the cheesecake filling provided a satisfying contrast of sweet piquancy with smooth sweetness—and the sour cream in the topping was just evident enough to evoke a cheesecake in the traditional style.

Her piece of cheesecake pie half finished, Nell looked up with a sigh. "If only you would confine your energies to cooking, Pamela," she said. "And knitting of course. This crime-solving is just too dangerous for anyone but the police."

Holly aimed a teasing grin in the direction of Nell's armchair. "But you want to know how she figured it out, don't you?" she laughed. "You *really, really* want to know."

Nell straightened her spine. "I absolutely do not," she declared. "Let sleeping dogs lie."

Pamela stifled a laugh. Wilfred was usually the one to apply old sayings to current circumstances.

A second response to Holly's question came from a surprising quarter. Roland set his coffee cup on the hearth and said, "I have to admit that I'm slightly curious."

"Yes! Yes!" Holly flashed a smile that brought her dimple into play. "Three against one." She turned to Karen. "You're curious too, aren't you?"

With a glance at Nell, Karen nodded.

Everyone was looking at Pamela. Where to begin?

"I was sitting in here," Pamela said, "on the sofa, and working on Bettina's sweater, and Precious was batting a ball of yarn around on the carpet . . ."

And she'd had a sense of déjà vu. As she struggled to figure out why the image seemed so familiar, a question from Penny had reminded her that Ginger and her sisters all looked like each other and all the females looked like their father, a dashing ginger-colored tom who had roved the neighborhood that year.

She had pondered: daughters resembling each other. Helen and Jenny had both been tall, attractive, and dark haired. At the reception after the funeral, poor Janice had even had a jolt when she thought she saw Jenny coming through the door—but it had been Helen.

And daughters resembling their father. The same handsome dark-haired man appeared in a photo on the shelf in Janice's town house and in a photo among the clutter on Helen's coffee table. Pamela had gotten a glimpse of the photo when Precious dispersed the clutter onto the carpet. When she and Bettina visited Helen to claim the cat toys and cat food, her real aim had been to check the photo again.

That had been the last puzzle piece.

"But what made you even think . . ."—Holly's smile was quizzical, not dimply—". . . think . . . to think those things went together?"

"Helen was from Minnesota," Pamela said. "She told Bettina and me that when we went to pick up Precious. And Jenny's father, Janice's husband, was from Minnesota too. 'Minnesota nice,' Danielle Hardy called him."

"Those details came out in her confession." Holly directed an admiring gaze at Pamela. "But you noticed the coincidence before that and figured out what it meant. That is *awesome*!"

"Helen was very mistrustful of men," Bettina commented. "We were talking to her at the reception after the funeral. Such a beautiful young woman. It was just sad."

"I can see how she would be"—Holly nodded—"with

a father who deserted her mother. That was in the *Register* too."

"Precious and the ball of yarn, though." Roland had been listening with the same intensity he might have devoted to the details of corporate lawsuit. "How did watching Precious and the ball of yarn complete the puzzle?"

Pamela smiled. It was actually rather fun to lay out the details of her sleuthing for such a rapt audience. "Helen was very adamant that she *did not knit*. She told Bettina and me that when we went to pick up Precious and she told us again at the reception."

Bettina chimed in, "So it would seem she couldn't have had anything to do with a murder committed with a knitting needle."

"But," Pamela went on, "I noticed clippings with knitting patterns on her coffee table. *And* I realized the reason for my déjà vu was that Precious had been chasing a ball of yarn across the carpet at Helen's."

"Well, my goodness." A teasing smile played around Nell's lips. She checked her watch.

At that moment the doorbell chimed. Pamela and Bettina looked at each other. Pamela shrugged and rose to answer the door.

Bathed in the porch light, Harold Bascom greeted her with a grin. He was a tall and fit man in his eighties, with a thick head of white hair that strayed onto his forehead in an unruly forelock. He was bearing a very large basket, like an old-fashioned laundry basket. The contents were covered with a colorful dish towel.

"Come in!" Pamela pulled the door all the way open and stepped back.

Harold advanced to the center of the living room, where he set the basket on the carpet. Watched by six pairs of curious eyes, he lifted the dish towel to reveal—a mountain of rhubarb, long thick stalks, glowing red and stacked to the rim of the basket.

"Only Pamela and Bettina's Wilfred have claimed a share," Nell said, rising from the armchair. "Holly and Karen"—she bobbed her white head toward where they sat together on the sofa—"I hope you will claim some. And Roland, if you like. But this whole basket"—she crossed the room to put an arm around Pamela—"is for Pamela. She's shown us tonight what creative things she can do with this often-ignored vegetable—yes, it is a vegetable, not a fruit."

She gave Pamela's waist an affectionate squeeze.

"I think we'd all agree that, much as we admire her crime-solving abilities, cooking is a much less dangerous use for her imagination. And"—Nell gestured toward the basket with its garden bounty—"when you've used all of this, there is a great deal more where it came from."

KNIT

Cozy Tea Cozy

Pamela and Bettina are coffee drinkers, but Nell and Karen drink tea. A hand-knit tea cozy is fun to knit and makes a great gift for a tea drinker. Cloth tea cozies often resemble tents that cover the whole teapot and are removed when the tea is poured. This knitted tea cozy is formfitting but stretchy and it slips on and off like a sweater. It leaves the handle and spout uncovered and can stay on during the tea service, but it can be removed easily when it's time to add more hot water.

The Cozy Tea Cozy is created from two almost identical halves that are then sewn together, leaving openings for the teapot's spout and handle. These directions make a tea cozy that fits a teapot about 21 inches around and 6 inches tall.

Use yarn identified on the label as "Medium" and/or #4, and use size 6 needles—though size 5 or 7 is fine if that's what you have. The tea cozy has contrasting stripes, like the one pictured on my website. You will need about 80 yards of color #1 (the main color) and 20 yards of color #2 (the stripes).

If you're not already a knitter, watching a video is a great way to master the basics of knitting. Just search the Internet for "How to Knit" and you'll have your choice of tutorials that show the process clearly. The tea cozy is worked mostly in the stockinette stitch, the stitch you see, for example, in a typical sweater. To create the stockinette stitch, you knit one row, then purl going back the other direction, then knit, then purl, knit, purl, back and forth. Again, it's easier to understand "purl" by viewing a video, but essentially when you purl you're creating the backside of "knit." To knit, you insert the right-hand needle front to back through the loop of yarn on the left-hand needle. To purl, you insert the needle back to front.

With color #1, cast on 32 stitches, using either the simple slipknot process or the "long tail" process. Allow for a tail of 7" or so if you use the slipknot process and add an extra 7" to your long tail if you use the long-tail process. Casting on is often included in Internet "How to Knit" tutorials, or you can search specifically for "Casting on." After you've cast on, start creating the ribbing that will form the bottom edge of the tea cozy. Ribbing is the basic knit 2, purl 2 concept. For your first row, knit 2 stitches, then purl 2, then knit 2 more, purl 2 more and continue like that to the end of the row. On the way back, knit 2, purl 2 and so on again. If you've cast on a multiple of 4 (which 32 is), you'll see that now you're doing a knit where you did a purl, and vice versa. This effect is what creates the ribs. After you do a few rows you will see ribs starting to form and this concept will become clearer. One important note: after you knit the first two stitches, you must shift your yarn to the front of your work by passing it between the needles. After the two purls, you must shift it to the back, and so on back and forth. If you don't do this, extra loops of yarn will accumulate on your needles and you will have a mess. Do the knitting and purling for five rows.

Now switch to the stockinette stitch for three rows. To do this, knit a row, then purl going back the other way, then knit another row.

To make the stripes even more interesting, it's fun to vary the texture. You do that by purling where you would knit and vice versa. Graft on your second color of yarn, color #2—there's a picture of how to do this on my website—leaving your main color attached too. Now knit a row and then purl going back the other direction. You can see that you've created a raised stripe that stands out against the flat stockinette stitch.

Switch back to color #1, leaving color #2 attached, and proceed for four rows, starting with purl and ending with knit. Pick up color #2 and knit one row and purl going back the other direction to create another raised stripe. Alternate four rows of color #1 (purl, knit, purl, knit) and two of color #2 (knit, purl) until you have four stripes of color #2. Clip color #2, leaving a tail of a few inches. Proceed with four more rows using the stockinette stitch (purl, knit, purl, knit) and then begin decreasing to shape the rounded top of the tea cozy. You will do this on a purl row.

To decrease, insert the right-hand needle into two stitches on the left-hand needle instead of just one. Do this twice at the beginning of the row, purl until there are four stitches left at the end of the row and then repeat the decreasing process. You will have 28 stitches on your needle. Knit the row normally going back the other direction. Decrease by four stitches again on the purl row, to end up with 24 stitches. Knit going back the other direction. Continue this process until you have 16 stitches left on your needle.

Now knit two stitches together, knit three normally, knit two together, knit two normally, knit two together, knit three normally, and knit the last two together. You will have 12 stitches left on your needle and you will be on a purl row. Purl two stitches together for the whole row to end up with six stitches. Cast off, leaving a tail of about 7".

You have now completed the first half of your Cozy Tea Cozy.

Repeat this process for the second half except for one difference. You want to make a buttonhole. Proceed as you did for the first half until you have completed three stripes. Purl one row with color #1. On the knit row, knit one stitch, cast off two, and continue knitting for the rest of the row. Going back the other direction, purl 29 stitches, cast on two, and purl the last stitch. Knit another row with color #1, make another stripe with color #2, and continue as you did for the first half. This buttonhole will fit a button about $\frac{5}{8}$" across. I used a shank-style button rather than one with holes.

Hide the tails of color #2 by threading a yarn needle (a large needle with a large eye and a blunt end) with each tail and working the needle through about half an inch of the stripe. There's a picture of this process on my website. Pull the yarn tight and cut off the smaller tail that remains.

Now it's time to sew the two halves of your tea cozy together. Smooth out the two halves and lay one over the other, wrong sides together. Thread the yarn needle with a tail left from casting on—there's a picture of this on my website—and use the whip stitch to sew the two pieces together, starting at the bottom edge and sewing to the top of the first stripe, catching only the outer loops along each side. Pass the needle through a loop of yarn to make a knot and hide your tail as you did with the stripes. Repeat this process on the other side with the other tail left from casting on.

Next, sew together the "shoulder" seams of the cozy. You can use the tails left from casting off or thread your yarn needle with a new piece of yarn. Depending on the shape of your teapot's handle and spout and the shape of its cover, you might want to make these seams shorter or longer. Basically you are sewing together the sides where the decreasing happened, but leaving an opening in the middle for the knob on the teapot's cover. For my teapot, I sewed a two-inch-long seam on one shoulder and three-inch-long seam on the other, as you can see in the pictures on my website.

Finally, using a regular needle and sewing thread, sew the button on the side that doesn't have the buttonhole. Position it close to the edge, between the third and fourth stripe.

For a picture of the finished Cozy Tea Cozy, as well as some in-progress pictures, visit the Knit and Nibble Mysteries page at PeggyEhrhart.com. Click on the cover for *Knitty Gritty Murders* and scroll down on the page that opens.

NIBBLE

Rhubarb Cheesecake Pie

People don't find rhubarb very exciting these days. We can get almost any fruit or vegetable we want at almost any time of year, with produce shipped from all over the world to our modern supermarkets. But in earlier times, people were dependent on what grew locally. Long before any fruit came into season in the spring, rhubarb plants would be sending up their shoots. The prospect of eating any fresh growing thing and getting the benefit of its vitamins must have been very thrilling to our forebears, and if one added enough sugar rhubarb could be quite palatable—even delicious.

Rhubarb is often called "pie plant" because it makes a great pie filling, sometimes in combination with strawberries or other fruit, in a flaky pastry crust. Just for fun I decided to have Pamela try something a little different. It's the same shape as a pie, but it's a rhubarb cheesecake.

This recipe includes directions for making your own graham-cracker piecrust, but you can use a ready-made one from the supermarket if you wish.

Ingredients

For the rhubarb compote:
2 cups of raw rhubarb, sliced thin (about ½ pound)
½ cup sugar
1 tbsp. water

For the graham cracker crust:
12 whole graham crackers (the rectangles, not the
    squares)
4 tbsp. butter, melted
3 tbsp. sugar

For the cheesecake:
16 oz. cream cheese (2 8-oz. packages), allowed to sit
    out and soften for an hour or so
⅔ cup sugar
2 eggs
½ tsp. vanilla

For the topping:
½ cup sour cream
1 cup heavy cream or whipping cream
2 tbsp. sugar

Directions

Make the compote. In a small saucepan, gently cook
the rhubarb, ½ cup sugar, and 1 tbsp. water, covered, until
the rhubarb is soft and jam-like, about 15 minutes. If the
rhubarb is soft but the compote is still soupy, boil it at
high heat with the cover off for a few minutes at the end.

Remove it from the heat and let it cool while you work on the cheesecake. The compote can be made ahead and chilled or even frozen. If you freeze it, thaw it before adding it to the cheesecake.

Heat the oven to 350 degrees.

Make the graham-cracker crust. Reduce the graham crackers to crumbs by putting them in a ziplock bag and rolling over them with a rolling pin. You will probably have to do this in two batches depending on the size of your ziplock bag. In a small bowl, mix the crumbs with 4 tbsp. melted butter and 3 tbsp. sugar until they resemble moist sand. Press them onto the bottom and up the sides of a pie pan using your fingers and the back of a spoon. There's a picture of the result on my website. Refrigerate.

Make the cheesecake. With an electric mixer, beat the cream cheese in a large bowl until it's smooth. Beat in ⅔ cup sugar, then the eggs and ½ tsp. vanilla.

Pour or spoon the cream cheese mixture into the graham-cracker crust and spread it evenly. Use a spoon to drop the rhubarb compote here and there on top of the cream cheese mixture. Pull the blade of a table knife in long random strokes through the rhubarb and the cream cheese mixture, taking care not to push deeply enough to disturb the graham-cracker crust. You want to create the effect of the rhubarb being marbled through the cheesecake. There's a picture of this on my website.

Bake the cheesecake pie for 40 to 45 minutes or until the center is almost set and the edges are slightly brown. Let it cool and then refrigerate it for at least 3 hours.

Make the topping. Pour the cream into a medium-sized bowl, add the sour cream and 2 tbsp. sugar. Beat on high speed until the mixture holds soft peaks. As you serve the cheesecake pie, add a few spoonfuls of the topping to each piece. Refrigerate leftovers of the cheese-cake pie. Cover the leftover topping with plastic wrap and refrigerate it too.

For a picture of the Rhubarb Cheesecake Pie, as well as some in-progress pictures, visit the Knit and Nibble Mysteries page at PeggyEhrhart.com. Click on the cover for *Knitty Gritty Murders* and scroll down on the page that opens.